T0208023

THE
ANSWER
IN ACTION

Claudia Helt

The Center for Peaceful Transitions

BALBOA.PRESS

A DIVISION OF HAY HOUSE

Balboa Press books may be ordered through booksellers or by contacting:

Balboa Press
A Division of Hay House
1663 Liberty Drive
Bloomington, IN 47403
www.balboapress.com
1 (877) 407-4847

Because of the dynamic nature of the Internet, any web addresses or links contained in this book may have changed since publication and may no longer be valid. The views expressed in this work are solely those of the author and do not necessarily reflect the views of the publisher, and the publisher hereby disclaims any responsibility for them.

The author of this book does not dispense medical advice or prescribe the use of any technique as a form of treatment for physical, emotional, or medical problems without the advice of a physician, either directly or indirectly. The intent of the author is only to offer information of a general nature to help you in your quest for emotional and spiritual well-being. In the event you use any of the information in this book for yourself, which is your constitutional right, the author and the publisher assume no responsibility for your actions.

Any people depicted in stock imagery provided by Getty Images are models, and such images are being used for illustrative purposes only. Certain stock imagery © Getty Images.

Print information available on the last page.

ISBN: 978-1-9822-3988-6 (sc)
ISBN: 978-1-9822-3989-3 (e)

Library of Congress Control Number: 2019920128

Balboa Press rev. date: 12/09/2019

OTHER BOOKS
Presented by Claudia Helt

The Answer Illuminated
2019

The Answer
2018

The Time When Time No Longer Matters
…continues…
2018

The Time When Time No Longer Matters
2016

The Book of Ages
2016

Messages From Within:
A Time for Hope
2011

Messages From The Light:
Inspirational Guidance for
Light Workers, Healers, and
Spiritual Seekers
2008

~ ACKNOWLEDGEMENT ~

For all who have been involved in the presentation of *The Answer* series of books, gratitude abounds. This outreach has long been in the making and it is with great happiness that this final book has reached its birthing process.

We hope the Readers of *The Answer in Action* will find it a worthy addition to your daily routines as you actively pursue becoming people of peace, as well as advocates for the wellness of the Life Being Earth.

Many have been working on her behalf for a very long time, but more participants are needed. Those of you who see the merit of becoming involved with this project of healing the Earth are most welcomed to this Mission of Rescue. As many of you already know, the planet is in extreme need of assistance. Her health is waning and her ability to sustain vibrancy under present conditions is limited. She needs help, not from just a few, but from many. We hope you will choose to be part of the many.

As a Reader of *The Answer* series, you are aware of the premise of these books. The idea of healing others, including the Earth, is within our means. Humankind has the ability to alter the course of Earth's wellness. For the sake of this remarkable Life Being and for our own future, we must become involved. All about the planet, activities to reduce our maltreatment of the Earth are coming forward. This must continue! And there is more that can be done by every individual residing on this incredibly generous Being. She has given her all for us. It is now time for us to give of ourselves on her behalf. Please read *The Answer in Action* and discover how easy it is to be a participant in her recovery process. So little is required of us. From the comfort of our homes, we can assist her. By addressing our own issues of unrest and by actively pursuing a life style that embraces peaceable ways, we will alter her declining health. The means is within us. Will you help, please?

In peace be, now and always!

~ Introduction ~

Welcome, Dear Readers, to the opportunity of a lifetime! Beloved friends from near and afar, please be with us if you are able. The time is now. The sun advances forward this day bringing Light to all who are in her view. We are most grateful for this remarkable event. In gratitude we gather on the Life Being Earth's behalf and we offer her our love, our Light, and our positive affection. Within each of us lies the energy that enlivens the universe. We are not unique in this quality, but merely the recipients of all that is, was, and ever will be. With this gift of life essence, we have the good fortune to assist self and others. And with this gift, we come forward to assist the Earth at this time.

Breathe deeply, Dear Friends, and empower the particles of Life's Essence within you at this time. Increase its power, and with the imagination of the mind and body, send your particle of life essence to the Mother Earth. Give generously of this powerful life source for it is capable of restoring her strength and vibrancy back to full health. Offer your essence to her for the sake of all who reside upon and within her. So much has she given to us. Share a particle of this life essence with her now so that she can recover from the years of generosity she has provided to so many.

We do so now, Dear Old Friend. Please receive this gift of rejuvenation and use this energy to heal yourself. We are most grateful for all that you have done for all of us and we stand ready to assist you again and again until your life essence is at its maximum once again. With the next breath that we take, we enliven our own life essence and with the next exhale we send this particle of Pure Source Energy to you. Accept this please and take time to revel in the love in which you are held. In peace be, Dear Old Friend!

Dear Readers, we begin our introduction to *The Answer in Action* with an action of love and kindness for She who has given her life's breath for the residents existing upon her. With this small action of generosity, her health can be improved. By repeating similar actions of good will, she will be restored to good health once again. So little time and energy can accomplish so much. Please consider participating in these small acts of generosity for the sake of our incredible host. She needs our help. And we desperately need her to continue. For the sake of our future we must come to her aid.

Imagine, Dear Readers, if you contributed a particle of your life energy to the Earth just twice a day. And then imagine your effort being compounded by billions of others who also offered similar acts of kindness from all around the world. Imagine the Earth receiving all these loving acts of generosity every day. What might happen from all these doses of medicinal particles of loving-kindnesses? Within each of us resides the ability to heal others. Although our awareness of this ability long ago was forgotten, the powerful energy still remains within us. The time is now, Dear Friends. We must awaken to the reality of that which lies within us, and we must access this gift for the sake of the Life Being Earth.

You are the answer to Earth's recovery. Please take action now. Save the Earth by focusing your attention upon her wellness, and remember: she is a very large Life Being. One dose of loving-kindness is beneficial, but it is not enough to heal a Being of such enormous size. Offer your healing powers to her daily and provide her with several doses throughout the day, if you can. Invite your family and friends to do the same. By generously sharing your powerful love with her, your own energy will be revitalized. She will respond to this tender care and we will benefit from her wellness once again.

Please join the effort to save the Earth. By participating in her recovery process, everyone benefits.

In peace be, Dear Readers!

PART ONE

~ 1 ~

"**W**elcome, Dear Friends! It is so wonderful to see you again!" Dee and Frank's delight was obvious. As their family of friends approached through the serene backyard garden, they both beamed with happiness. Although little time had passed since this group's last gathering, a passerby would think it was a reunion long in the making. Many hugs and warm greetings were exchanged before everyone made themselves comfortable around the table that was already lovingly prepared.

"My, oh my! How wonderful it is to see your bright, smiling faces!" Dee sighing loudly shook her head in disbelief. "How blessed we are!" Her brief words of gratitude inspired similar comments around the table.

For your edification, Dear Reader, the family of friends being alluded to is indeed the friends that you have come to love and appreciate in the previous adventures shared by these good people. They are, as you know so well, the Smiths, Jan and Everett, the Joneses, Bill and Pat, and the walking buddies, Marilyn and the nameless narrator. Perhaps, you wonder why this individual who is so actively involved in our story remains unidentified. Simply accept that there is a reason for this anomaly.

"Thank you for inviting us!" the one of which we are speaking announced. "The garden is glorious as usual, and this setting is simply the perfect place for us to gather." Frank, who typically did not accept compliments well, rose to the occasion when the focus was upon the garden.

"You know it's been a long time since the garden has been this lush. I think it's because of the youthful energy that it's receiving. Guess that sounds odd, but I really do believe the flowers are responding to the tender care of our young friends who are managing the garden for us. And just look at the vegetable garden," he said pointing to the area of the yard that had been offered to the young couple in exchange for their help with all the flower beds. "There is a special relationship developing in our backyard and I think we are witnessing the results of this collaborative effort." Frank's sensitivity to the exchange of energy transpiring in the garden that he and Dee had lovingly cared for over the decades was descriptive of his relationship with nature. His connection began at an early age through the lessons learned from his father who was also exceptionally connected with all things natural. And like his father, Frank's love for nature never waned.

"Has it been difficult to allow someone else to attend your masterpiece, Frank?" The question asked by Marilyn was one that everyone at the table was thinking at the same time. Even Dee was curious how her husband would answer the question. She had her own reactions to spending less time in the garden, and often reminisced about the hours of labor and love that went into that sacred space. She was not surprised when Frank's response included her feelings as well.

"You know Dee and I loved working in the garden." He turned and smiled at his beloved of many decades, "Remember in the beginning, dear, when we strategized the design of the backyard and then worried over which flowers would be best suited for each particular bed. Those were great times, weren't they, Dee?" Her smile acknowledged his sentiment. "But I think our new young friends appeared on the scene just at the right time. We don't have the physical strength we used to have, so we wear out rather quickly. And quite honestly, we are so happily engaged in our new passion with this outreach program we are sharing with all of you that we just don't have as much time anymore to focus on the garden. Oh, we still love this remarkable beauty, and we are very grateful that it is being maintained for us, but I believe at this stage in life, we are here to appreciate our garden rather than providing it with the tender loving care that it deserves.

Dee and I laid the foundation for this little patch of heaven." Frank's mind seemed to travel elsewhere as he looked over the various flowerbeds that flowed seamlessly from one end of the yard to the other. He and his beloved had created this colorful showpiece together. A single tear glistened in his left eye. "And now," he slowly continued, "it's time for us to allow someone else to take her to another level. The garden needs new energy and new collaboration with someone other than us. We've grown so accustomed to the way she has looked for so long that our imaginations have become limited. But look at her! She remains vibrant and still has so much more to offer. Yes, the garden is continuing to fulfill its life's purpose. And these young folks can help her to reach a new phase that will surpass her present glory. She deserves new energy!" Dee reached across the table and placed her hand upon Frank's.

"Well said, dear! And you're right. Those were good times, and right now in this moment, I love you more than ever. Our garden keeps moving forward...and so do we! Thank you for this wonderful adventure called life. How sweet it has been!" As the elder couple tenderly clasped hands, their friends bore witness to this intimate moment of connection.

"You two are role models for all of us," whispered Jan. Her husband

Everett nodded in agreement and followed the couple's lead by reaching over to seize his beloved's hand. He clutched it tightly and silently mouthed 'I love you.'

"Wow!" he exclaimed aloud. "You certainly know how to start a meeting!" Everyone present at the table…and beyond…applauded Everett's response to their hosts' demonstration of love. The elders blushed a bit and then quickly regained their composure. Dee took the lead by inviting her guests to do a brief check in and Jan was the first to respond.

"Well," she began. "Everett and I have…Oops! Sorry! There's that four-letter word again! Wellness to the Earth, my friends!" Jan paused briefly as similar exchanges were shared. The group's newly formed commitment to acknowledge the Earth each time one of them began a sentence with the four-letter word "well" was thriving. "It seems," continued Jan, "that old habits are truly difficult to break, but I think our decision to convert these moments into opportunities to honor the Earth is very clever. And by the way, Everett and I have continued our commitment to send energy to the Earth twice a day. It has become part of our morning and evening rituals."

"Wonderful!" acknowledged Pat. "It's been easy for us as well, I'm happy to report." The friends quickly assessed that everyone had merged the new commitment into their daily routines with very little effort.

Marilyn acknowledged that she was surprised how easy it was to bring the energy transfer meditation into her overcommitted life style. "At first, I was hesitant about introducing another task into my day, but truthfully, I find this daily engagement with the Earth to be one of my favorite activities. I'm so grateful to be part of this healing process!" Her comment received similar responses from other group members.

"I'm not surprised to see this reaction," stated Frank. "Engaging with nature is always a humbling experience and having these deep, heartfelt connections with the Earth during our energy transfers is particularly meaningful. I'm glad this is working for all of you." Frank recognized the sense of gratitude that his friends were enjoying with their new commitments and he was pleased. And also, good host that he was, Frank realized that it was time to turn the conversation back to Jan. Looking in her direction, he invited her to continue.

"Oh, thank you Frank! Yes, let me see if I can begin without the use of that overused four-letter standby. I want to update everyone regarding recent conversations between Everett and me. We've thought a lot about our mutual project and particularly about the development of the book that Dee so amazingly designed for us. And we came to the conclusion that it is time for us to develop an approach to this work. The last time we were together, we all agreed that the outreach program needed to move forward before the book is completed." Jan looked around the table to see that her friends were all still onboard with that idea. They obviously were, so she continued.

"So, what we would like to discuss this evening is our first outreach meeting. Actually, this will be our second meeting," she said acknowledging that the first attempt at outreach had successfully been implemented. "Our initial effort was so easy and comfortable that it inspires us to take the next step. As we," she pointed to her husband, "reviewed and discussed our first session, we agreed that the basic format was on target, but we also realized that we had the luxury of greeting newcomers who were already connected to one or more members of our group. So they were strangers to some of us, but not to all of us, and we suspect that made the evening run more smoothly. We anticipate that our next meeting may truly have guests that are strangers to all of us, and we would like to keep that in mind as we plan our activities.

We're very excited about moving forward and feel we can focus both on the upcoming event, as well as the activities that will be included in Dee's book. As we prepare for our first session, the activities we agree upon can also be composed and assembled to blend into our book project."

"Goodness!" declared Dee. "You have given this a great deal of consideration. I am both grateful and pleased at the same time. And curious!" she quickly added. "In your deliberation process, how did you see the book unfolding? What do you think should be the first entry into the book?" Dee's question aroused interest among her friends. Eyes sparkled around the table and the energy level of the group, which was already high, ignited. The shift was visibly noticeable. Dee giggled with delight inspiring similar responses from her friends and future contributors of the upcoming outreach manual.

"Actually, Dee, we're just following the outline you created for the book," Everett responded. "You really did a stellar job! The material is precise and flexible at the same time. And now, it's time for us to take the next step." A look of modesty crossed the elder's face, but Jan quickly intervened.

"Yes, it's true, Dee, your outline propelled Everett and me into a lengthy discussion about the opportunities that await us in this 'coming out party' that we're all planning. You know we were so fortunate in our initial session with newcomers. Of course, we don't think it was a coincidence that the first session went so well; however, our review accentuated the reality that we were truly united with a lovely, responsive group of folks. And quite honestly, we are excited about who we will meet in this upcoming event as well, but because we are cautious planners, we were trying to anticipate all possibilities that might lie ahead. Bottom line is this," asserted Jan. "Our hospitality efforts for the first meeting served us well. And our openness in sharing our own stories laid a safe foundation for the newcomers to share their stories with us.

I think," Jan paused briefly to take in a deep breath, "actually, we both believe that we must proceed with the same intentions for this event as we did the first. We must be open, hospitable, humble and gracious to the best of our abilities. And we must never lose sight of how uncomfortable we were when we first shared our own stories. As we become more relaxed with these presentations, we may have a tendency to forget how it was for us in the beginning, and we mustn't. For the sake of those newcomers who are sharing their stories for the first time, we must always remember what that initial experience is like. We were so fortunate to have each other for support and we must provide that for those who come to our presentations."

"Indeed!" replied Dee. "This is a very important and timely reminder. I must admit I simply take it for granted that we can openly discuss these unusual topics. How far we have come in such a short amount of time!" She shook her head in disbelief, as did others who also experienced memories surfacing from the past.

For your edification, Dear Reader, a gentle reminder is provided regarding the series of events preceding this present gathering. Dee and Frank, as you may or may not remember, had held their unusual encounter in secrecy for some 50 plus years. Their dearest friends, including those currently sitting around their table, never knew until recently what had happened to them when they found themselves 'lost' in the woods decades before. The Smiths also had held their unusual experiences closely to their hearts until they could no longer live in silence about it. When Jan and Everett finally revealed their secret to these same friends then more secrets, regarding unusual experiences, were disclosed by other members of the family of friends as well. The remarkably similar experiences reunited these old friends, and the many conversations they shared about their strange encounters opened the door for more unusual encounters to unfold. Suffice it to say, these experiences profoundly altered their lives, and as a result, our eight friends chose to embark upon a delightful journey intended to assist others who also had similar experiences awakening them to the reality that we are not alone in the Universe.

Through the many stories shared in the previous two books, our group of friends discovered that they were intricately linked with one another and with all other life beings, including the one that is most obvious, but who is in truth rarely regarded as a life being at all.

It is most unfortunate that such a truth must be brought to humankind's attention, but indeed, it must be done. We speak of the Life Being Earth, who is desperately in need of assistance from those who have had the privilege of existing upon her for a very, very long time. One wonders how oblivious the human species can be. Nevertheless, let this be a reminder to all who read this book. The Earth is a Life Being to whom extreme gratitude is owed. So much she has given and so little has been given back. The time to reciprocate her generosity is upon all who have been the recipients of her good will.

Silence fell, as it often does with this group of good people, as each individual pondered the circumstances in which they found themselves. In recent weeks their awareness of the Earth's decline had become so vividly real that they could no longer deny her condition. Like so many of her inhabitants, this group of dear friends had recognized changes happening around the planet and in their own immediate environments, but the idea of Earth's failing health was so grossly incomprehensible that the fearful mind stilled the normal human response. Rather than reacting immediately to assist another who was in jeopardy, humankind became overwhelmed by the enormity of the task. And as is often the case when faced with an unbearably fearful event, shock inhibits what one normally expects of his or her self. The people of Earth were paralyzed by the reality that their planet was in peril.

Humankind's initial reaction to the Earth's circumstances was understandable; however, fear and its corresponding inaction can no longer be the guide. The time for action is upon everyone. Even now as the lovable characters in this story ponder their own commitments to the Earth, changes are happening. People across the planet are awakening to her situation and are taking actions to create sustainable co-existence. Each day, advances are being made and there is reason for hope. These actions of goodness must be participated in and supported. Everyone must take a stand to assist the Earth. No act of kindness is too small to offer. Step up, Dear Reader, Dear Friends! Do whatever you are capable of doing, and do it diligently and loyally; for one act of kindness is not enough. As already noted, the Earth is a very large Life Being and her recovery demands persistence. Daily persistence! One might ask how long her recovery will take and the answer is simple. Forever! As long as she exists and offers residence to other life beings, she must be attended with care. Mutual loving co-existence is essential for her wellness. Those who have the privilege of calling this remarkable Life Being home must accept the reality that their future depends upon her good health.

Although this may be shocking news to those who are obsessed with the illusion of ownership, the truth is, no one possesses any part of existence. We share existence with all others in existence. By accepting this reality, humankind will come to understand our place in existence. It is time for everyone to accept that by abiding in loving kindness and living in peaceable ways, all in existence will continue for all existence. The path of peace is the way for continuance. Hopefully, Dear Reader, each of you will choose this path for it will render good health and happiness for all who participate.

As the fellowship of friends sat quietly together, many thoughts raced through their minds. Each in his or her own way wondered about the task that lay before them. The outreach program being planned was invigorating, and each member of this family of friends felt called to participate in the project. And yet, the minds of these good people created doubts.

"My friends, may I interject a thought?" The narrator of the story took the lead with the group's permission. "I sense a shift in our energy. Doubt is setting in. Before it takes us any further down a path of nonsense, let's stop it now." Hands instantly reached out to one another until the circle was completed. How comforting this small action was. Their clasped hands reminded them that they were all here for a reason. "We have a plan! And it's a good one! So let us recognize our doubts for what they are, a brief moment of insecurity. As I look around this table, I am so grateful to be a part of this gathering. Look at us! We are just ordinary people, and we have a plan to assist the Earth! Let's not allow a moment of doubt to derail us.

Human nature will always be a factor in our efforts. We will have moments of confidence interrupted by moments of insecurity. Such is life! But we are so much more than our doubts, and together, we can quickly bring a halt to the downward spiral of these inner distractions. In fact, we just did!"

"Brava!" declared Marilyn. "Thank you for recognizing and immediately addressing that shift in energy. Well done!"

"The doubting mind is insidious," interjected Jan. "We were having such a joyous moment, and in a blink of an eye, the shift occurred. Oh, goodness! Another lesson learned and another idea to add to the To Do List."

"Why does this happen?" asked Bill. "What inspired that reaction?" Bill's question returned the group to another encounter with silence. In fear that his question might instigate more doubts, he quickly explained that curiosity was the basis for his question. "Please understand that I am simply curious about this process. How does it happen? Why? And what can we do to prevent these incidents?" Bill's questions, intended to open conversation, led to more silence. Eyes glazed over, as they so often do when one is in deep thought.

"Those are very good questions," Marilyn replied pensively. "My own thoughts about this are somewhat muddled, but I believe it has to do with being present. It is the wayward mind that takes us off on these excursions of disillusionment, and when the mind is under its own direction, I don't think that we are truly present. We're too busy wandering about with the mind that has a mind of its own. My point is this," Marilyn noted with hopes of providing clarity. "We are not here in the present moment!" Pausing briefly, she sighed and then hastily added, "I'm afraid my words are not helpful. I don't really know how to articulate what I'm feeling."

"Actually, I think your words speak a truth that can help us prevent these unwanted and undesirable distractions. Being present in the moment maintains and sustains our mission of purpose. It is in those moments that we feel clear, confident, and joyous about our work. But as you said, Jan, it only takes a second for insecurity to sneak in. Welcome, to the human condition!

We are really very fortunate to be aware of this tendency, and our conversations about this inclination will help us override these evitable detours when they surface."

"Agreed! Now that we have that trail of nonsense out of the way, let's talk about the manual."

Frank's manner seemed insistent and purposeful. Before anyone could respond, he elaborated upon his intentions. "Friends, I think we can applaud ourselves for our newly found ability to recognize when one or more of us plummet into the hole of doubts, fears, and insecurities. And I also believe we can feel good about our ability to discuss and explore where these intrusions take us. However, now if I may be so bold to say, it is time for us to move onward. Let's put the distraction behind us and move forward. Obviously, we must reflect upon these incidents, but in my humble opinion, we don't need to linger there. We must trust ourselves! Now, unless there is something still causing anyone of us a problem, let's look to the future. We've got a book to write!"

"Well said, Frank!" The remark from Pat made the elder man blush, but he appreciated her compliment nonetheless. Truth be known, half way into his explanation, Frank began to doubt himself. He wondered if he was being too forceful and then feared he might be completely off the mark. Although he was not one that leaned toward presumption, he wondered if he had erred in that direction. He silently questioned whether he should bring his bout with doubts into the conversation and then his dear wife invited him to do so. Smiles were exchanged between the two before he quickly took the hint.

"Okay, folks, as you can see, the lovely lady over there was eavesdropping on the misdirection of my mind. So I will very briefly acknowledge that while I was attempting to explain myself, doubts came roaring in. Bottom line, fears rose to the surface and I was concerned that I had made an error in judgment. But I still believe my intentions were correct and my present situation is a good example of it. I just had an incident with insecurities, but I'm okay, and I hope no one was wounded by my forward manner." He looked about the table and assured himself that everyone was all right. "So, I wish to move on. There is no need to linger with the doubts; to do so, only gives them more attention than they deserve." Frank glanced over to Dee for reassurance. Her smile was all that he need. "Let's talk about the book! How shall we begin?"

"We already have!" Bill's declaration captured everyone's attention. "But before Pat and I share our quote-quote achievements, I want to thank you, Frank, for that lesson in wisdom. There is necessity and merit in discussing our experiences with emotional frailties, but your point is well taken. We must strike a balance. Acknowledge whatever the situation is in the moment, learn from it, and move forward. I think we have a good operational strategy... thanks to you Frank!" Although Frank didn't enjoy being the center of attention, he was grateful for the feedback. Such validation countered any hope a lingering doubt might have for creating another episode of disillusionment or discontent. He nodded a thank you to Bill and then invited him to take the lead.

Bill happily did so.

"Well," he began and then immediately rolled his eyes. Chuckling at himself, Bill turned to his friends and invited everyone to join him in the appropriate response. "Wellness to the Earth!" The entire family hailed the newly established mantra at the same time.

"Know that you are loved and cherished, Old Friend!" added Marilyn.

"And know that we are working on your behalf, Dear Friend!" chimed in Pat. "You are in our hearts and on our minds, as we gather here today. As we compose the pages for the book that will enlist others around the world to come to your aid, please hold on, Mother Earth!" Pat's impromptu prayer resulted in a brief moment of silence followed by a number of deep breaths and utterances of amen.

"Isn't it wonderful how we have turned that old habit of beginning conversations with the overused four letter word into an opportunity for healing prayers and intentions. I'm so glad we are doing this. It lightens and brightens our time together." With a gentle, sweet look upon her face, Dee reveled in the moment and then turned to Bill and urged him to continue.

"Thanks, Dee. Pat and I are eager to share our thoughts and ideas… and we do want feedback of course." As Bill spoke, Pat passed around copies of their rough draft to everyone. "We approached our outline for this project in the same manner as we personally lived through the experience with all of you and with our children and grandchildren. As you can see, we began with the unusual event. We both agreed that the story of the incident and the incredible impact it had and continues to have on our lives must be told fully. We attempted, hopefully successfully, to elaborate upon the incident so that the reader and our future audiences truly can understand the significance of these events. Our goals are multifaceted. We want others to know about our experience so that they may feel inclined to share their own. We also want them to know how nervous we were about sharing our story with anyone else, and how grateful we were when we finally did share it with all of you. That moment of disclosure also changed our lives! Having the privilege of sharing our story with you was a critical factor for us. It propelled us forward to the next necessary step. It helped us realize that we had to find a way to involve our children. We could not keep this secret from them, nor could we advance forward until they were aware of our situation.

So as you can see from our rough draft, we include our angst about sharing our story and we also plod through the decision-making process that we went through. We feel confident about sharing our experiences in person, because as you well know, interactions of this type are rich with possibilities. However, we have less confidence about reaching the folks with whom we will not have personal contact." Looking about the table, Bill's demeanor changed. It was subtle, but his friends noticed the shift. A deep breath was taken before he continued. "This is where our insecurities surfaced. The truth is, we don't really feel comfortable with our literary writing skills. And we don't want to blow this opportunity! We both realize the potential this book has and we want to be sure our commentary enables the reader to fully understand the ramifications of our experiences. Indeed, we've all had some incredible experiences, which led us to more remarkable experiences, but the true story lies in what we have learned as a result of these seemingly unusual events." Bill's eyes scanned the table reuniting with each of his friends. With a full face smile, he gently announced, "We are here to help the Earth! That's the real story that must be presented to the reader.

While sorting through all of our ideas, we realized that our first attempt at this rough draft was founded in the assumption that other people will have had similar experiences, and that they would naturally be inclined to work on Earth's behalf. But then we realized we must also address and welcome those people, who have not had such an experience. We want to reach everyone! And we assume, perhaps incorrectly, that most people for reasons that we do not yet know haven't had these encounters. The point is we do not want to limit our outreach. Our ultimate goal is to inform everyone that they have the ability to assist the Earth through this remarkably easy practice. Even those who are already involved in serving the planet can add this healing exercise into their daily encounters with the Earth. In fact, we believe one of the possible benefits from our outreach program will be an infusion of additional ideas from others folks that are already attending the Earth in similar yet uniquely different ways than we are suggesting."

"Our hope," added Pat, "is to extend an open invitation to everyone to assist the Earth. We suspect that many people feel a sense of hopelessness regarding Earth's situation. They may want to help her, but they don't really know what to do. Hopefully, our idea of infusing her with daily doses of positive healthy energy will spark other ideas around the word. Just look how compatible this energy work is with those who already have some type of daily devotions. In essence, when we focus our intentions upon sharing positive energy with Earth, it is simply our version of praying for her good health. An invitation to the millions of individuals who hold prayer in high regard to add the Earth as a recipient of their prayers seems appropriate, welcoming, and beneficial to everyone."

"Oh my!" Dee's excitement was barely audible. *Of course,* she thought to herself, *"reaching out to people of faith, all faiths, is a grand idea.* "Once again," she spoke aloud, "I am stunned by the possibilities that lie ahead. Earth's health crisis has the potential for uniting peoples all across the globe. We face a shared problem that demands everyone's cooperation. As the crisis worsens, our petty differences will become irrelevant. Although many continue to believe in the illusion that their circumstances will not be affected by this crisis, they are wrong, and their denial will not serve them well. All who inhabit this planet will experience the inescapable consequences of her decline and they will quickly learn that they must work together for her survival and for their own. Because of this tragic situation, people will learn to look beyond their perceived differences and come to appreciate one another in ways not known before. This dilemma will cross all boundaries. The true meaning of loving thy brothers and sisters will be realized while the people of Earth strive for their continued existence. In truth, the mission to heal the Earth may finally manifest peace on Earth." Dee fell silent, as did her friends. The words that came from her were startling to hear, and yet, everyone knew the truth had been spoken.

"My goodness," she declared. "I have brought a dark cloud to our gathering." She looked to her husband for reassurance and saw his left index lift slightly. Not certain of its meaning, she peered into his eyes. *What should I do?* Her question was internally spoken, but she knew that Frank would respond.

Give them time to mull over your comments. No reason to intercede now. Give them time. And with that heard, Dee was able to take a deep breath and follow his guidance.

"Dee, I know you are worried and concerned about what you just said, but just trust us, please." My words seemed to be effectively consoling, which was my intention. I suspected she was bewildered by the words that had come from her, so I added, "And trust yourself too!" A subtle smile crossed her face.

"I agree," declared Marilyn. "And if the rest of you are able to resume our conversation, I have some thoughts to share." Her friends urged her to proceed. "Dee, I want to give you some feedback, if you are open to that." Dee responded immediately.

"Yes, please do. I must admit I have mixed feelings about my actions, so I would really appreciate your perspective." Marilyn knew that Dee needed to talk about what happened and was grateful for the opportunity to do so.

"I empathize with your mixed feelings, Dee, because I experienced mixed feelings when you were speaking. I went from agreeing with everything you said to feeling you had really ruined my day. Of course, these emotions and numerous others all transpired in an instant and it took me a moment to sort through everything. Dee, this is my explanation of what happened for me. You spoke the truth and I didn't like hearing it. That was the visceral, instantaneously reaction. And then, my truth came forward. Even though I didn't want to hear the truth spoken truthfully, I am very grateful that you did. It's hard to hear the reality of what is transpiring, and for a brief moment, I wanted you to hush. My own denial system was fully operating, and then, my truth came forward again. I know that I must face this truth. We must all face this truth," Marilyn declared to her friends. "Because if we don't, the

Earth's crisis will worsen. What you said Dee was the truth, and it inspired me to take action. If we live in denial and do nothing to assist her now, then unspeakable disasters are going to happen around the globe. But, if we continue to aid her with positive energy infusions and if we can encourage others to help with that, then we can break this cycle of decline.

Dee, I know it was difficult for you to bring those words forward, but it was necessary. And I want you to know that I'm grateful. I heard you! My previously avowed commitment to help the Earth was ignited once again. We have to continue our daily practices and we must move forward with completing this book so we can maximize our outreach." The word 'agreed' echoed around the table as if it were the 'amen' to a prayer.

"Marilyn, you just described my own reactions perfectly, so there is nothing more for me to say other than thank you." Looking in Dee's direction, Jan praised their elder friend. "I am so grateful Dee. Please don't worry about us. You spoke the truth and we needed to hear it."

"This has been very helpful," replied the one who had spoken the words of truth. "I was indeed taken aback by the words that seemed to flow through me. Your feedback has been a relief, and I wish to hear more if anyone is so inclined." Her husband Frank had a great deal to say but he decided to wait. If necessary, they could have a conversation about Dee's pronouncement later, after the gathering was over. He remained silent but looked in my direction. His silence was remarkably loud and his look was definitely a call to action.

"Dee, I'm curious. What was it like for you to deliver that message of truth?" My question gave her pause. She closed her eyes and breathed deeply while a solitary tear made its way down her cheek. Part of me wanted to take my question back and another part of me knew without knowing how it was known that it was exactly the right question and the right time for Dee's personal development. I glanced toward Frank for reassurance, and once again, saw the subtle movement of his left index finger. I wondered if he knew how powerful that small gesture was.

"It is, isn't it, dear?" Dee's response to my unspoken wonderment took me by surprise. "Sometimes," she added, "I wonder what I will do if that old finger wears out. That small act of love and reassurance is immeasurably significant to my everyday sense of wellness." The rosy color of her cheeks returned as she spoke of her beloved.

"Your question is timely, dear. I appreciate the opportunity to talk about that experience." Dee looked in my direction and seemed to peer into my soul. *"You know what this is like, don't you?"* My nod was as subtle as Frank's

13

gesture of lifting his finger. *"Of course, you do. This happens to you frequently, doesn't it?"* Again, I nodded in agreement. Our friends around the table listen intently. Their heightened focus indicated to me that they were aware of the unspoken dialogue that had transpired.

"It was odd," she began again. "I heard the words coming out of my mouth, and yet, they didn't seem to be my words. I believed what was being said and they could have been my words if I had given the topic consideration, but the point is I had not done so. The words just started flowing from me, and as I listened to me, I had concerns about what was being said and how it was being delivered. Again, I must admit that I believe what was said, and I also believe it was necessary, but I'm not sure I would have been so blunt about the crisis. I was concerned about the impact this message was having. And my concerns took me down the same path we discussed earlier. It's really remarkable how quickly the downward spiral can happen." Before Dee concluded, another idea arose that she believed needed attention.

"This experience brings to mind another thought. What if these free flowing incidents happen while we are hosting others? It's one thing to have this happen among us, but if it happened with strangers, what might they think?" Dee's question revealed her deep concern about what she presumed had happened. It became clear to me that another perspective needed to be explored.

"Dee, you know how we all feel about coincidences…well, I believe this experience happened for a reason and I don't think it was a coincidence. So, I would like to present a similar, but different perspective of what transpired for me during your pronouncement as Frank referred to it. My initial reaction was the same as Marilyn's and Jan's. I did not want to hear the truth, even though I knew without any doubts or questions that the truth was being presented to us. However, now that I've had some time to review our discussion, I believe there is a much greater truth that is being given to us through this message and we must review our process of listening, interpreting, and misinterpreting such messages." The family of friends came to attention as curiosity and excitement ignited around the table. Marilyn leaned forward and urged me to continue.

"What I want to do now is what Dee has frequently and skillfully demonstrated in recent weeks when she seized upon each and every teaching opportunity that crossed our paths. My friends, we have another learning experience here that I believe will be an extremely important addition to our repertoire of helping aids."

"Yay!" declared Jan, whose joy of learning was inspirational to everyone around her. "Let's do it!" I was amazed how quickly Jan's energy could uplift the energy of those around her. Her smiling face was contagious.

"I agree! Let's do it! So, this is what I witnessed. First, let me acknowledge that I can speak of this retrospectively, but I was now aware of the process, as it was actually unfolding.

When Dee began to speak of the Earth's crisis, she captured our attention. We were drawn into the reality of this situation and our minds fixated upon the possible disastrous outcomes of her continuing decline. Are we all in agreement with that?" Mutterings of validation indicated I was on the mark. "However, what our minds neglected to hear was the equally powerful messages of hope that were also expressed. This actually makes sense when you recognize that our initial attention was still focused upon the crisis when the second equally significant message was presented. We heard both, but the mind lingered in the field of tragedy. We must each be aware of our mind's reaction. I believe we were stuck in the undesirable zone where thinking the worst consumes the mind when the powerful optimistic message was presented to us; and because of that, the significance of those messages passed by us.

Assuming that my observations are correct, I believe this means we must be alert to similar reactions that may unfold in our future interactions, and we definitely need to be aware of the possibility of this type of reaction transpiring in our outreach events. Essentially, we must find a fine balance of speaking the truth about Earth's situation and at the same time emphasize that there is reason for hope." I started to pause and then realized it was time to practice what had just been said.

"My friends, there truly is reason for hope. We know this! We believe this! And what happened just now gives me even more hope. Dee experienced a remarkable event of receiving and speaking a truth, and she did so with her usual grace and dignity. And the message she brought forward had impact. We experienced it and we also recognized that our energy shifted because of it. But we didn't stop there! We explored the process and have learned from it and now we will be more capable of assisting others when they fall victim to their fears.

I think we handled this well, and I am very grateful for the experience." Frank, who had been closely monitoring his companions, quickly stepped up to facilitate the next step.

"That was nicely done," he began. "And it helps me to sort through my own reactions and thoughts at the time. Does anyone else have any thoughts about this experience?" Several additional comments of gratitude were expressed before Frank turned to his best friend.

"How are you doing, Dee?" His question pulled his wife back into the present. She was still reliving what had transpired and wondering if it could have been done differently.

"I'm fine, dear. You know how I am...always micromanaging. I don't need to discuss this now, but sometime in the future, I would like to have a conversation about 'receiving' messages." Dee accentuated the word receiving by indicating quotation marks with her fingers. "I have much more to learn in this area," she admitted.

"Why don't we discuss this now, Dee? It's a very important topic, and I think we all agree it happened for a reason. I think it's doubtful that this was a one-time event." The group responded to my suggestion immediately. Words of encouragement came flowing forth, except for Everett who spoke from a place of sincere interest.

"Dee, I do not wish to push you into further conversation, if you don't feel ready to do so; however..." he said with a smile. "I am intrigued by what we just witnessed. I believe it is safe to say that all of us are aware that you are a woman of wisdom. Your words have inspired us and propelled us forward countless times, and we have all benefitted from your presence. In all honesty, Dee, we've grown accustomed to the privilege of having access to your wisdom. But today was different. You had a unique experience! And we had the good fortune of witnessing your experience. If this situation had happened to one of us, you would be the first one in line encouraging that individual to process the event." Everett's comments were a salve for Dee's heart. She knew he was right and while she appreciated his efforts, she still was reluctant to continue. She wondered why?

"May I be of assistance, my dear friends?" The familiar voice brought instant happiness to the family of friends. To add to their surprise and delight, the voice was accompanied with a body. Everyone immediately jumped up to make room for their Beloved Elder Friend. In other circumstances, hugs would have been exchanged, but present circumstances did not allow for such an interaction. Nevertheless, everyone experienced the intimacy of an imagined warm embrace. Bill quickly grabbed another chair from the other end of the deck and placed it conveniently for their new arrival and soon everyone was comfortably seated again. Frank could not contain himself. Tears filled his eyes as he welcomed their elder friend into the circle.

"You've been missed, Old Friend!" He reached over to pat the elder on the knee, and then realized the futility of such a gesture. He drew his hand back to his lap, and said, "It is so good to see you again!"

"I am most happy to be in your presence once again. While I am often near, I must admit it is remarkably satisfying to be seen. Visual connection does indeed heighten the joy of the experience. I am grateful for the opportunity to be with you." His smile literally made the sunny day seem even brighter. Frank wondered how that was possible, but didn't need an explanation. It was what it was, and he was content with that.

"I expect you are here for a reason," exclaimed Frank who longed to have unencumbered time with this old friend. He wondered how many times they had enjoyed long walks together and also if there were to be future opportunities for such interactions. His desire for connection was so heartfelt that his friends could not help but overhear Frank's thoughts.

"Old friend, I am honored by your sentiments and I too would enjoy extended time together. Indeed, we have had countless long walks and endless conversations throughout our lifetimes, and there are more to come. Always, there will be connections at exactly the right place and exactly the right time, because this is our commitment from long ago." More tears escaped from Frank's eyes as he listened to this friend from the past. Outwardly, he appeared composed except for the few tears that trickled down his cheeks, but internally his heart ached. Dee could feel the depth of his pain; she was in awe.

"You have assumed correctly, my friend. I am here for a reason. As you well know, many from afar watch over the Circle of Eight. Your work pleases all, and all are most grateful. You have made great strides, and still there remains so much more to do. Many are here today enjoying this review of your personal contributions. This gathering provided an opportunity for connection to be made, and also, for old skills to be reinserted into your current abilities." The elder gentleman turned his attention specifically to Dee.

"As your friend noted, you have had a unique experience. Shall we take advantage of this opportunity to discuss your experience?" Before Dee could answer, the elder continued. *"How may I be of assistance, old friend?"* She remained silent. Although her beautiful mind was filled with thoughts, she was unable in the moment to grasp just one. She tried without success to narrow her train of thoughts. Then she contemplated starting anew with a completely different set of ideas, which quickly led to another group of thoughts overtaking her.

"Perhaps, my dear friend, it would be wise to take a long deep breath. Shall

we all join with this process, for it is indeed a most gratifying experience?" The family of friends immediately responded. Eyes closed as the deep breaths were taken and released, and within seconds, the peaceful mind returned. Dee relaxed with the first exhalation, and her husband and friends who sensed her relief were able to let go of their concerns for her. The blessing of this simple exercise was a great reminder for everyone. Within a brief moment, Dee regained control over her restless mind and was able to respond to the gracious offer of assistance.

"My goodness! How good it is to see you again. What a sweet surprise this is! And of course, your timing is impeccable. Thank you, my friend; you have successfully assisted me. I am very grateful." Frank was pleased to see the change in his wife. She was back.

"I am pleased my presence was of assistance. But in truth, all I did was to remind you of that which you already know. The blessed breath is the path to peace and quiet. Once there, the confusion and agitation is easily released. And now, may I assist you in processing your unique experience?" Dee's eyes turned upward to the sky, and the sight was one to behold. She consumed another long deep breath.

"Life truly is a miracle!" she whispered. "Look above my friends. Beauty surrounds us from the ever-changing sky scape to the beauty of Mother Nature, and to the beauty of our precious relationships." Embracing her friends with her eyes, she added, "I am so grateful to be on this journey called life, and even more so to have such wonderful companions along the way." Turning her focus to their unexpected guest, Dee declared, "That includes you, my fine friend! Although you are rarely visible, I know you are always with us. And because of you, all of us know we are not alone. So thank you, and also, please share these sentiments with all those other invisible friends that we have not had the pleasure of meeting...yet!" A look of complete satisfaction washed across his face and another deep breath was taken as he savored the moment.

"I assure you my friend, the companionship to which you refer is ongoing, never-ending and I too am most grateful for these relationships. In regards to those whom you have not yet seen, they ask me to relay a message to you." His smile grew larger as he glanced about the room. *"They wish you to know that they are deeply grateful for your kindness and your generous participation in the mission of mercy. They look forward to the day when all of you will be able to see their presence. And that day is coming soon!"* The message created a stir about the table. Frank immediately took the lead.

"What exactly does that mean?" His question was precise and demanding. Frank, the man of few words wanted and expected an answer to his question. He was not surprised by what he heard.

"I am sorry my friend, but I have no more information other than what was offered. Like you, I am very curious and excited; however, what you just heard is all that I know. We must be patient together."

"So this is just a peek into the future," Everett's disappointment revealed itself. Frank was equally disappointed and frustrated. His feelings rushed from his mouth.

"At my age being patient can be a tall order. I know this sounds selfish. I openly admit it and maybe some day I will feel guilty about my behavior, but right now, I refuse to feel guilty about it. If the Companions are coming forward, I want to know when and where this is going to happen. I want to be present when this transpires! I want to be in the welcoming party and I want a front row seat for the occasion." Frank's outburst caused Dee to quietly chuckle, which had a ripple effect. Soon everyone was laughing, including Frank who had turned several shades of pink. Their guest also participated in the boisterous relief.

"My old friend, your words are heard by many more than just me. And I assure you all are delighted with your desire to be part of the joyful reunion. They reassure me that they share your impatience."

Dee leaned forward in her chair and smiled at her beloved. "I'm sorry, dear, for setting off that round of laughter, but I was just so proud of you. I was tickled with delight. I too share your frustration and concern about missing this opportunity, but I'm also extremely optimistic about this news. How kind it was of them to apprise us of this possibility. Like you and Everett, I also want the specifics, but for some reason, I am content with just knowing that the day is coming. And perhaps," she faced the elder gentleman, "we may be able to fast forward this great happening by pushing our work ahead more rapidly. Am I correct in thinking this?" Her question was well received.

"Indeed, your supposition is correct. Many details are being orchestrated as we speak, all of which must come into alignment for the greatest good to unfold. Your work is just one of the details being addressed. My friends, you are not alone. Many are working on behalf of our Dear Friend Earth, and in order to assist her to the fullest, all matters must be attended simultaneously. Creating peace is an extremely complicated factor within all the initiatives that are in process. Surprising it is, how elusive peace can be. As peace of mind and heart is reached in one individual, the opposite erupts in another. Conflicts rise and fall about the

planet's surface as if they have a life of their own. This has been true for millennia. Our good intentions have been met with resistance for reasons that are perplexing. Still, we have hope in humankind. You are much more than you presently realize, and because of this truth, we persevere. You are all invited to share this hope with us. Have faith, dear friends, and know that you are more than you appear to be." His invitation gave pause to the family of friends.

"Believe in yourselves as much as we believe in you. Trust yourselves as you trust each other, and please accept that those who came before you trust you as well."

"Those are profound words," whispered Jan. "Both comforting and challenging at the same time." She looked around the table, her eyes filled with awe. "Can we really do this? I trust each of you without doubts, without reservations. But can I trust myself? That's the real question! And the fact that I am asking this question reveals my doubts." Jan's facial expression changed from awestruck to frustration. "Why am I doing this? I am a trustworthy person. The fact that I have wonderful friends who love and trust me is evidence of this. Why does the mind insist upon disrupting one's confidence? I just do not understand why this happens." Facing the elder gentleman, Jan pursued an answer. "Do you know what this is about? Perhaps, I'm being presumptuous, but I don't think my self-doubting behavior is uncommon."

"Your perception of the prevalence of this behavior is accurate. For reasons yet to be clarified, humankind, at some point during their developmental history, came to regard their doubts dubiously. This was and remains a most unfortunate misinterpretation. In truth, the doubting mind has always been an asset. If you perceive your doubts as cumbersome, they will be so; however, if you accept your doubts as the asset they are intended to be, then this process of deliberation actualizes into an extremely beneficial skill set. When the process of doubting was misinterpreted and judged as an action of indecision, its usefulness became restricted and limited.

I invite you, dear friends, to create a new relationship with your doubting mind. Because you have grown accustomed to believing that the doubting mind is a diminishing factor, you no longer give your doubting mind the benefit of a doubt. What if, my dear friends, your doubting mind is indeed trying to assist you with whatever is being addressed in the moment? Perhaps, the doubting mind has another option that is actually worthy of your review. Trust yourself to be able to engage with the doubting mind. Listen to what it has to say and then determine if you can use this information. Such an interaction can be very informative even if the option provided is not a preference you wish to pursue. As long as you trust yourself, dear friend, such interactions can be very helpful, for they can strengthen your understanding of a situation, thereby resulting in an increase of self-confidence regarding any decisions that you face.

We are concerned that there is confusion related to the doubting mind and the distracted mind. The former is an avenue for assistance and clarification, where the latter is a path that draws one away from the focus of attention. Each engagement with either of these inner components of your mind demands that you, the possessor of this beautiful, intricately complex mind, must trust yourself to manage it. Trust yourself when the doubting mind disrupts you to share its latest idea that you will be able to discern its relevance; and also to let go of it if need be. Doubts are not intended to override your preferences or decision; they are intended to assist you in gaining clarity and confidence about your decision-making process.

Likewise, trust yourself to engage with your distracted mind. If it leads you in a direction that is actually productive and helpful, trust that you will recognize the benefit of the detour. However, if it leads you down a path that has nothing to do with the moment of intention, trust yourself to abandon the excursion. You need not fear the distracted mind, but you must be willing to manage it. Left to its own devices, it will attempt to overtake your preferences. Again, there is no reason to fear this part of you. Simply know the impetuous nature of the distracting mind and set limitations accordingly." The elder gentlemen specifically sought eye contact with Jan and reassured her that she was more than capable of managing the wonderful aspects of her mind.

"You, dear friend, sense emotions exquisitely. This sometimes leaves you feeling at a loss when great changes occur suddenly within. In the moment, it is most unsettling; however, as you become more open to these changes, you will feel your strength rising within you. Your sensibility is a gift, not a diminishment. You will come to appreciate the blessings of this gift when you understand its full potential. My friend, the doubts that bubbled up within you were those of a person of humility. They were the natural response of someone who was awestruck by the idea that she was worthy of the trust of her friends and of others whose names she no longer remembers. The feelings of their respect and admiration overpowered you. The feeling was so strong that you had to break the connection. When you retreated from the intensity of their love for you, the change was misinterpreted as doubts. My dear friend, your doubting mind played no role in this situation. What you experienced was the joy of being loved so fully and so dearly that it was overwhelming. The time will come dear friend when you will be able to sit with this feeling of love and be restored by it. Today, you experienced a hint of divine

love. Much more is coming your way and you will in turn share this love with others.

What I say to you is also true for all of you, my friends. As you continue to move forward with your work, you will find greater connection and love surrounding you, for as you reach out to others, others will reach out to you. Your work is of divine goodness. Please accept this as truth, for it is indeed so." Eyes glazed over as each individual attempted to grasp the elder's prophecy. As was often the case, Dee was the first to respond.

"You do have a way about you, my old friend. You arrive, you capture our attention, and you give us great pause." She broke into laughter. "What a great guest you are!"

"I am most pleased to be in your company once again. It is a joyous occasion for me as well." The elder gentleman's sincerity was not doubted, but the mystery of his presence often tempted the curious mind. Frank, quietly observing, wondered about their friend's origins. His appearance hadn't changed in over fifty years. Everett's thoughts were similar but with a different time frame. His experiences with the elder had been more recent but questions about this mysterious man's comings and goings often surfaced. Who is he? Who had he been? How long ago was his most recent lifetime? Questions, questions, questions.

Indeed, the questions were as fluid as the appearances of the well dressed, gray haired elder gentleman. Sometimes curiosity arose and the desire to know more about him surfaced with the same intensity as when the initial contact was made, and then, equally as rapidly, one's insatiable curious nature would quiet itself, and one was simply grateful for the moment.

"Some day, will you tell us more about your life?" Like her friends, Marilyn's desire to know more about their remarkable companion occupied her mind.

"I too have the desire to sit and reminisce with all of you. As much as you wish to know more about me, I wish that you could remember all of our times together. So many experiences have we shared!" His eyes turned downward, as he seemed to retreat to another time and place. *"That luxury is not ours today, but I promise you the time awaits you. The memories lies within you and the time will come when they will surface and all that was known will be known again."*

"I look forward to that day," Frank softly spoke. He could say no more than that because he knew what was coming.

"Yes, old friend, you anticipate correctly," replied their gentle friend. *"Our time together passes so quickly, and once again, I must take my leave*

of you. Please remember, my friends, you are deeply cherished and you are greatly needed. Much remains to be done, and you are more than capable of managing all that is coming. Stand firm in your commitments, reach out to one another for assistance, and remember you are not alone. Also, please remember, my absence is merely an illusion. Always, I am but a breath away. I bid you farewell, dear friends. In peace be!" As was his way, the companion from unknown parts faded into nothingness. His departure, although witnessed many times before, demanded their attention. Every time his disappearing act unfolded, they were reminded that their experience with this seemingly ordinary fellow was much more than it appeared to be. Over time, they had adjusted to his comings and goings, delighting in his unexpected arrivals and anticipating the news he might bring. Their relationship with the elder gentleman almost seemed commonplace until the time of his departure came into play. Then their encounters with him shifted into the realm of the unusual. One moment he was with them and the next moment he was not. Simply stated, Dear Reader, the time spent engaging with the elder was extraordinary.

"Wow!" declared Jan. She started to say more, but instead just shook her head in amazement. Several others at the table mimicked their versions of her reaction while others remained silent. These were not unusual responses to the elder's departure. Often each individual would travel about in his or her respective mind processing what had occurred. It is appropriate to say that the elder gentleman made lasting impressions.

"Are we in agreement that our dear friend has once again left us in a state of bewilderment?" Her question inspired giggles and affirming remarks. "Why are we so blest?" she mused and then quickly brought herself back to the present. "Where are you my friends? Do you have the energy to continue our meeting now or shall we adjourn and reschedule?" Feelings appeared to be mixed. Energetically, the answer seemed obvious. The friends were tired, but they enjoyed each other's company so much that no one really wanted to bring the meeting to a close. As the energy worker of the group, I decided to accept responsibility for making the decision.

"Friends, our energy levels are low. Just check in with yourself and you will be able to make this assessment. In my humble opinion, it is in our best interest to reschedule." Turning to Dee, I invited her to give us a homework assignment, which she quickly did.

"Okay, then!" she acted in her capacity as the team coordinator. "Let's all face our fears regarding our literary skills and take the next step. Please bring in outlines, summaries, fliers, etc. for the next meeting. And do not worry about perfection! Bring in 'something' and the rest of us will offer suggestions. This part of the process will become easier with practice. Let's just take the next step."

~ 2 ~

"**H**ello, dear house of mine! You are looking exceptionally well today. Guess who made an appearance at the meeting today?" I waited for a response, but as usual the house remained noncommittal. Assuming my house knew exactly who I was referring to I shared with her that it had been lovely to see him again. "My only regret is that you missed his unexpected visit. Hopefully, he will visit us here soon." Before heading to the bedroom to change clothes, I apprised the heart center of the house of my plans to take a walk. Just as I did so the phone rang. It was no surprise when Marilyn's voice announced that she was headed for the trail. Our thoughts were in alignment. "Oh yay! I'm changing clothes now as we speak. Will meet you at the intersection in ten minutes." Rushing to be on time, my goodbye to the house was minimal.

"I'm off, dear house of mine. I will convey your greetings to Marilyn. Will be back before dark!" And out the door I went.

"Is that you?" called the familiar voice on the other side of the hedge.

"Of course, it is!" My reply came just as we avoided colliding into one another at our favorite designated intersection. Anyone witnessing our reunion would have assumed that we were long lost friends who had not seen each other for ages. Our excitement and the huge hugs shared certainly indicated such a conclusion.

"Oh, it is so good to see you!" We both declared at the same time. That set the stage for more opportunities of synchronicity. We giggled like children as we hurried to our favorite trail head and the hills beyond. We chatted about this and that, refreshing each other on the latest news since our last visit. This was the small talk that set the stage for the more important conversations that were yet to come. This seemed to be a routine that worked well for us. We would chat about little things as we walked through the neighborhood towards the trailhead outside of our small community. Once we reached and entered the trail, our energy would shift and the heartfelt discussions and revelations would begin.

"Marilyn, tell me everything! Including how you felt about our friend's appearance today?" She shook her head and pointed her index finger at me, but decided not to pursue the fact that it was really my time to go first. So often did we fuss about this with one another, but today, Marilyn was eager to go first, so she accepted my invitation.

"I'm delighted to go first, even though I am keenly aware of the fact that it is not my time to do so. Just giving you notice, my friend. I know what you're doing and I'm holding you responsible for our next two walks." We exchanged smiles, and walked a bit further down the path as Marilyn collected her thoughts. "Do you have any idea who our friend is?" Her question surprised me. Before I could respond, she added, "Surely, you must wonder about this."

"Yes, of course, I do. I often think about it, but I have no answers. I feel such a strong sense of connection with him that it makes me believe that we've had special times together. I can't be any more specific than that. There's no recall or intuitive awareness about previous lifetimes together. And yet, with all that I am, I believe we are old friends. Not unlike when you and I first met, Marilyn. Remember how we were back then? Completely and totally at ease with one another! I suspect we've all had previously lives together. We share such an incredible camaraderie with the Sandersons, the Smiths, and the Joneses that it makes you wonder." A loud sigh seemed to indicate a conclusion to my response, but instead led me to another thought.

"What about you, Marilyn. Why has this question come up now? Has something happened?"

"I'm not sure. Seeing him again reminded me that our adventures with him were real. And I am not saying that I have any doubts about all the incredible times we shared with him, but the truth is, being able to see him makes such a tremendous difference. I don't want to think of myself as one of those people who must see to believe, but goodness, it really helps. I'm embarrassed to acknowledge this out loud, but it's true. I feel totally reenergized by his appearance."

"So do I! And I suspect everyone else does as well. It was a boost to see him." My words seemed to console Marilyn, but there was still something bothering her, so I nudged her a bit.

"What's going on? You seem to be out of sorts with this." Although my friend was taken aback by the idea, she did not oppose my suggestion.

"How do you do that?" she asked while gently poking me in the arm. "How did you know I was out of sorts, when I didn't even know it myself?" I just smiled and winked at her.

"Maybe, it's because we both know each other better than we know ourselves." She nodded in agreement, but added that she was uncertain about the source of her concern. We walked in silence for a while, and then a thought struck me.

"Marilyn, are you afraid that you are becoming dependent upon our friend?" Once again, she was surprised by my question and so was I.

"Geez, that never occurred to me, but you may be right. I was so glad to see him, and because of his presence, I actually believed we could accomplish what is being asked of us." She seemed frustrated, but I chose to remain silent. She just needed time to work her way through this. "Wow! This sounds like I'm doubting myself and everyone else in the group, but that just isn't true. I really believe we are making great strides and I do think we can reach our goals."

"But do you think we can do what needs to be done without his assistance?"

"We are intended to do our part!" Marilyn's response was resolute. "Remember what he has repeated to us so often. We are part of a much larger team and all our efforts are needed. We are not intended to do this alone, but our contributions are essential. Our friend's guidance has been immeasurable, and I'm certain that he will continue to provide us with assistance if needed.

So, this is not about feeling dependent upon him. But something is going on…I think it is about missing him." Emotions rose and a tear slipped down her cheek. "Yes, that's what this is about. I miss him! Even though I know he is near and I trust that he will be available if there is an emergency, the truth is, I miss him!" She looked to me without shame or embarrassment and repeated, "I miss him!"

"Thank you, Marilyn." My tone reflected my sincere appreciation. "Your good work is providing me with clarity. You're absolutely right! There's a hole in our lives when he is gone. And like you, I know he is still near, but in those moments when I really, really miss him that knowledge isn't particularly useful. It's just a big heartache that cannot be denied or avoided." Marilyn remained silent, but nodded her agreement. It was obvious that she was processing our conversation.

"What are we to learn from this?" she mused. Her question was an invitation to go deeper, which we did each in our own way. Our walk became a quest for greater understanding. Marilyn ventured down her necessary inward paths, while I pursued mine. We each had a unique solo journey, and yet, we were not alone during our experience. I remember feeling the comfort of her presence even while I was alone within my own journey. She was there, and she was available if needed, but I was alone in my own experience.

"Fascinating!" We both announced at the same time. And then we came to an abrupt stop.

"What were you just thinking?" Again the question was asked simultaneously. We both stood still, shaking our heads in amusement.

"This is amazing!" We announced together. At that point we could no longer contain ourselves. An exhausting giggle episode commenced and was uncontrollable until it ran its course. Gasping for air, we agreed in was time to continue our walk.

"Wow! That was a hoot!" Marilyn's joyous expression, stated without my echo, could not go unnoticed. "Ah, we're finally back-to-normal!" She breathed deeply, before she concluded her thought. "That spree of absurdities could not have been a coincidence! I think we are in the midst of a teaching moment. The question is…will we learn the lesson?"

"I think we were provided a microcosmic view of an existential experience. Please excuse my choice of words; they may be lacking, but my point is this. We just experienced our own singular life journeys while we were in the company of each other. This is not unlike our experiences with our invisible friend. As we walked in silence just now, Marilyn, my solo journey was intimately experienced without you, and yet, all the time it was transpiring, I was acutely aware of your presence. You were not with me within my journey, but you were accompanying me from a near by vicinity. I think this is exactly what the elder is attempting to teach us. Even though we cannot see him, he is nearby! Just as we were for each other now, as we walked separately into the depths of our own heart space.

Oh, goodness! I'm not expressing this well at all, but the point is, he is here! He accompanies us! And yes, we do and will continue to miss his visible presence, but we must remember that he is here. We must learn to trust this reality and somehow, we must come to accept our moments of sadness when we long to see him. Perhaps, during those times when the heart aches to see him, we should breathe deeply and access our memories of times when he appeared before us. We should remember that incredible smile of his and the marvelous sound of his voice, and of course, his laughter. Oh, we must remember his laughter! Those images are embedded in our brains. Dare I say those memories are there for a reason and we should use them wisely.

We are so blessed to have this awareness, Marilyn. Not only do we have each other and our family of friends, but we also have awareness of a much greater network of friends who accompany us and assist us in our life journeys. We are so blessed to know this!" My words, which were poorly descriptive of my heart's intention, were received and understood nonetheless. Marilyn wrapped her arm around mine as we continued our walk up the hill.

"Thank you," she whispered. "I know you feel your words were inadequate, but they weren't. Let's face it! How can one describe the indescribable? But you did, and it was extremely helpful. The beauty of this synchronicity is precious and astounding. We were provided with a personal experience that demonstrates the ongoing presence of the elder friend in our lives. This new insight will, of course, find its way into our outreach program. Amazing! How many people will be served by this small, yet expansive walk we just shared?" We paused to take in the views, and again, were at a loss for words. Every direction offered another scene that literally took one's breath away. We reveled in the beauty of Mother Earth.

"What do you think would happen if everyone on the planet awakened to the reality that we are not alone?" Marilyn's question came just as I was wondering the same. My smile indicated to her that we had just shared another synchronistic moment.

"As an energy worker, I believe it would profoundly change the negative energy generated by humankind, which in turn would redefine out attitudes towards one another. Because violence and distrust have been so prevalent for so long, we seem unable to open our hearts to others. Instead, we are suspicious of anyone who is different or unknown to us. We don't seem able to give strangers the benefit of a doubt. We are quick to judge folks that we don't even know. I'm afraid fear was the instigator of these misunderstandings and still remains the primary force that drives our misbehaviors.

And there is another factor that has recently come to mind. I think there is an arrogance among many people that leads us to believe that it is the other person's responsibility to prove his or her worthiness, while at the same time we demand that they (the others) regard us with the highest esteem. It's a curious and entitled attitude that I fear is more prevalent than we know.

Marilyn, I believe there is goodness in everyone, but for reasons that began longer ago than any of us can remember, we lost our way. So much meanness and injury has occurred over the ages that it is difficult for most people to have any objectivity about the possibility of peaceful relationships in the present. We are rooted in the heartaches and atrocities of the past, therefore we are unable to see or accept the goodness of the person standing before us. At some point, it would be very interesting to discuss this with our circle of friends because I believe this may be another topic for our outreach mission."

Marilyn nodded in agreement. "This would be a very interesting subject to pursue and I would love to hear our friends' viewpoints on it." She paused briefly as a gorgeous hawk screeched from above. "Hello, dear friend, I hope you are well. Fly safely, dear one." One of the similarities between Marilyn and me is our love for nature and all her inhabitants. Her greeting to the hawk made me smile: such a kind gesture from one species to another. Her thoughts strayed for a moment, before she returned to our conversation. "So, I have another question for you," she announced pensively. "Are you saying that we, meaning all the billions of people living on this beautiful planet, may be able to open our hearts to one another again?"

"Goodness," my reply was accompanied with a deep breath. "Actually, this sounds like a question for our elder friend and his Companions. I'm afraid I am way out of my depth here, but I will share my opinion, if you like." Marilyn welcomed my thoughts. "I believe if we could allay our fears and our impulsive judgmental nature then anything and everything could be possible, including recognizing the goodness in everyone everywhere. If we learned to manage our kneejerk reactions to people we've never even met, then we would have the space, and hopefully the grace, to see the beauty in all others. Rather than focusing on our differences and immediately making judgments about those differences, we could instead recognize the similarities that we share. So yes, Marilyn, I do think we have the capacity of opening our hearts to one another again."

"Wouldn't that be wonderful?" she whispered.

"Indeed, it would!" hailed a familiar voice. The two dear friends came to an abrupt stop, both looking around to find the body that went with that beloved voice.

"My apologies, my friends, but materialization is beyond me at the moment. This morning's visit expended my reserves; however, I am in wellness in my present form. May I join you, please?" His presence filled them with joy. They were so delighted to be in his presence that his invisibility didn't matter. He was with them!

"We were just talking about you, but I guess you are aware of that." Not knowing where to direct her comments, Marilyn simply spoke to the empty path ahead.

"Yes, I have been present during your discussions. I am grateful for your lovely sentiments and for the clarity you have reached regarding my limitations. Obviously, I would prefer to be visible to you at all times, but this cannot be. However, please do not concern yourselves regarding my immediate location. Because my present form is formless, my location is nebulous. Wherever you are, I

am, and wherever you speak, I am. So it is best that you simply speak in a manner that is comfortable for you, because I will hear you regardless."

As he spoke I listened admiringly and wondered what it was like to be in his present state. Curiosity stirred within me. *This isn't a casual visit. Our friend is here for a reason.* Marilyn turned to me with a smile.

"Of course, he is!" she said responding to my unspoken thoughts. "He's always here for a reason. So what's up, dear friend? What's the purpose of this meeting?"

"Ah! Your existential communication improves. This is most gratifying. But we will discuss this more thoroughly at a later time when the Circle of Friends is gathered.

Let us speak of the present. Indeed, I am here for a reason. My friends, it is time for the book to be written. I come to ask your assistance in energizing the group for this task. Each of you is keenly aware of the positive impact of healing energy; therefore, I ask you both to take the lead in bringing energy facilitation to the forefront of our mission. As you know, healing energy clears the mind of nonsense, freeing the recipient to address challenges more expeditiously. It is time to move this project forward. Presently, fear is inhibiting our progress. Although the inner growth that is occurring is essential and noteworthy, we must entice the fragile ego to recognize its full potential. The family of friends are people of goodness and sincere intentions. We trust your desire to assist with the Mission of Mercy is sincere, and we also know that the human condition often interferes with one's ability to address tasks that are unfamiliar. The creation and publication of a book is new to all of you. While there is enthusiasm, there is also reluctance. Unfortunately, the seed of doubt is being sown in your minds, which will delay our progress. Although this is a common reaction, my friends, we do not have time for such a delay. So with your help, we will address this concern by initiating group energy sessions. Do you concur with this strategy?"

"I think it is brilliant!" Once again our responses coincided. Marilyn pointed to me to continue my train of thought. "As you can see and hear, Marilyn and I are on the same wave length. This has been happening during this entire walk. But you know that, don't you? Anyway, my friend, I believe your plan has merit. We have been confronted with a loss of confidence that has taken up a great deal of time. The detours are beneficial in that we are discovering more ideas that may and probably will require discussion in our outreach programs. These diversions are educational for all of us. Like I said, we are all learning a lot about ourselves, as well as each other, as we go through these bouts with doubts. But they are time consuming! Frank has attempted to move us along, but we will have greater success more rapidly if we are all engaged in monitoring the downward spiral. And we can counteract this tendency by facilitating energy sessions. I think this is absolutely a brilliant strategy."

"We are most pleased that you concur with this plan, for it is one that will aid the process that the Family of Friends pursues, and it is also one that will filter down to many others as the outreach program begins to circle the planet. Many will benefit from this shift in energy and the new awareness that it brings. Once again my friends, I express gratitude for your assistance. Please convey this message to our dear friends. I must bid you adieu now. In peace be, Dear Ones."

"Thank you for coming by," Marilyn whispered. *Always a pleasure to be with you!* Her internal communiqué did not go unnoticed, and her walking companion agreed with the sentiment. They continued up the hill in silence, as each processed their latest encounter with the elder gentleman.

"Marilyn, may I interrupt your thoughts?" My friend did not respond. This was unusual for her, but I trusted her reaction. I refrained from saying anything more, and returned to my own thoughts about the elder friend, our Family of Friends, and of the future. *So many questions; so few answers.* For a brief moment, my confidence waned, but then I remembered the recent encounter, and realized it was unnecessary. *I do not need all the answers. They will come when the time is right, but now in this moment, it is time for me to simply be at peace, knowing that I am not alone and trusting that assistance will be provided at the necessary time in the necessary place.* The realization of this truth gave me the peace of mind that was necessary for this particular moment. A smile came to my face when the poignant message was received and accepted. We continued without conversation until we reached our favorite spot, the one that always stopped us in our tracks. Below, down in the meadow, the deer were peacefully grazing. We had arrived just in time to witness their evening meal. Although they were aware of our arrival, these gracious creatures paid us no notice. They simply accepted us in their domain. I hoped and preferred to believe that they understood how fond we were of them.

"Their numbers are increasing," Marilyn quietly noted.

"Yes," I whispered in agreement. "Look how serene they are. I wonder what secrets they hold that we are yet to learn." She turned and stared at me.

"That is an interesting thought. Do you care to elaborate upon that idea?" Marilyn's inquiry sparked a topic of personal appeal. The part of me that wholeheartedly believes in the sagacious powers residing in the animal kingdom was eager to pursue such a conversation; however, another part of me quickly squelched my enthusiasm. Visions of past diminishments flooded my consciousness. Drowning in the immersion of old insults and injuries, my mind went blank and embarrassment quickly followed. Marilyn immediately sensed the change and came to my rescue.

"Stay with me!" she projected loudly. "Your energy has totally shifted. Look at me, please!" Her intervention instantly pulled me back to present.

"Oh my goodness, how quickly the mind can derail you! Thank you, Marilyn. Fortunately, your reaction was so swift that I didn't have time to dwell in the nonsense that the mind was recreating into my consciousness." Taking a deep breath, I returned fully into the present. "I'm so grateful this happened. Once again, I feel we have been provided with a demonstration of the topic we just discussed." Marilyn listened carefully as I explained what had just happened.

"So, the painful memories from your past surged forward and literally overtook your present experience." I nodded in agreement. "Please excuse my forward manner, but are these issues that you struggle with on a regular basis?"

"No!" I replied. "I haven't thought of these incidents in years, and that is why my reaction is so astonishing. In the blink of an eye those events from the past resurfaced with the same force that was experienced when they happened decades ago. I remember the sickening feeling of embarrassment and shame as if it were yesterday. No wonder my enthusiasm and energy plummeted so rapidly. I'm surprised and shocked that these events could extract such a profound reaction. Obviously, these painful memories were never properly attended. Now that this has been brought to my attention, I promise that I will address this necessary inner work at an appropriate time. But for now, Marilyn, let's discuss what we have learned from this incident."

"I've been reminded of two very important elements of engagement," she responded immediately. "First, pay attention! And stay alert while practicing the art of the active listening. Second, trust yourself. If we are truly actively engaged with someone and we think there has been a shift in his or her behavior, we must trust our intuition. We must respectfully check in with that person and confirm whether or not they are all right. The worst that can happen is that we simply misread the situation. Acting quickly, as we did today, can save someone from spiraling down into the depths of unpleasantness. I agree with you, my friend," Marilyn affirmed, "we just experienced another demonstration of what we should look out for not only in our small group, but also in the larger groups that will be unfolding soon. We've witnessed what can happen and we've learned at least one rescue technique for the future. I'm certain that other opportunities will arise, which will expand our repertoire of helping skills."

"Well spoken, Marilyn. And thank you again for assisting me through that misstep and also in articulating this synopsis. I think we are sufficiently prepared for handling future situations. Dee will be very pleased with this new addition to the To Do List." We began meandering up the hill again enjoying the beautiful scenery that surrounded us. Marilyn repeated an often-made statement regarding our good fortune. Living in this area and having access to the views and to the trails was a gift. It was comment worthy of repetition. Minutes later, she did what Marilyn does so well.

"Are you sure you're okay?" she asked quietly. "We moved through your experience so rapidly that I'm a bit concerned. We can take time now to do some processing, if you like." Her kind manner was always present and upfront. Never, in all the years of our friendship, had she fallen short in being a loving, caring friend. I trusted her without reservation and relied upon her wisdom and guidance. So, when Marilyn suggested reviewing or processing a situation, I gave it careful consideration.

"Thank you for being You! Your generosity doesn't surprise me at all; however, I do appreciate the offer to explore this incident more carefully. Actually, I feel really good about what just happened. I was given the opportunity to witness my mind at work, and it was amazing. Of course, we both know that our minds are functioning nonstop. But how often are we actually aware of what it is doing? I must admit that I simply take my mental acuity for granted. I don't regularly pay attention to how my mind is functioning. I just accept that it is working in collaboration and cooperation with my intentions. Well, what I witnessed today tells me I need to start paying more attention. It took the lead and I followed. Marilyn, if you hadn't taken action, I would have found myself in an abyss of disruption and despair. Instead, I had the good fortune of witnessing what was transpiring and where it was leading without actually experiencing the hardship associated with such event. I'm really fine! And I'm grateful. This was an important learning experience, and I can use this, Marilyn. I can use this information to help others. Reviewing the past doesn't mean you have to literally relive it. It's too shocking to one's health and well-being. There has to be a better way, and perhaps, we have seen a glimpse into a healthier approach. What I witnessed today demands much more consideration, but for the moment, I feel at peace with this. Thanks to you, dear friend!" Feeling complete with this discussion, my attention turned to my dear friend and walking buddy.

"How about you, Marilyn? How are you feeling about our brief encounter with our elder friend?" Thoughts of the elder brought a smile to her face.

"His presence brightens my day. He has such a positive energy about him and it's contagious. Whenever he shows up, I feel hopeful, reassured, and excited."

"Then, all is well!" I whispered.

"Yes! All is well!" Marilyn replied.

~ 3 ~

"**E**verett, dear, are you awake?" Jan's husband considered remaining silent, but in that fleeting moment, his beloved's impatience rose. A gentle nudge on his shoulder urged the situation forward.

"Are you aware of the hour, dear?"

"Yes, dear, I am."

"I assume this is urgently important and cannot wait another second."

"Your assumption is correct," she nudged him again. "Everett, dear, we have company. Will you please be hospitable?" Her husband immediately turned over and sat up. Jan was already upright with the bedcovers tucked tightly around her.

"My goodness, this is a surprise and a delight," his voice was welcoming and revealed no signs of someone suddenly awakened in the middle of the night.

"I have arrived at an awkward time, my fellow travelers, and for this I apologize; however, as you so accurately stated, this is an urgent and important matter." Both Jan and Everett repositioned themselves in an attempt to demonstrate some level of respect and dignity for this unusual occasion.

"Please make yourselves comfortable, my friends. I have interrupted your slumber; please do not feel that you must accommodate my unexpected arrival.

The time has come, my friends. The book that is being discussed must come to fruition. Your plans are exceptional and extensive. Now the plans must be actualized and presented in a desirable format. Enough conversation has transpired, my friends. All that is needed is available. The written word must now begin.

I beseech you my friends, face the challenge. Allay your fears about writing this book and face the task from another perspective. You are here to assist the people of Earth. Presume you have arrived to a setting that is in an impending crisis situation and imagine how you would participate in aiding the inhabitants who are in denial of their dilemma. Imagine this my friends, and then accept your truth. This is the situation that you are facing and you cannot allow fear to be your guide. Every action taken on behalf of the Earth is important. Your participation in writing and presenting this book to the people of Earth is important. Your role in assisting the Earth matters. Your role in helping the people of Earth matters. My dear friends, the Earth matters, and she desperately requires your assistance.

I come, my friends, to encourage you to move forward. The ideas you have amassed are plentiful; no more are required at this point. Because this situation continues to worsen, we cannot delay the project. You and your associates will continue to discover more information to be shared, as the Earth's wellness continues to decline, and this new information will be relayed through various media opportunities and through the outreach project that is in development. The project as it is progressing allows for future distribution of information. But for now, the task that is essential to complete is the writing of the book. The time is now, my friends. Action must be taken.

Similar conversations will be had with your Family of Friends. The message of urgency will be delivered. Once again, my friends, I am most grateful to be in your presence. Rest well now, please. You will find that sleep will come quickly and you will awaken refreshed in the morning. I bid you adieu, my dear friends."

"Are you awake, dear?" The question often issued in the Smith household came by way of another voice the morning after the unexpected visit during the night. Jan instantly jumped in response to Everett's question. She was shocked by their role reversal.

"Oh, my goodness!" Jan's eyes sparkled in the sunlight filtering through the window into their bedroom. "What time is it, Ev? Have I missed something?" Chuckling quietly, Everett wondered how his wife and best friend could awaken so energetically from a sound sleep.

"The time is later than usual, dear, and no, you have not missed anything, but I would like to talk if you are available." Jan quickly rose, assumed her usual position, and poised herself for their early morning discussion. Alert and available, she pronounced her readiness to proceed.

"Please tell me what's on your mind, dear. I am eager to hear what you have to say. And I do apologize for sleeping late this morning, Everett. Don't know what's wrong with me. As you well know, this is not my style."

"No need for an apology, Jan. Actually, it was nice sleeping in for a change." Readjusting his own position to accommodate hers gave Everett additional time to figure out how to broach the yet-to-be announced topic. Because Jan was the one who typically spearheaded their sunrise conversations, he was feeling odd about his present situation. She sensed his discomfort but chose to remain quiet. She knew her husband could manage the awkwardness. "This may sound nutty, Jan, but I think something unusual happened last night. Well, as we both know, a lot of unusual things happen in our lives, but the point is, I'm not sure if something really happened or if it was just a dream. So, I wanted to know if you remember something unusual happening last night." Jan's puzzled face was not the answer Everett was hoping for. He attempted patience, but it was a wasted effort. Again, Jan's intuitive sense was alerting her to his uneasiness.

"Tell me more, Ev. Obviously, something happened so let's talk about."

"Well," he began, and then stopped himself. Recognizing this was the second time that he had used the overused four-letter word, he addressed his personal commitment to the Earth. "Wellness to the Earth! Old friend, we are here, and we are aware of your circumstances. Please hold on. More will be honoring you soon, Dear Friend, but in this moment, may Jan and I send you a particle of our God Pure Energy? With your permission, we will do so now." And this they did, each in his and her own way, and when the energy transfer was done, they each took a long deep breath. A relaxed state took over their bodies as they sat resting next to each other.

"That was wonderful, Everett. Thank you for bringing an energy session into our morning connection."

"Yes, we must remember our commitment to the Earth, Jan. She needs us! And we cannot allow our own personal matters to distract us from this reality. I am shocked how easy it is to forget about her situation. Her health issues are the most important issue transpiring on this planet and yet, we go on with our lives as if her life, her health, is not a priority. I'm speaking in generalities here, but for the most part, I believe my statement is founded in truth. If a family member or a dear friend were in the hospital, we would adjust our schedules accordingly to provide assistance in whatever ways we could, but that isn't happening for the Earth. We go about our days as if this issue is not really an issue. What is it going to take to make us wake up about her crisis?" Everett's frustration with himself and with people in general was evident. His discomfort with the Earth's situation reminded him about the unusual experience he had during the night.

"Jan, this takes me back to what I am wanting to talk about. I think our elder friend came to me in a dream last night. Or maybe it really happened; I'm not sure. Do you remember having a similar experience, dear?" Everett's question triggered a memory. The expressions that crossed Jan's face were worthy of a photograph. Surprise, recall, recognition, and gratitude, all transpired in a matter of seconds.

"Oh, my word!" she whispered. "Thank you, thank you, thank you. How could I have forgotten this? Oh, Ev, this was not a dream! Our friend really visited us and he delivered his urgent message about completing the book. It was real, dear! It really happened!" As Jan spoke, her husband's memory returned. They sat quietly for a moment as the powerful message actualized within each of them, and then, as if mutually orchestrated, they both exited the bed, grabbed their respective journals, and situated themselves in their preferred chairs.

Time passed as personal issues unfolded upon the pages in front of the Smiths. First, the concerns were addressed…and released. And then the book came into focus. Each wrote for several hours before a period of rest was necessary. Jan looked up initially, but was quickly followed by Everett. Smiles came forward as they both realized the book had been initiated. Deep breaths were taken, and sighs followed. They had faced their fears and met the challenge.

~ 4 ~

"**A**re you ready for a break, dear?" Dee waited to be certain that her husband had heard her request. She was confident that he had when the hum of the lathe came to a halt. She quietly closed the door so that he could have a private moment with his work before coming up for breakfast. Dee knew Frank well, and she assumed rightfully so that he would require a moment of conversation before exiting his workshop. This was his sacred space and it demanded courteous and respectful intentions at all time. Frank never presumed he had dominion over the pieces of art that he pursued. Instead the process was one of mutual consent between the selected piece of wood and the design that Frank saw in his mind. Because the wood could intuit his imagery and vice versa, a design was cooperatively developed and decided upon before the first cut was taken. But the collaboration did not end there. With each step taken, consultation was sought and considered before the design of the object was finally reached and executed.

He turned the mounted piece of maple slowly in one direction and then the other, carefully observing the black irregular lines that were surfacing. Revealing the spalted areas of a piece of wood was a delight for any woodworker. It gave one the illusion of enhancing that which was already beautifully created by nature. Frank was pleased thus far, but knew it wasn't his opinion that matter. "So, how are you feeling about this?" he asked the work in progress. "I can take several more layers off, if you prefer. That will reveal more of the spalting, which is always pleasant to the eye. The shape itself is forming nicely, but again, this is your decision. I'll just let you think about it for a while why I go up and spend some time with that lovely lady who's waiting for me. I'll leave the light on. Take your time; there's no hurry." And with that said, Frank headed upstairs to greet his beloved. "Good morning, dear!" His greeting came as Dee was in her own process of revealing a masterpiece. He arrived just in time to witness the orange cranberry scones being removed from the oven. "Oh, my goodness! The aroma is intoxicating!" Dee giggled and agreed.

"So, how's everything going down in the workshop?" she asked as they situated themselves around the breakfast table. Ordinarily, Frank was reluctant to speak about his creative endeavors, but his shyness seemed to be

41

losing its grip upon him. A smile immediately crossed his face and his eyes were twinkling, which was a very good sign.

"I think we have another winner in the making!" he declared. "I'm so grateful we went back and retrieved more pieces of that remarkable maple. It has graced us with such beauty…talk about fulfilling one's life purpose." Frank paused as he pondered the tree's passage through its lifetime. He marveled at the life of a tree, first as a seedling, then as a picture of beauty in the forest, and now, even after its passing, the tree nurtured the forest bed while also providing beautiful artwork for those fortunate enough to be the recipients of its remaining form. "This tree has served well." Frank's tone revealed his admiration for the splendor of Mother Nature. "We're very lucky to have the privilege of hosting this tree in our home for a brief moment before we gift it to someone who will also cherish it as we do." Again, Dee nodded in agreement. She always enjoyed listening to her husband talking about his collaboration with Nature. His appreciation was heart rending and touched her to the depths of her innermost being.

"Sounds like you are having a marvelous morning, dear." Her comment coincided with his first bite of scone. He smiled happily. Frank was indeed having a good day.

"So, what's on our agenda today?" Dee asked. Frank chuckled quietly. He knew this question was an indication that his beloved had a plan. "I heard you chuckling under your breath and I know you think I'm up to something," she paused for just the right amount to convince him that he was indeed accurate in his supposition. "And perhaps, you are right, dear. However, it's not an agenda, as much as it is a yearning. I woke up this morning with a hankering to go to the scenic overlook. I think we are supposed to go there, Frank. Can't really explain it, but I think we are intended to go there this morning!" Frank immediately got up and started pouring the remaining coffee in a thermos. Dee took the cue and gathered the extra scones and put them into a container. In mere minutes, they were ready to travel.

"Good morning, my friends. I see you have received my message." As always, the elder's arrival was impeccable. The Sandersons were delighted, and quickly welcomed him to the small breakfast table.

"So, I was right!" declared Dee. "We were supposed to meet you at the overlook, weren't we?"

"It is true, I desire your company this morning. However, it seems more expedient for us to meet in this location. I am most pleased that you are available."

"As are we," responded Frank. "Of course, we are always glad to see you, but it seems you are on a mission this morning. What's going on, friend?"

"I come with urgency in my heart." The elder friend's visits were always intentional and purposeful; however, this visit had a qualitative difference. Both Dee and Frank intuited their friend's sense of urgency before he mentioned it. *"As you both know so well, the Earth's situation demands attention now. Although positive strides are being made, her health continues to decline. Her need for immediate assistance grows. I come this day to ask you both to take leadership roles regarding the development and publication of the book that you and the Circle of Friends are pursuing. The time is now. We must move forward and this must be done rapidly. My friends, action must be taken. Please hear me and know that what is spoken is the truth. The time is now. She can no longer endure delays. Prepare the book now, my friends."* His sense of urgency was palpable. The Sandersons accepted his appeal without hesitation or question.

"Have you spoken to the others?" Dee assumed he had, but desired verification.

"I have connected with everyone but the Joneses, and will meet with them after leaving your company. They will of course be as cooperative as you, but the process demands leadership. Do not allow the group to fall into doubt and/or despair. Push them forward and bring this book project to completion. I trust you grasp the importance of this, my friends. I will be available to you at all times. Do not hesitate to reach out for assistance. As you will reach out to the masses, so too will we reach out to assist you and your Family of Friends. The time is now, my friends. I cannot adequately impress upon you the significance of these four small words. The time is now.

I bid you adieu. Know that I am near at all times. In peace be, Old Friends!"

And with that said, the elder friend faded into nothingness.

"Do you still want to go to the overlook, Dee?" asked Frank.

"No, I don't think it is necessary now. I think the message was delivered and received." Dee pulled out two scones from the container and placed them on the plates that still remained on the table. Likewise, Frank unscrewed the thermos and filled their cups with coffee. They ate in silence, each lost in the meanderings of their respective minds. Eventually Frank asked if they should initiate a meeting. They agreed to give the elder some time to connect with Bill and Pat before doing so.

The Joneses pulled into the overlook just about the same time that Dee and Frank had been packing their breakfast goodies for the same destination. As always, the view captured their attention. They held hands as they looked out over the meadow below. "I'm so glad we both had the urge to come here this morning," signed Pat.

"Me too!" responded Bill. "Actually, I think this site was in my dream this morning just before I woke up. It was strange. Just felt like we were supposed to come here, so I guess it wasn't a surprise when you brought it up. But I'm glad you did!" Bill squeezed her hand tighter and she responded in like manner.

"Such a small but lovely gesture," she whispered.

"What's that, dear?" he asked.

"This," Pat replied while raising their clasped hands. "I just love holding hands. I hope we never tire of this, because it is one of my favorite ways of expressing our connection." The couple did indeed love to hold hands. Although Bill had never really thought about it, Pat's comment made him realize how he had taken this gesture for granted. Truth is the Joneses are so accustomed to holding hands that it is second nature for them. They hold hands in the car. They hold hands while walking, and at night when they go to bed, they fall asleep hand-in-hand.

"Thank you for bringing this to my attention, Pat. You're right! It is a very comforting gesture. I'm glad we do this." Pat squeezed his hand tightly again and lifted his to her heart.

"Yes, me too!"

"Indeed, a loving gesture, it is!" The familiar voice took the Joneses by surprise. They turned about immediately to greet their old friend.

"Come join us," invited Pat. "The view is breathtaking as always!" The elder gentleman approached the railing and responded accordingly. A deep breath was taken and a corresponding sigh was released.

"A beautiful view complemented by a loving gesture of connection. You model for others the quiet love that thrives between you. I am most grateful to be in your presence." The couple was flattered by their friend's kind words. Bill wondered if he was responsible for their urge to visit this locale this morning. An answer to his thoughts came immediately.

"Yes, I must acknowledge that a suggestion was implanted into your dreams during the night. I am so grateful that you received my invitation to meet at this favorite spot."

"How do you do that?" Bill's insistence overrode good manners, but the elder understood the impulsivity of the inquisitive mind, and he accepted that Bill was particularly curious about unusual events.

"My friend, some day, we will have ample time to speak of such matters, but today is not that day. I come with urgency as my guide and I bring you a message that must be heard and addressed. My friends, the time is now! As you well know, this beautiful planet is suffering from the environmental changes that are transpiring all about her. She struggles to maintain sustainable functionality but her efforts are hampered by those who reside upon her. The blatant disregard for her well being brings her to the brink of a catastrophic possibilities." His message came to an abrupt halt. Delivering such a message takes a toll upon the messenger. The elder friend breathed deeply while the recipients of the message stood fast, wanting to assist but not knowing how to do so.

"Your patience and your kind intentions are gratefully received." After another long inhalation, the elder began again. *"My friends, the challenge that lies ahead must be addressed. The completion of the book that the Family of Friends is pursuing is strategically significant to the recovery process of this remarkable Life Being. Many projects are underway and all of them are essential to her wellness. The book plays a vital role in her healing process. Please accept this truth even if you cannot yet comprehend its importance. Begin today, my friends! Lay your fears aside and begin writing your portion of the book. Take the first step and the rest of the task will follow quickly and easily. I do not make false statements. The task awaits you and you are ready to meet this task. Please begin, my friends. For the sake of your children and all others on this planet, please take the step. Your contribution is essential to the recovery of our beautiful Mother Earth. The time is now!*

I am most grateful for this time together, but now, I must take my leave, for other tasks await me. Please know that you are ready for this mission of extreme importance, and also, please know that I am but a breath away. In peace be, my friends." And with that said, the elder faded away. The Joneses took his departure in stride. They had grown accustomed to his disappearing acts. But his message gave them pause. Each stared out over the vista contemplating the magnitude of the message they had just received. Pat was the first to break the silence.

"We should probably return home, Bill. I imagine another meeting is in the making." Her husband nodded and reached for her hand as they walked towards the car. "You knew I was going to say that, didn't you?" Bill nodded again.

"And did you know, Pat, that I was marveling at the life we are living?"

"Yes, and you were also thinking about stopping at the bakery to pick up some goodies for the gathering even though we don't know when the meeting will be scheduled." They both giggled about their improving telepathic abilities. Whether it was intuition or just common sense in this situation, Bill concluded the obvious.

"I suspect Dee's message will come through once we get out of the hills. I feel certain that she and Frank are already on this. Thank goodness for those two!" The Joneses left the scenic overlook, both lost in their own thoughts. It didn't take long before they reached an area that had phone service. Pat's cell phone alerted them to a voicemail; it came as no surprise that Dee had reached out to the group for an emergency meeting. However, what was a surprise was Dee's suggestion that they meet the following evening. The couple looked puzzled, and then, a smile crossed Pat's face.

"She's leaving the day open for us to start working on our project. Brilliant!"

~ 5 ~

"**T**hanks for hosting tonight, dear! It's always a pleasure to be in your lovely home." Dee and Frank marched through the front door with arms filled with various treats and placed them carefully on the dining room table that was prepared for the evening's fare. Before I could even greet them, Dee surprised me with her intuitive capabilities. "Has your house started conversing with you yet, dear? It wants to, you know. It delights in your pleasantries and appreciates your acknowledgements of its beauty."

"Dee Sanderson, how do you know this? I have not shared this secret with you. How do you know this?" Her look stopped me in my tracks.

"Your house knows dear, and it does not keep secrets!" Before the conversation could go any further, the other members of our Family of Friends entered the door. Greetings and fond hugs were shared on the way to the living room. And then the meeting convened.

"Dear ones, thank you for coming. I believe this is going to be a very interesting evening." Smiles and quietly spoken comments circled the room. "Before we begin our work, I would like to ask Frank to lead us in a meditation for the Earth." Frank had come prepared for this. He snatched a piece of folded paper from his shirt pocket, opened it, and appeared ready to start when he stopped and looked in my direction.

"I believe you are better suited for this evening's meditation. Will you gift us with your wisdom?"

The word 'wisdom' gave me pause and old tendencies were wont to take action. I battled to keep my eyes from rolling about in their sockets and refused to follow the misleading tangents of my mind. Instead, I remembered the repetitive message from our elder friend…the time is now!

"Thank you, Frank. I am happy to facilitate a meditation." I took a deep breath and my friends did the same. A smile came to my face as I witnessed their immediate reaction. This was becoming second nature for us. After several more long breaths, I sensed the readiness of my familial group.

"Beloved friends, far and near, please join us now as we quiet our minds and open our hearts to the potential that lies within us. Let us be embraced by the energy of All That Is so that we may share this essential energy amongst ourselves and with the beautiful Life Being Earth. All who are listening, regardless of your location, you are invited into this circle of healing intentions. We come together on behalf of the Earth. We join our energies so that she may benefit from the healing energy generated from and through us. Her wellness is our highest priority…and all who wish to participate in this healing session are welcome.

Please prepare yourselves everyone. Each of you has your own preferred way of moving into the silence. Make yourself ready now, as you are so inclined to do. Take the necessary deep, prolonged breaths. Quiet your mind…and open your heart to participating in this act of energy transference.

As we prepare ourselves, rest comfortably with the energy source that lies within. As does this energy serve you so too can it serve others. Trust this reality, dear friends, for it is a universal truth, a gift that is granted to all in existence. Breathe this awareness into the depths of your innermost being. Sit quietly as the energy within accepts the opportunity to assist another who is in need." Time passed, and in its passing, the energy within, aware of the intention to aid another Life Being, grew more powerful.

"Beloved Earth, we gather on your behalf. Our combined energies amass in preparation for an energy transfusion. Old Friend, caretaker of all for whom you provide residence, we are aware of your present situation and we wish to offer our healing energies to assist you with your recovery process. With your permission, we will proceed." Again time passed. No resistance to our offer appeared evident.

"Unless anyone senses differently, we will now begin our efforts to share our energy with the Earth. My friends, I remind you to send only one particle of your healing energy. As we all learned, our source energy is extremely powerful, and we must be mindful that our combined energies are even more potent, therefore we must be gentle in our transmission to the Earth.

Access your beautiful mind now, my dear friends, and picture your favorite place on this remarkable planet. Imagine yourself in that special location, the one that captures your heart each time it comes to memory. Be in that place now as we follow through with the energy transmission. Imagine your particle of source energy rising from within you and allow it to manifest to even a greater size than it already is, and then, when you are ready offer this energy to Mother Earth. Release your source energy into the Earth, and trust in the power of this healing energy. Trust that this energy infusion will assist in restoring her back to full health.

Believe, dear friends! Believe in the healing energy that resides within you and within all, and trust the power of this universal source energy. And with your intentions fulfilled, gently disconnect your energy from the Earth's and return to your own body. Rest in your body, knowing that your act of generosity is deeply appreciated. Rest."

Time passed as it always does. Eventually, movement began to stir within the Circle of Friends. Eyes opened, limbs were stretched, and a sense of well being radiated from the group. Frank turned in my direction and winked. I accepted his action as the compliment it was intended to be.

"Well done!" expressed Bill. Numerous other comments were made about the meditation, all of which were complimentary and hopeful. Jan's description of her experience was most indicative of the group meditation.

"I just loved participating in that process. The connection I felt with all of you was so heartwarming. Once again, I was reminded of how important this family is to me. Everett and I are so grateful to be sharing this experience with all of you. We really do think of you as family and it gives us great comfort to do so." Other comments attested to similar feelings, but Jan had more to say. "And there was more," she declared. "I felt a much greater connection during this meditation than I have before. I know this may sound crazy, but I truly felt connected to the universe. We were not alone!" she insisted. "Others joined us during this process, and I felt like they were family as well. It was a remarkable experience. I'm so glad to be part of this. I feel like I'm doing exactly what I'm supposed to be doing. And it feels great!

Thank you for facilitating that session for us. It was lovely."

"Thank you, Jan!" Dee's insertion into the conversation indicated we were moving into another direction. "I think your summary of your experiences resonates with all of us." Dee turned to me and smiled. "I hope you are feeling good about this feedback. You did a lovely job, dear." Once again, she was intuitively correct. I was feeling good about the session. It had gone well. And I too enjoyed the company of our companions. Indeed, we were not alone.

"By the way," added Dee, "I do trust that our efforts were beneficial to the Earth. And I believe we provided her with a significant dose of good energy today. It makes me happy to know we can serve in this way."

"Yes, so do I!" Frank's voice began softly but then became more exuberant. "In fact, I think she is very grateful for our kindness. And I believe that we will be even more helpful to her when we publish this book that we're intended to address. So, shall we shift our focus to the issue of the moment?" He glanced about the room making eye contact with everyone. "I think it is safe to say that we've all had an encounter recently. And I'm presuming that we've all received a similar message. The time is now!" His voice accentuated the last four words. We all know these words speak the truth, so let's just jump in now and get this project moving." Turning back to his best friend of over fifty years, he urged her to take charge. "We need your guidance, Dee! Help us walk through this chapter of our lives with grace and efficiency."

Dee remembered every word their elder friend had conveyed. She had all the tools and materials that were needed. And she had the best associates to work with that anyone could possibly desire. Indeed, this group was ready… and so was she. Although she did not need to rise to take the next step forward, she did need to bend down to gather her notebook that had been at her side for the last twenty-four hours. And in so doing, the proverbial next step was taken. "My friends, I am so happy to be with you. We are so blessed! We are gifted with each other's company and we share a life purpose. How lovely is that?" Her smile brightened the room. "Isn't it wonderful to have an invisible friend who unexpectedly appears and helps us to understand that we have an important mission to accomplish? Sounds like make-believe, doesn't it? And yet, it is really true. So, again I say…we are so blessed!

My friends, let's get focused. I assume each of you has had a conversation with our dear friend, and I also assume you have been on task since that connection. So, let's begin with a progress report." Dee's work model was streamlined, to the point, and end goal oriented. Bill and Pat responded immediately.

"We're ready if that suits everyone," announced Pat. Within minutes, their update was succinctly presented and a rough draft was handed out for review. Initially, the shuffling of papers was the only sound heard in the room. Then murmurs of excitement raced around the circle while the Joneses sat rigidly waiting for some dreadful literary critique. When it didn't happen, they started breathing again, and actually realized their friends were reacting positively.

"Pat," nudged her husband. "The disapproval we were expecting didn't happen!" The couple laughed with relief and gave each other a high five. Everett, observing their reaction, understood the stress his friends were releasing, for he and Jan were also apprehensive about sharing their work.

"You know, I recognize the anxiety that you two just went through, and I want to say thank you. Thank you for going first. And thank you for doing such a great job. You deserve high fives and applause from all of us!" Congratulations and praise were hailed about the group before Everett continued his thought. "Even though our wonderful elder friend instructed us to disregard our fears and doubts, it is difficult to eliminate old habits. I felt for you Pat as you were birthing the project, and then, my heart ached for both of you while you waited for what must have seemed like an eternity for us to provide you with feedback. And by the way, in case you missed any of the feedback, which you probably did, it was good. In fact, it was excellent.

You've really brought your ideas regarding family connections forward in a way that will aid everyone who experiences what we have gone through. Your section of the book will resonate with folks and it will be very comforting. Great job! I have a much greater appreciation now for what you two have gone through with these unusual adventures, and I truly mean this when I say that your contribution is significant."

"I agree!" added Marilyn. "I've always felt favorable about your ideas to include families into this outreach process, but your materials really exemplify the importance of doing so. After all, the goal of outreach is to increase awareness! That goal would be diminished if we elected to keep information from our families. You two have been wonderful examples of how to carefully approach familial connection and your materials inspire ways to successfully facilitate healthy and mindful communication. The added factor of this inclusive process is the expansion of information that results because of it. This is really good work. Thank you both!"

Dee observed in silence. *They proceed well. They are acknowledging doubts and fears, but they are not dwelling in the uncertainties. The elder was right. There is no time for such digressions. You apprised them well, dear friend.* Her thoughts were not hers alone. Others from afar noted her observations and concurred, but they did not convey their thoughts to those on the Island in the Sky. Their thoughts remained their own, as did their joy and appreciation.

"Well," inserted Frank, who quickly recovered from his oversight regarding the use of the overused four-letter word. "Wellness to the Earth!" he declared rambunctiously. "And wellness to all of you, my friends, who are so successfully remaining on target and refraining from taking trails that lead us down into the distractions of our fears and doubts. We have acknowledged our susceptibility to them, but we have not been misled into the depths of that discomfort. We are indeed making progress." Turning back to his dear wife, he urged her to continue with a wink of the left eye.

"Thank you, dear. And who would like to go next? I am excited to hear more." Without hesitation, Marilyn leaned forward in her chair as a sign that she was ready to take the lead.

"I openly admit that the Joneses are a hard act to follow; however, I am so taken by the loving atmosphere in this room that I feel absolutely safe to proceed. Thank you my dear friends for being such a remarkable family. How often I listen to folks who cannot say the same for their families. I recognize how blessed we are, and because I do, I am comfortable sharing my ideas.

My time with all of you has been so rewarding. Words fail me! Suffice it to say that I am grateful to be part of this incredible journey and so happy that we are sharing this experience together. As you may imagine, I have often wondered what my role in this adventure was intended to be. While I have been very excited about the possibilities, I felt clueless about what my contribution would actually be. And in many ways, I still feel some uncertainty; however, my reaction to the uncertainty is now very different. I no longer feel that I have nothing to offer. In fact, I am certain that I have something to offer, even though, I may not know exactly what that will be until the moment arises. My goals at this point are to show up, to be a calming presence, and to have patience. I trust myself to do this, and I also trust that opportunities will surface for my gifts to be shared."

Like the Joneses, Marilyn had a folder with copies of her rough draft. She handed one set to her left and another to the right and then watched her private papers circle the room. A moment of anxiety captured her when she awakened to the reality that a significant part of her life story was being shared for the first time. The moment demanded a deep breath. *They already know this*, she thought. *But others will not!* The mind continued to conjure up reasons for concern. Marilyn did what Marilyn does so well. She took another deep breath, she showed up, she became a calming presence, and she sat patiently waiting for a response from her friends. *There is nothing to fear.* Marilyn wondered if the words heard were her own or another's and then realized that it really didn't matter. The intention was accurate. There was nothing to fear from these beloved friends or from the readers in the future. Her story was hers, and it was real. She didn't have to prove her story to anyone, nor did she have to justify its relevance. Marilyn simply shared the truth of her experience with the elder gentleman and the remarkable impact that it had on her life. She shared her bewilderment, her skepticism, her joy, her vulnerabilities, her ecstasy, and her desire to know more. She openly, lovingly, and wholeheartedly shared this life-changing experience including the ongoing effect it had upon her. Her hope in sharing this story was that it would aid others who were having their own experiences. Acknowledging that everyone's experience was different and honoring that truth was part of her desire to assist others. Recognizing the similarities of the journeys was another aspect that she wanted to focus upon, which hopefully would help others know that they are not alone in their process. Marilyn shared her soul in her writings, so others would benefit from her calming presence. She opened the door and invited people into a space of safety where they could share their own stories. Marilyn's contribution would assist others in trusting themselves while also teaching them to open their hearts to these life experiences that people all around the world were experiencing. Marilyn's quiet, yet powerful way of telling her story would pave the way for others to do the same.

She sat patiently while her friends read her story. Silence consumed the circle of friends. Even the turning of pages was done so carefully that a sound could not be heard. As each person finished reading her story, eyes would close and the silence would continue. Peace befell the room. Marilyn remained patient. Finally, in unison, a deep breath was consumed, and eyes opened. "Welcome back," she whispered.

Frank, who was not one to quickly embrace sentimentality, spoke first. "My heart is full." As he raised his head to face Marilyn, tears glimmered in his eyes. "It was a privilege to read your story, Marilyn. "I am deeply honored to be here at this moment. We are the first readers of the book we've been called to bring forward. That in itself is a remarkable story, as is your story, dear. People will read this, Marilyn, and they will live your experience. I'm very grateful to be a part of this." Frank pulled out a handkerchief, as only a man of his generation would do, and wiped the tears from his eyes. He could speak no more.

Dee looked on and shared her husband's tears and they were not the only ones with moist eyes. She started to speak, but chose not to. This was a time to let the others take the lead. She just sat, holding the space for her beloved Frank.

"I can't add anything more to what Frank just said, but I do want to express my appreciation, Marilyn. Your story summarizes the experience we've all shared during the last few months. And it needs to be told! You did a marvelous job. This story matters, and it will make a difference! Thank you!" Everett's words warmed her heart, as did the nods and smiles from those who concurred with him. Marilyn's walking buddy who would normally reach out and touch her on the knee sat remarkably still. The stillness emanating from her friend could not go unnoticed.

"Are you okay?" asked Marilyn. I seemed to return from a faraway distance. I was present, and yet, I was elsewhere. It took a moment for me to ground myself.

"I'm fine." The comment demanded more, but in the moment I was still trying to find myself.

Marilyn's question brought me back from a place I do not know, and yet, while I was in this undisclosed location, I remained here among my family of friends. I remembered reading Marilyn's story and hearing Frank's emotional response, and Everett's as well; however, as I experienced everything that was transpiring around me, I was elsewhere. And while in this other place, I had an experience that I also remembered clearly.

"My friends, I believe it is safe to say that I just had an unusual experience. Where I was, I do not know, and I am incapable of describing the setting; however, I do remember the encounter and the message that I am to deliver to all of you. Please be with me, my friends, for this is a new experience for me." I turned to face my friend and walking companion and attempted to explain my situation.

"While I was reading your beautiful story Marilyn, I was taken away. Forgive me, but I do not know how to describe this in any other way than I just did. Obviously, my body was still here with all of you and I remember everything that happened, but at the same time, I was somewhere else. And in this other place, I was given information to share with all of you. So let me do that now, because I am afraid, perhaps unnecessarily, that I may forget something.

First, let me quickly report that while in this other place, I was aware of the presence of others. Even though I could not see anyone or anything specifically, I sensed their presence. Actually, their presence could not be missed, because their energy frequencies were so profoundly high that I was absolutely certain I was accompanied. My goodness, they are such powerful life forces. I suspect they are the Companions of our elder friend, but that is pure speculation on my part. My imagination may be working overtime regarding this.

On the other hand, there are no doubts about the message received. It was as easily heard as the conversations we shared with our elder friend when he was in invisible form." A deep breath was taken as I prepared to present the message. A twinge of anxiety gave me a moment of queasiness, but it was readily released when words of truth fleeted through my mind. *You are among dear friends; there is nothing to fear.* Whether this was my own thought or a message from those beyond, I do not know, and it didn't matter, because the truth had been heard regardless of its origination.

I reached out to Marilyn on my left and Frank on my right, who both did the same until the circle was complete. And with the circle intact, I invited everyone to share and enjoy a deep, elongated breath. I began with the same sentence that was first spoken to me. "Old Friends, we are deeply grateful for your participation in the Mission of Rescue. Our beloved friend, Earth, is in great need as you well know, and your willingness to assist in her recovery process brings great joy to all in the Universe. She is a beloved Life Being who is deeply cherished by all in existence and we are relieved that you are willing to assist with her rejuvenation process.

Many gather on her behalf and also for the human species; however, we cannot intrude upon another's evolutionary path. Humankind must make decisions about their future. Either they choose to continue in peaceful harmony with their gracious host and benefactor or they choose a route that is not in their best interest. To those who bear witness to this unfolding crisis, the answer is simple. Why would you choose the latter when peaceful coexistence with the Life Being Earth is the obvious way of continuance?

Beloved Friends, many residing upon this planet are beginning to change, and there is still time to assist the Earth back to a place of wellness, but time is the critical factor. Every delay in her restoration process matters. Every absurd pretense that her condition is not an issue creates more delays. There is no longer time for delays. The time to come to her aid is upon you. The time for her survival and also for yours is now. The truth cannot be spoken any more truthfully or simply. Humankind's future is dependent upon the survival of the planet Earth. Assist her now or your future will be limited and most unpleasant.

Dear friends, we take no pleasure in bringing this terrible news to the good peoples of Earth; however, we must do so because you refuse to face the evidence that blatantly lies before you. The truth is available to everyone. One does not need to be a person of science to recognize that she is suffering. One does not have to wait for political action to take action oneself. A Life Being is in distress and each of you is capable of assisting her. You turn to others expecting them to address this situation when you are capable of addressing her wellness yourself. You act as if you have no voice in this situation, yet you have more than a voice. You have the power within you to assist this planet. You have the power to heal her, and yet, you disregard her circumstances as if she is of no consequence. Let us speak bluntly. Without the vitality of this planet, you will not survive. Those who live in denial regarding this truth will cease to exist.

Dear friends of Earth, we gather around your planet in hopes that you will choose to continue your existence. We hope you will choose to emerge from your shameful lack of regard for another Life Being, and we hope you will choose to assist the one that has assisted humankind since long before you came into existence. The choice is yours. We pray you will make the right decision.

Those who have loved and cherished this remarkable Life Being since she came into existence will remain to assist her, for her continuance is essential to all others in existence. We will not abandon her. We hope that humankind will choose to do the same. The Earth can and will continue beyond your wayward ways, but you cannot and will not continue without her vital life energy. Please ponder this, dear friends, as you make your decisions.

Old friends of the Circle of Eight, we speak bluntly with you in hopes that you will fully comprehend the magnitude of this crisis situation. Our hearts ache as we share this devastating news with you, and yet, for the sake of all humankind, the truth must be spoken. Your assistance brings us great hope. Through the messages shared in your book, the truth has the potential for reaching the masses. Old friends, within you and all other beings, lies a healing power that can restore the Earth's health. She is a very large being, but there are over 7 billion people on this planet with the innate ability to heal self and others. The ability has been within the human species since it came into being, but the truth was long ago lost to your memory. It is most unfortunate, but the gift still resides within, and with very little direction it readily awakens to its full potential. Old friends, your assistance in sharing this news with the people of Earth will greatly aid us in restoring her back to full health. Your work is critically important. Your assistance is essential. You must continue, dear friends, and you must make haste. The Earth is depending upon you. We hope our words do not burden you. The truth is, you are capable of the tasks. Everything you need to assist the Earth lies within you. Because of your efforts, the children of Earth will be reminded of their inner abilities. And because of your own experiences shared within the pages of this book, they will recognize that there is more to existence than they presently remember. Hopefully, they realize they are not alone, and with all these new awarenesses, we pray they will realize the necessity of their participation in the mission to save the Earth.

Old friends, the roles you play in this critically important mission are substantial. We are sorry so much rests upon your shoulders, and yet, we must ask more of you. We beg you to continue. We beseech you to spread the word to all who will listen. And we implore you to make haste. The time is now."

With a deep breath, I came to the end of the message that was received from the unknown messenger or messengers. I sat in awe and disbelief. *How could these words have come through me so easily and accurately?* I remembered hearing the words that were spoken to me while I was absent during Marilyn's presentation. I remembered coming back to be present with my friends, and I remembered sharing the message with these friends in the same exact way that they were presented to me. I was not summarizing or paraphrasing the message. I was repeating it exactly as it was spoken to me. *How could this happen? How could I have done this?* My mind raced in many different directions trying to discern what had just transpired. As I scrambled for answers, my friends remained silent. *Oh my goodness, I've been so lost in my own meanderings that I did not notice that everyone was perfectly still.* Embarrassed by my lack of consideration, I instantly regained my sense of self. My observations told me that they were not in distress, although the intensity of the message certainly could have led them into a state of concern. I watched carefully. Their breathing was steady and relaxed. There were no visual signs of discomfort. I was puzzled.

Dee was the first to open her eyes. She glanced around the room and then focused upon me. *"Everyone is fine, dear. We are meditating. Will you please join us?"* We simultaneously closed our eyes and followed our companions into a state of peaceful tranquility. How long we remained in the quiet, I do not know. But it was lovely. Eventually, my favorite Tibetan bell welcomed us back into the present. Movement was heard as we shifted in our chairs and stretched our bodies, as each was wont to do.

"Well, my dear friend, you've had an adventure," Dee's attention focused upon me. Everyone noticed her use of the four-letter introduction and inwardly praised the Earth for her continued assistance. The practice was advancing, sometimes outwardly, sometimes within. The point being, the Earth was being acknowledged for her contributions.

"Yes, I have and it's a bit confusing, but I'm fine. And I hope all of you are as well."

"We're okay!" Frank declared for everyone. "Perhaps, I'm being presumptuous, so let me just speak for myself. I'm fine, and I'm grateful. Once again, I must say that it is a privilege to be here this evening. Goodness! That was a monumental experience, dear. From my perspective, you managed this incredible event really well, but I'm curious. How are you dealing with this internally? I imagine your mind is still reeling from this experience?" Jan's energy was pulsating from across the room. Even though she was striving to contain herself, she simply couldn't. I looked in her direction and welcomed her thoughts.

"Oh, please excuse me. Frank, thank you for broaching this conversation, because I too am very curious about what just happened. My goodness, friend, you were amazing. If I hadn't witnessed this myself, I'm not sure that I would have believed it. The words that came from your mouth sounded remarkably similar to those that we have often heard from our elder friend. How did you do this? How did it feel to have the words flowing through you?" Jan knew her energy was boundless, so she stopped herself. "Oh, please forgive me. This is just so exciting. Please just tell us how you are and what this experience was like for you."

"Tell us everything!" Marilyn's declaration lightened up the room. Everyone burst into laughter, which was a well-needed release. Playful chatter circled about the room. I imagined that my house was delighted with the banter. The delightful distraction gave me time to collect myself. *How will I speak of this,* I wondered.

"Well," I said, pausing briefly, "and I choose that word intentionally and purposefully, because this conversation, this gathering, is about the wellness of our planet. We are here for a reason and acknowledging our gratitude to the Earth should enter our conversations often. So, Dear Mother Earth, thank you for everything that you do for us. Thank you for providing us with a place to live and for all the beauty you bring into our lives. We are so grateful!"

"Amen!" echoed through the living room.

"Peace and wellness to the Earth," whispered Pat.

"And to all her inhabitants," added Dee. "Particularly to all those who are too afraid to face the truth."

"Nicely stated," was my response. "And it's true. We must hold those who live in fear about the Earth's crisis in loving-kindness. This is one of the challenges that we will have to face. Their fear worsens the situation. We must help these folks to understand that there is reason for hope. Perhaps hopefully, the book will inspire others to join the Mission of Rescue." Nods of approval were noticed, which seemed to conclude that train of thought. It was time for me to address the unusual experience with my family of friends.

"May I turn the focus back to my unexpected encounter?" Everyone urged me to do so. Indeed, they would. Their curiosity was still burning, as was their concern for me. *How grateful I am to be a part of this family.*

"So are we, dear!" Dee's telepathic skills were stunning. "Now, tell us about your experience, please."

"What I can tell you is this." Although my desire was to make eye contact with each person individually, it is difficult to do that when the words you wish to share are so specifically intended to reach the collective. I expressed this to my friends, who immediately encouraged me to just relax and not worry about them. Once again I was struck by my blessings. *They are such good people.* "My friends, I want you to know that I am fine. I still feel a bit flushed by the experience, because…well, quite truthfully, it was awesome. So, I'm excited, almost giddy about it, and I am also amazed that this has happened. And very curious about how it actually transpires.

The words that came through me were exactly the way I had heard them when I first received them. I cannot imagine that those words could be remembered perfectly, and then in turn, repeated word for word to all of you. How could that possibly be, and yet, it happened.

And because it did, I feel deeply honored. It was a privilege to bring the message forward. And of course, I wonder if this will happened again. Is this going to be a way that I can be of service? I don't have any answers to all the questions that are racing about in my mind, but I am open to anything that happens, and I would love to hear your thoughts and comments.

Frank immediately reacted to the invitation. "I think you should fasten your seatbelt! My intuition, or my gut, or whatever this inkling is, is telling me that this is just the beginning. And it thrills me!" His smile lit up the room and warmed everyone's heart especially the one under the spotlight. "And I suspect everyone here would agree with me that it just makes sense that this skill would develop within you. You are the quintessential listener! If the words of wisdom that flow through you on a regular basis are any indication of this type of innate ability then I would say you are a prime candidate for existential communication, if that's what we're talking about." Frank laughed at himself, and acknowledged that he didn't have a clue about these unusual experiences, but he also admitted that he had grown very fond of encountering them. He leaned towards me to add another comment. "You know as well as I do that something very special is happening here, so just open up to it and enjoy the ride."

"As you can tell, dear, Frank is tickled pink about this, and so am I." the Sandersons' reassurance was very comforting. "Actually, I'm very curious about your practice as an energy worker, and I wonder if that has assisted this process for you. Don't you also receive messages for some of the clients that you work with or am I mistaken about that?"

"It's similar Dee, but this experience was definitely different. I can't actually articulate how it was different. Perhaps, I will be able to after I have more time to process it. But I do think my years of being a listener have somehow prepared me for this new adventure.

Do you have any thoughts about this, Marilyn?" She smiled at me and shook her head in feigned disbelief.

"Of course, I have thoughts about this!" Her laugh was delightful. She, probably more than anyone else in the room, understood what had really happened during my unusual absence. Giggling again, she indicated that she probably had 5 miles worth of thoughts and wonderment.

"Oh, goody! Tell me everything!"

"My friend, this is who you really are! You've been training for this since you were a youngster listening to all the stories of your fellow classmates. Remember the story you told me about the time when you were six years old, and you and another little friend were on the merry-go-round. Remember that story? Remember how you listened to that child's story. Even then, you were the quintessential listener, as Frank just referred to you. And I would add to that by saying you are also the quintessential counselor, always knowing when to be quiet and when to voice the exact feedback or pose the perfect question that the person needs to hear. You're a natural, friend, and always have been." She gave me a Marilyn look and mumbled, "Makes me wonder how many times in the past you've been a listener in some way, shape, or form." She paused. And my mind raced another cross-country marathon.

"I have more to say, if you can quiet your mind long enough to listen." Our friends chuckled, enjoying the playful way that we interacted with one another.

"Goodness, is everyone tuning into my overactive, runaway mind?" I feigned embarrassment to cover-up the real self-consciousness that I was feeling. My mind really was out of control. So I took several deep breaths and motioned to my friends to join me. After our joint activity, Marilyn asked me if I was ready to be present. Assuring her that I was, she leaned forward and stared me down.

"I have something to say to you, and I need you to be present, because it is important." Her manner grabbed my attention.

"I'm present and I'm ready to listen."

"Dear one, please quiet your mind and open your heart to what I have to say. You are here for a reason and it time for you to accept this reality. The time is now, old friend. Your reason for being is more than you have allowed yourself to imagine or to believe. You have lived your life well and you have served many. Many have benefitted from your presence; however, there is much more for you to do. There are many more for you to address. A single client can no longer be the way of outreach. You must reach outward. You must touch the masses. This is the way that you can best serve the Life Being Earth. She requires your assistance and you must come forward. Old Friend, you are not alone, but you must step forward. Within you exists the ability to reach the masses. Although you do not yet understand this, it is your truth and you must open your heart to this reality. The time is now. You must speak the truth truthfully. Do not shy away from this responsibility; it is your charge to do so. Once again, I say to you, you are not alone. You are blessed with companions who are equally charged to assist the Earth. You must take the next step and you must bring this book into fruition. Take the lead, my friend, and be the one you are intended to be." Marilyn fell silent, as did I, and so did the rest of our companions.

"Old friends, may I join you?" The familiar voice brought fervor back into the room. As always, an empty chair awaited their guest. Not knowing if or when he might join them, the chair was always available just in case. The visitor materialized in his usual fashion, which still had the impact of an unusual event.

"Geez! That never fails to amaze me!" Bill's friends shared his wonderment. The comings and goings of their beloved friend was indeed a delight to witness.

"It is a joy to be in your presence once again my friends. My time here must be brief, so if I may take the lead, I will confirm what is already known by all of you. You are called to a mission of higher purpose. Long ago, before any of you can remember, you made a commitment to aid in the recovery of another Life Being. Each in your own way has been reminded of that commitment, and your willingness to serve this purposeful intention pleases all who are also involved in this Mission of Mercy. My friends, your assistance is greatly needed. As you well know, you are not alone in this quest. Many on the planet are already serving in various capacities and all activities taken on her behalf are necessary. Her needs are great at this time and there is no time for delays. Tonight you gather to share the progress each of you has made in the last twenty-four hours and as each contribution is presented, you are stunned by the magnitude of your gifts. Those who are your oldest and dearest friends are not surprised for we know who you really are.

My friends, I come to remind you that you are more than you appear to be. Within each of you resides the Presence from which all come. This simple truth is what it is. You are more than you appear to be, and so too is every other Life

Being. When one becomes consciously aware of this truth, life changes. One can no longer live as if one stands alone. One can no longer live as if one is more than another. These misunderstandings are the root of discontentment and unwellness upon this beautiful planet. The idea that some are more valuable than others is a profound misunderstanding with far-reaching consequences. All in existence are equal. This truth includes everyone! This reality extends throughout all existence." Our friend paused allowing the powerful message to reach our innermost being. His internal time clock was impeccable. Just the right amount of time was allotted before he resumed.

"Dear Ones, your situation is unique. You have the luxury of each other's companionship and you have a mutually shared mission to which each of you are contributing. Within this circle of eight are eight leaders and eight followers. Together you can bring this project forward quickly. And this is needed, for as you well know, the time is now. Remember, you are not alone. Already your outreach has touched others who are also interested in participating in this mission of mercy. Inform them of tonight's progress. Provide them with the materials gathered and invite their involvement. Inclusiveness is vital. The more that know of this work, the greater potential there is for the information to spread, and that is the goal. The messages and ideas fostered in this book are intended to reach the masses. The people of Earth must be reminded of their innate abilities and they must be taught to use their abilities on behalf of the planet. With their help, she can be restored to complete wellness. Old friends, your work is vitality important.

Assist one another. Help each other to grow into your full potential. As you develop, so too will the efforts being made on the Earth's behalf. All are most grateful for your participation. You bring hope to those who are also working on her behalf.

In peace be, my friends. I bid you adieu."

"There he goes again," whispered Bill. As was always the way with their elder friend, it required time to recover from his comings and goings. Frank retreated to the dining room and poured glasses of water for everyone. Marilyn joined him and prepared small plates of goodies that she and Frank delivered to the others who were still contemplating the latest visit for their friend.

"Oh, good!" Dee said in appreciation of the treats. "Have some protein friends. We all need it." The sense of urgency resonating in the room would not allow the snacks to be a time of rest. Jan announced that she would contact the out-of-towners in the morning and apprise them of the current state of affairs.

"Should we tidy up our rough drafts before we distribute them?"

"I don't think so," replied Dee and Frank simultaneously. Dee urged her husband to elaborate upon their thoughts. "These folks have great ideas. Let's get them onboard as quickly as possible. In fact, we need to push for another meeting and include them in the process. Jan can you try to schedule that when you talk to these folks?" A quick nod in response was all the affirmation that Frank needed.

"Yes," interjected Dee, let's give them time, let's say forty-eight hours to address their ideas just as we did, and while they are doing their preparations, we can continue to expand and edit our own materials." Dee's ability to streamline tasks was impressive…and a Godsend. "Now," she asserted. "Where are we?" She looked toward Marilyn and me, "Are you two done? Anymore thoughts or conclusions to discuss?" Before either of us could answer, Jan intervened.

"I have a question, please, before we move on. My curiosity is gnawing at me." She posed her question to Marilyn, "I'm confused. The message that you gave to our friend here," she said pointing in my direction. "Were those your words or were they words that you were receiving?"

"I don't know, Jan. Perhaps, it was both. All I know is the words flowed from my heart, and possibly my soul. I just knew our friend had to hear this message." Marilyn took a deep breath as she often does when contemplating an issue. "I felt compelled to remind her that she is here for a reason. It felt as if I was being driven to reassure her of the purposeful nature of this life experience. Were these my words? I honestly don't know, but truthfully, I don't think I could have done that by myself." Jan had many more questions, but she stopped herself. As interesting as the conversation was, she knew it was time for the meeting to move along. She thanked Marilyn first and then turned to Dee.

"Everett and I are ready to proceed, if that's okay with you?"

"Please do!" she responded excitedly. "I am eager to hear about your project. Tell us everything!" Those three words were beginning to take on a life of their own. I must admit it was an interesting experience to hear them used repeatedly during our meeting. For so many years, I had used those three words to encourage people to share their stories with me. Now, I was witnessing others accessing these small but powerful words. They were words of invitation that opened doors and allowed people to truly get to know one another. Until this moment, I did not realize the full potential of these influential words. I wondered when they entered into my daily life. Who was the client that first heard them flow from my mouth? Whose story was

I blessed to hear because of this small enticing phrase? My thoughts quieted as the Smiths began their presentation.

"Well, my friends, we are excited about sharing our work with you, and of course, we are a tiny bit apprehensive, but that's just stage fright. As Jan and I prepared ourselves for this grand debut, we realized that our main discomfort about presenting our stories had to do with public speaking. That was not the case when we first came out about our experiences. Then we were nervous about sharing our stories, because we didn't know how people would react, but that's not the case anymore. Our group meetings have given us time to adjust to the feeling of being exposed, as did the first outreach meeting. Coming out to strangers really helped diminish our concerns about people's reaction. We are comfortable with that now, but public speaking is still an obstacle for us. So we wanted to share that with all of you this evening in hopes that the disclosure will relieve our anxiety." Everett glanced about the room and saw the support in their friends' eyes. "Although, we never discussed this among ourselves, we figured all of you would relate to this nonsense." Nods and a few mutterings validated his assumption. "Shyness, self-consciousness, and limited opportunity to do public speaking all play a role in this discomfort. We figured if it is an issue for us, it might also be for some of the folks we have contact with, so we intend to come clean about this the minute we introduce ourselves. Hopefully, it will quiet our own heebie-jeebies and also any similar reactions that our guests may be experiencing." While Everett spoke, Jan passed around their rough draft.

"As you can see, our presentation begins with the encounter we had with our elder friend, and reveals the sense of urgency that overwhelmed us, as we felt more and more compelled to move to the Island that we had been frequenting for years. We believe the story introduces our passion for wanting to assist the Earth, and also speaks to the calling that we believe reminded us of our commitment to do just that. We also address our ideas of taking our outreach program on the road. Because we love to travel and are comfortable doing so, we feel we can assist in spreading the messages entailed in the book by actually taking our presentation to various locations that are interested in starting up their own outreach programs. We definitely need to do research regarding avenues for publicity, and hopefully we can find folks who will know more about this than we do, but in the mean time, we will begin reaching out to people we know around the country and overseas that may be open to hosting a presentation or a series of presentations. We can start on that process now, even before the book is published. What's important is that we take action now rather than waiting to have the book in hand. We'll learn more about our possibilities as we start exploring our options and as we acquaint other people about our plans. Truthfully, we are feeling much more optimistic about this now that we have put our thoughts together on paper."

"Yes, that's true," interjected Jan, "as we made a list of people we know in other settings, we were surprised and comforted by how many potential possibilities are available. We are going to initiate conversations with several couples we know and see what kind of responses we get. Hopefully, our discussion will lead to more. We envision going to people's homes and sharing our stories and our outreach initiatives with them. And of course, we will apprise them about the healing capabilities that we have learned about, and we will lead them through healing sessions for the Earth. We have one couple in particular that we want to target, because we think they will be very open to everything we've experienced. Ideally, this couple will respond positively and hopefully, they will invite friends to participate in our initial conversations. This is our ultimate goal. Meet, inform, plant a new outreach center, and move on to the next possibility.

As we have so often discussed, our mission is to spread the word and to find others who will carry on the process. Our book will assist folks in creating their own hubs, and hopefully we can track all the new startups so that centers can network with one another. Again, we will need assistance with the technology for all this, but it will come." Jan repeated her prediction with conviction. "Whatever assistance is needed will be provided. We need not worry about this."

Applause broke out from the first readers of the Smiths project. "This is awesome!" declared Marilyn.

"You're going to be very busy people, but you can do this." Frank was astonished by the synchronicity of passion and calling. "In fact," he stated in his usual logical manner, "this is a perfect utilization of your skills. You are seasoned travelers, you love traveling, and you've already established a network of people with whom you can connect. What a wonderful combination of preferred passions and innate abilities. There are no coincidences! I am so enjoying this." As he chuckled quietly to himself, another came forward with equal enthusiasm.

"I don't know why this surprises me," exclaimed Pat, "but it does. Everything is falling into place! And the different components of our projects are blending beautifully. I'm so excited about your rough draft; it's a riveting tale. And it will inspire the reader to keep reading, which is exactly what we need to have happen. Not only is this going to be an important teaching tool, but it also going to be a sweet, loving book that will warm the hearts of all who read it. I am so grateful to be part of this. Thank you all for being here and for being our family. We are so blessed."

"Indeed, we are," added Dee. "I too am amazed at what we are witnessing here this evening. My friends, we've taken the next step and this book is ready to be formatted. I had no idea we would progress so rapidly. Jan, I hope you and Everett were able to take in all that wonderful feedback that you received. It is a lovely document of mystery, wonderment, and possibilities. You did a remarkable job of articulating your experiences in such a way that it is a joy to read."

Dee's words successfully broke through the wall of tension engulfing the Smiths. They had sat quietly with hands tightly clasped throughout the entire time that their friends were providing them with feedback. Even though the comments were extremely positive and complimentary, they were unable to relax until Dee broke through their shell of disbelief.

"My dear friends, please come back to the present. You are lost in that dreadful place of self-doubt and disbelief in one's own merit. Hear me, dear ones! Your presentation was a success! And your rough draft is excellent and demands little if any editing. Applause! Applause! Applause!" Cheers and praises accompanied Dee's comments. The reality of their achievement finally sunk in. Their locked grips released and the couple embraced one another. Tears were shed and more followed, when their friends realized the depth of emotion that was being shared. It was a powerful moment for everyone, because each person present could identify with the Smiths' reaction.

"Oh, dear friends, you honor us with your tears. I so hope you can now take in the compliments and the praise that were offered you."

"Thank you, Dee, for helping us through that relapse into old behaviors," responded Jan. "That was an interesting moment of vulnerability. I felt good about our presentation of our ideas, and I think you did as well, Ev," she glanced towards her husband to be certain that her comments were accurate. He nodded in agreement. "But when the feedback began, old fears rushed forward. Even though the feedback was gracious and kind, fear overrode the compliments. Wow! That was salutary. One must be aware that these situations can arise even when things are going well." Again Jan turned to Everett and inquired about his reaction. His experience was similar.

"I can honestly say that I'm glad this happened. We were prepared for this possibility because of old habits, and we did successfully overcome the intrusion of fear during our presentation, but it sneaked up on us afterwards, and that is important information. I will be more vigilant in the future, and Jan and I can do some strategizing about managing this if it happens again."

"Well done!" praised Frank. "You two handled that efficiently. I think we can all be pleased with ourselves tonight. We have not been delayed by our vulnerabilities. Good for us!"

"How about you two?" Bills question focused the attention towards the elders of the group. "What are you up to? Tell us everything!" Frank and Dee turned to each other and enjoyed a quiet conversation.

"I think you should go first, dear," urged Dee, but Frank declined.

"No! You're the one with the plan. You take the lead and I'll monitor everyone's reactions."

"Okay, Dee. You drew the short straw. So, tell us everything!" Marilyn grinned cheerfully. She was obviously enjoying showing off her telepathic skills.

"You rascal!" responded Dee. "Your skills are developing nicely, dear. Okay then," she declared. "As Frank distributes our handout, I will bring you up to date on my thoughts about the book format. I must admit that tonight's conversation makes me want to chuckle out loud and also to sing Hallelujah!!! I've been working on this since our visit with the elder and I think all of you will be amused with the changes that I have incorporated into the book draft." Dee paused briefly as her companions breezed through their copies of the rough draft.

"This is amazing, Dee! Your outline follows the structure of this evening's meeting. I can't believe this. You have drafted the book format in alignment with what transpired here this evening. Geez! This is incredible!" I had more to say, but decided to quiet myself. My friends needed to express themselves as well.

"Were you guided to do this, Dee?" ask Jan. "Did the elder friend have something to do with this coincidence. How are Earth did you know to structure the book in this format?" Similar questions arose, but Dee had no answers. Eventually Frank put his hand up to stop all the commotion.

"No more, please! Dee would you like to explain your process to our friends." As was often the custom among this group, the matriarch paused and took a long deep breath, and as she indulged so did her companions.

She started to speak, then laughed at herself, and then began again. "My friends, I'm finding it very difficult to engage with all of you lovely Beings without our famous four-letter word. So, let me just say in advance...Wellness to our Beloved Earth! How wonderful it is to be with you and to feel the marvelous energy that you're creating. Isn't life grand?" Dee was beaming with joy. She was a different person, or perhaps it is more accurate to say, she was herself again. Radiant, bright, and sharp! Frank looked on with awe and gratitude. They weren't worried about the future anymore. The present was occupying their time and they were living life fully.

"I must admit," continued Dee, "that I'm tickled by your questions. When the meeting began to unfold this evening, I couldn't believe what was happening. As each of you spoke, you fulfilled the plan that had been prepared earlier. Isn't that amazing?" She glanced about the room exchanging smiles with her friends and cohorts. "Now in answer to your questions as to whether or not I was guided to alter our previous plans, all I can say is this. I don't know. As I reviewed my notes that were distributed a while back, it seemed to me that the format needed to be changed, so I did. Was that guidance, assistance, or Divine Intervention? I just don't have an answer. But as you all know, I don't believe in coincidences. What you see before you was reconstructed yesterday, and tidied up this morning, and we all know how the meeting unfolded this evening.

Do I feel as if I prepared this work alone?" She posed the question to herself. "At the time, I certainly thought it was my own work. In all honesty, I know that I'm capable of preparing such a document, but after seeing what has happened here tonight, it makes one wonder. And to be perfectly honest with all of you, I rather like the idea that I was assisted. It pleases me to think that our wonderful companions were helping to prepare this project in alignment with their preferences and needs. Astonishing!" She lost herself in wonderment for a moment and then came back with another question.

"Can this actually be happening? Can we actually be living a life where we are assisted and lovingly guided by companions from another realm of existence?" Dee turned to her husband with sincerity and asked, "Is this really happening, dear? Or have we grown so old that we no longer know what is real?" Frank did not hesitant with his response.

"We don't have to have all the answers, Dee. We have enough confirmations about the things that are happening around us to know that this unusual life we are living is real…and it's wonderful. The truth is, the unusual experiences that we keep encountering are exciting and invigorating, so let's just enjoy what is happening and keep seeking answers to the mysteries that continue to unfold. We're having a great time! And we have purpose and meaningfulness in our lives again. I don't think we can ask for anything more than that!" Frank's strength and confidence nourished Dee.

"Well spoken, dear!" Then she turned and faced her friends. "My friends, I believe we are being assisted in many ways. And sometimes we may actually be aware of it when it's happening, but probably most of the time, we are clueless. Whether we are consciously aware of friendly helping hands or not, we should always be thankful for the help we are provided. Let us give thanks now for all the assistance we were given before and during this meeting. And for those who are in listening range, we are giving you notice…we will be needing a lot more help in the days to come. Thank you for your loving care of us." Gratitude echoed throughout the room and far beyond. *And the energy of gratefulness infused the Earth with wellness.*

"What's our plan now, Dee? How do we keep this powerful momentum energized?" Jan's questions stated what was on everyone's mind. Before Dee could answer, I found myself speaking out. At first I was embarrassed by my bold manner, but then I realized something important was happening so I desperately tried to get out of the way.

"We take the next step," I stated confidently. "Excuse me for interrupting Dee, but I believe it is important that we all accept the reality that once again, we must take the next step. Tonight's achievements speak for themselves, and we all have reasons to be happy and to be grateful; however, our work is not finished. We achieved one big step and now we must discern what the next step will be. And then, we must make another giant leap. My friends, we cannot dwell in our satisfaction. Remember, the time is now. We must continue moving forward. We must reach for the next goal." My words were followed by another deep breath and then silence took over the room as it often does with this clan. Time passed and eventually the Tibetan bell brought us back together again.

Dee sat with a welcoming smile upon her face and with a small stack of papers on her lap. "My friends, I think we all know that we are called to move forward. This morning, I was guided to share this with all of you. Please just take it home and give it a glance before you go to bed. Be safe, dear ones, and thank you for all your good work." And with that said, my friends quickly helped with the clean up of the house and then went their separate ways. *What an evening!* I thought to myself as I waved goodbye to Marilyn as she turned the corner leading towards her house. The moon was bright. It was a lovely night for a walk, but fatigue had set in and I was ready for bed.

"Well, dear house of mine, I hope you enjoyed the gathering this evening.

It was an amazing event! Don't you agree?" Once again, the house remained silent. I wondered about Dee's comment when she arrived this evening. *Hmm, we never had a chance to finish that conversation.*

"If you are trying to connect with me, please reach out. I would love to hear your perspective about our meetings and anything else that you might wish to talk about." Again, there was no response, so I said goodnight and moseyed back to the bedroom. Once there, I realized the handout that Dee had given us at the end of the meeting was still in my hand. I turned on the light, sat down in my favorite chair and stared at the page.

"Oh my goodness, I don't believe this." My mouth literally dropped open, and then just as suddenly slammed shut when the phone startled me out of my stupor! I knew without looking who was calling.

"Have you seen Dee's handout?" Marilyn sounded out of breath. I surmised she had rushed to grab her phone after seeing Dee's notes.

"I'm staring at it right now, and I'm speechless. I haven't had time to process my feelings about this, because I'm still reeling from what I'm seeing? What about you? How are you feeling about this quote-quote coincidence?"

"Well, if memory serves me, which it often doesn't," she openly admitted and then proceeded with her bold pronouncement. "We, you and I, and the other 6 wonderful people in our group do not believe in coincidences. So, I can say with absolute confidence (and also with absolutely no authority whatsoever) that this situation is not a coincidence." We both broke into laughter. Marilyn's playful antics helped us to settle into the reality of Dee's remarkable To Do List that she had created for the group before the meeting occurred.

"Okay, so the question is, how are we feeling about what has happened? Let's get focused!" I looked in the direction of Marilyn's house as if she actually could see me peering at her. We both remained quiet for a bit while we tried to wrap our minds around this situation. Eventually, Marilyn responded.

"You know, with all the unusual occurrences that we've encountered lately, you would think we would be accustomed to this by now. But the truth is we're not. And least, I'm not! Dee's handout really rattled me, not in a bad way, but it just took me aback. Now that we've had a few laughs, I'm able to appreciate the wonder of all this again. I don't know how she managed in advance to create a To Do List for our next meeting that is perfectly devised for each one of us. It's remarkable. We each have a succinct guideline to follow. So, how do I feel about this? I'm amazed. And I am so grateful to be a part of this. We are being helped in the most incredible ways, and it's real. Who thought life could be like this? And it makes me believe that this is really how life is supposed to be." She stopped briefly and then apologized for going astray.

"No apology needed, Marilyn. I agree with you. What is happening is real, and it's a privilege to be involved in this. It's a hoot! I believe everything that is happening is happening for a reason, and at the same, it seems unbelievable. So once again, I think we are in sync when it comes to the mysteries we are encountering." Knowing that we were in agreement seemed to settled us both down. We decided to rise early to greet the sunrise and scheduled a 5:30 a.m. meet up at our favorite intersection.

"Good night friend. Sleep well."

"You too!" And with that said, we both put our phones to bed.

~ 6 ~

In a faraway place, known to but a few, conversations regarding the progress of the Circle of Eight were underway. Excitement filled the space. *"Our plans at long last are reaching fruition. There is reason for hope."*

"Indeed, this is true," said another, *"and still, we must be vigilant. Our Beloved Friend Earth continues to decline. Her condition is most worrisome. As she continues to show signs of increased temperature, her immune system is weakening. Violent storms attempt to assist her by bringing forward cooler temperatures and extreme rainfall. Both serve to assist temporarily, but the effects do not last long enough to create significant changes. And as she fights for her life, the residents continue to worsen her situation by stripping her of vitally important internal fluids, while at the same time, continuing to pollute her surface fluids thereby diminishing her ability to restore and heal herself. Their actions are foolish and selfish, and as a result of their misguided deeds, they suffer the consequences of her declining health. She nears the point where she will be forced to recede into dormancy. Although, she valiantly resists this option, if her situation does not improve immediately, there will be no other choice available to her. This reaction will have a devastating impact upon all her residents.*

Humankind must awaken to this crisis. They must come to her rescue. With their innate abilities, they have the power to reverse this situation. They have the power to heal her. Unless they participate in her recovery process, she will fall into a state of dormancy and without her vitality, they will cease to exist. This is not intended.

The Life Being Earth is intended to continue as the vibrant energy source that she has always been. This is her destiny. She graciously accepted the seedlings of the human race and willingly and lovingly provided for them since they came into existence. They too are intended to continue, but not at the expense of their host. Humankind can correct this unbelievable mishap. They can heal the Earth with the power that was gifted to them when they came into existence.

My Friends, there is reason for hope, but we must continue our efforts to apprise the people of Earth of their perilous situation. And we must also educate them to the power that lies within them. Unless they accept their true potential, and do so quickly, there will not be adequate time to reverse Earth's decline.

We must increase our efforts to assist the people of Earth, and our best avenue for doing this is by convincing them to accept and utilize the healing powers that they possess.

Greater assistance must be given to the Circle of Eight. Their role in the Earth's recovery process is vitally important."

PART TWO

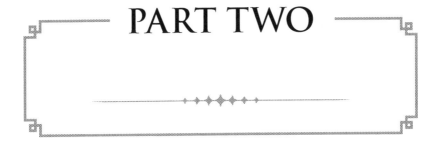

HEALING THE LIFE BEING EARTH:
A CALL TO ACTION

Dear Reader,

Your assistance is needed. The wonderful Life Being Earth has fallen into ill health. There are many reasons for this unfortunate reality; however, discussing the causes of her decline will serve only to incite more debates and more inflammatory remarks, none of which will facilitate the positive changes that are immediately necessary. While in the past these endless conversations have inspired some people to take action on her behalf, they unfortunately have had the opposite effect upon countless others. Inertia has been the primary reaction to conversations regarding the Earth's decline. This action of inaction can no longer be the way of the future.

To those of you who have already altered your lifestyle for the sake of Earth's well being, we express our gratitude for your courageous commitment. The leadership roles you have taken must continue. Because of you, she has managed to sustain herself, but as you well know, more assistance is necessary. The actions of sustainability that are now underway must multiply and expand across all lands. Everyone must participate. This is not a project for the few; it demands the participation of all the residents of this planet. As these words are read, there will be some who immediately reject the idea that they 'must' participate. Their individualism will override the reality of this situation. To those who engage in this ill-fated reaction, we invite you to open your heart to the truth. The truth, as it is, must be spoken truthfully and there are no perfect words that will make this truth any less cumbersome. The Earth's health crisis is real and this reality must be faced now. The shock of this truth has paralyzed the majority of Earth's population. Fear has closed the minds and hearts of those who are needed to assist her. This initial reaction is understandable. The prospect of losing one's home is undeniably frightening. But now we must move forward to aid the Life Being who has sustained us since we came into existence. We are a people of goodness who are capable of looking beyond our fears. We have done this is countless ways in our history, and we will do it again. The Life Being upon which we reside is our home and she needs our help. An invaluable trait of humankind is to assist one another when one is in need. We face such a situation now. Our planet is in need, and we must take action on her behalf.

Dear Reader, we come forward this day to invite you to participate in an act of generosity. We hope you will accept our invitation. The act of generosity suggested may initially cause you to raise your eyebrows. So be it! Our reaction was similar, but we assure you that we adjusted to the idea much more rapidly than we had anticipated. Because our introduction to this idea came about through relationships, our inclination is to foster a relationship with you now, as you read about our proposal. We hope you will open your heart to this invitation of friendship. In anticipation that you will, we will now include you in our circle of friends.

So, Dear Friend, we have a message regarding the truth of your existence that we are intended to deliver to you. We suggest that you take a very long deep breath, because this may come as a surprise to you. If it does, please know that you are in very good company. We anticipate that many of you will be as surprised as we were when this information was shared with us. We suggest that you simply be with the surprising news, and if you can, please observe the reactions of your mind. There is no need to squelch or tamper with your mind's responses, but do take notice, for this may be an extremely informative moment.

We share with you what was shared with us in hopes that you will accept the truth about your existence. Dear Friend, you are more than you appear to be. This statement laden with mystery may stir the mind's imagination; however, your attention is needed. Please stay focused just for a few more minutes.

The insinuation that you are more than you appear to be serves many functions, and these opportunities will be yours to explore, but again, for this point in time, we are here to provide you with one specific detail of this mysterious pronouncement. Dear Friend, you and all others in existence came into existence with an innate ability. This ability has always been, but for reasons unknown, the memory of this ability was lost to humankind. Nonetheless, the ability still exists and it can be restored to its fullest potential with awareness, acceptance, and practice.

Some of you from various faith traditions and spiritual practices already believe that this ability is a possibility, but few of you accept this possibility for yourself. You sometimes 'ponder' the possibility and you 'think' it might be true for some people, but your doubts do not inspire you to seek more information. Today, we will sidestep your doubts and provide you with the information that is truth for all in existence.

Dear Friend, you are indeed more than you appear to be, and in the context of the book, *The Answer in Action,* you are 'the answer' and you are being 'called to action' on behalf of the Life Being Earth. Within you, Dear Friend, resides the ability to heal self and others. This ability has always existed in you, as it as in all other Life Beings. You are reminded of this truth now, because it is necessary. If time had permitted, the human species would have regained their awareness of this innate ability through the natural flow of one's own evolutionary process. Unfortunately, there is no longer time to wait for this natural process to unfold.

The Earth's health crisis has reached a critical state. If she does not receive the necessary infusions of Source Life Energy, she will not be able to survive without a prolonged quiescent period. Inactivity will allow her to regain her vitality back, but such a recovery entails extended periods of time. Because all her personal resources will be focused upon recovery and renewal of the entire life system, there will be no remaining resources available to sustain other life forms. The ramifications of such a transition are too unbearable to ponder. Thus, we choose to focus our attention upon the obvious solution that is available. As stated, Dear Friend, you are the solution to this unthinkable problem. Humankind possesses the healing ability to restore the Life Being Earth back to her a state of youthful wellness. This can be done. It must be done, for the sake of this remarkable Life Being, and for the sake of all who reside upon her.

The healing energy possessed by all Life Beings is comprised of the same robust energy that exists throughout all existence. It is the energy that empowers all life in existence, and as such, the possessor of this energy has the power to empower other Life Beings who are in need. Dear Friend, please listen with the ears of your heart. You are one who possesses this power! Please pause for a moment and read the previous statement again. Although you may find this difficult to accept, it is the truth, and we bring this truth to you now, so that you have greater understanding of who you really are and why you have been invited to participate in this urgent act of generosity.

Please do not resist this truth about yourself. Instead, place your energy towards a more productive path. Give yourself time to adjust to this reality so that you can then proceed to gather more information about activating the ability within you. What is needed in this moment, Dear Friend, is open-mindedness and curiosity. Please do not automatically decline this opportunity to learn more about your potential. Open your mind and your heart to the possibility that this really is one of the truths about humankind's capabilities. Let your natural curiosity take the lead in this adventure of self-discovery.

To assist you in your process, this handbook has been created to expedite your journey. While it would be preferable to take one's time when exploring such a remarkable possibility, unfortunately, time is of the essence. Our Beloved Earth does not have the luxury of time. Her decline is rapidly progressing; therefore, it is essential that you pursue the truth about your healing abilities immediately. If our tone is insistent, please forgive us, but the situation demands that we speak the truth forthrightly.

Activating the healing energy within is a process that simply demands patience, commitment, and practice. If your mind is rapidly calculating how you will work yet another project into your already filled scheduled, please quiet that precious mind of yours. What is asked of you is a very small amount of your time! Nothing more! So little is required of you, and still, the benefits of your participation in this act of generosity will be globally life changing.

The healing energy within you, when activated, will not only improve your own vitality, but it will also profoundly alter the Earth's present state of decline. Perhaps, this is a statement that sounds too good to be true, but it is the truth nonetheless. Currently, there are many misunderstandings existing upon this wonderful planet that interfere with our abilities to make good decisions. One of these relevant and disconcerting factors is the expectation that an idea must be complicated and expensive for it to be worthwhile. Our innate ability to heal the Earth is neither of these, and yet, it is the most viable option available to humankind. Indeed, it is true that the sustainability changes that must be incorporated into our present and future lifestyles are costly, and these changes must be managed regardless of their expense. However, in this present moment, there are actions of change that can be initiated immediately that cost nothing but a few minutes of our time each day.

Simply stated, our planet has a population of over seven billion people, all of whom possess the ability to facilitate healing. Imagine what might happen if we all accepted this reality about ourselves. Just imagine what might be accomplished if we accepted this truth and decided to cooperate with one another for the sake of our Beloved Planet. Dear Friend, think expansively please. Imagine what might happen if the billions of people of Earth actually joined together emotionally, cooperatively, and lovingly for the sake of another Life Being. Stretch your imagination, please. Imagine rising at your usual hour and pausing briefly to share a particle of your powerful healing energy with the Earth. That's all it would take…just a few moments of your day. And then compound your action by seven plus billions of similar donations of energy. Think of it as a prescribed dose of medicine for an extremely large Life Being. Imagine this act of generosity. If you can capture this image in your mind's eye then you are drawing closer to the reality of humankind's capabilities. Dear Friend, please listen with the ears of your heart. Humankind has the ability to heal the Earth. We can do this! To achieve what is necessary, we must act immediately. While a single dose of our Source Life Energy can work wonders, we must take into consideration the size of this remarkable Life Being and we must also remember that she is severely compromised at this time. She requires more assistance than just one treatment, and fortunately, humankind has the resources to provide her with billions of doses of energy every day until she is fully rejuvenated.

The purpose of this book is to invite the peoples of Earth to participate in the most important act of generosity ever known to humankind. With our help, the Earth can regain her full vitally once again. This proposal is not intended to negate any endeavors presently underway. Every effort made to create a sustainable state of cooperation between the planet and her inhabitants is an action of necessity. The Earth desperately needs our help. Our proposal is one that complements the actions already being initiated.

Many issues have been brought to our attention as a result of the Earth's health crisis, and because of this, we, the people of Earth, have been presented with a most unusual opportunity. We have been given a chance to make amends. Because of our mutually shared global unpleasantness, humankind has had to review and assess our relationships with one another and with other Life Beings. In general, one might say that we have fallen short of our true potential when it comes to the development of healthy relationships. Our relationship with the Earth is a primary example of our misunderstandings about relationships. Abundant evidence reveals that we have not been good stewards of this planet. We have not treated her with kindness nor have we given her needs appropriate consideration. Our actions have been driven by greed and selfishness and we have behaved irresponsibly. Similarly, our relationships with other Life Beings also existing on this planet have been equally disrespectful and dismissive. Our behaviors thus far indicate that we have not yet grasped the idea of mutual co-existence. Other indicators of our relational immaturity are depicted by our maltreatment of those within our own species. The issue of differences continues to be a factor of great dissension within the human species. The ability to accept Beings of all kinds regardless of differences is a concept than humankind has not yet mastered.

Earth's crisis has brought all the issues to the forefront, and once again, she is playing a significant role in our evolutionary process. Long before any of today can remember, this gracious Life Being participated in an act of generosity when she welcomed the seedlings of humankind into her environment. Until this day, no other act of generosity equaled her contribution. Now, we have the opportunity to repay her generosity, by coming to her aid, as she did for us when we first entered into existence. So much she has done and continues to do for us! Her commitment to humankind's evolutionary development is humbling. She served as a remarkable surrogate parent, graciously accepting us into her womb and then allowing us to live and thrive upon her surface. And this we did...for better or worse, we inhabited this beautiful Life Being. During our maturational phase, we accessed and utilized the abundant gifts that she selflessly provided, while giving little thought to or consideration of our actions. We simply took her hospitality for granted. We were naïve. We presumed that her abundance would be endless and never imagined there might be consequences as a result of our indulgent behaviors. Now, we know better. We are responsible for the Earth's health crisis and we are responsible for her recovery.

If you are wondering what you can do to assist the Earth, the answer is simple. Become an active participant in healing this beloved Life Being. You are capable of this! Each and every one of us is endowed with this innate ability, so please do not dismiss an opportunity because it presently seems unbelievable to you. Instead, open your heart and your mind to the possibility and choose to participate in an act of extreme generosity. Take the first step, by continuing to read further. So little is asked of you in comparison to what was asked of the Earth when she accepted responsibility for hosting humankind. Take the step please, and learn how easy it is to participate in this healing process. For the sake of the Earth, take this small step and discover who you really are through your participation. For the sake of humankind and your continuance, please take this next step.

Dear Friend, please take a deep breath as you ponder what it being asked of you. After all, this is not an ordinary request. Rest assured that in recent weeks our Circle of Friends has taken many deep breaths, as we engaged with this most unusual topic. As you might imagine, we too were taken aback by the notion that we possessed healing capabilities. It is fair to say that we were skeptical and doubtful, but the desire to assist the Life Being Earth overcame our inclination to resist what seemed an improbable idea of action. We opened our hearts to the possibility that in some small way, we might actually be able to help this beautiful Being that we call home. What we discovered was life changing for all of us and we came to realize that the improbable was possible.

Each of us, Dear Reader, has a story that we wish to share with you. At this point in our lives, we doubt that our stories are unique, but at the time, we were deeply confounded by the unfolding events. By sharing our stories with one another, we came to know that others were also experiencing unusual events in their lives. This was a remarkably comforting awareness. We realized we were not alone in our mysterious stories, and found that our stories were curiously similar. All of this is to say that we believe many other individuals across the planet are also having similar experiences, and we personally believe this is happening for a reason.

We believe, Dear Friend, that we are being solicited to assist the Earth and that we are being apprised of our innate abilities so that we can unite our efforts and effectively rejuvenate the planet back to a state of wellness. As individuals, our contributions will be helpful, but en masse, our efforts will achieve the necessary energy infusions to heal the Earth. With this in mind and heart, we felt called to develop a handbook that can be used as a guide for revitalizing one's own innate abilities. The process is so simple that some of you may question its validity. We appreciate whatever reactions you may be having at this time. As you read our stories you will understand why we have great compassion for your introduction into this unusual adventure. We accept that many of you may regard the suggestion of humankind's healing capabilities as a preposterous proposal. Again, we ask you to open your heart to this possibility.

Read further, Dear Friend, for there is much too learn about the marvelous reality in which we live. Thank you for everything you are currently doing on behalf of the Earth, and whether you are inclined to join this healing mission or not, please continue your current efforts. She needs your help.

In peace be.

The To Do List

Breathe deeply...
>Open your heart to all possibilities...

Breathe deeply...
>Share your story...
>Face your resistance, your doubts, and your fears...
>Quiet your mind and simply accept all reactions that surface, whether they are of a positive or a negative inclination...

Breathe deeply...
>Listen with the ears of your heart...
>Compassionately react to your reactions...
>Strategize actions for change...

Breathe deeply...
>Implement your preferred actions...
>Review the outcome...

Breathe deeply...
>Implement necessary changes...
>Establish your commitments...
>Perfect your goals with consistent daily practice...

Breathe deeply...
>Increase your efforts as your abilities expand...
>Continue sharing your energy with the Earth until she is restored to complete wellness...
>Spread your awareness of your healing abilities with all you encounter...

Breathe deeply...
>Live respectfully and gratefully with the Life Being Earth...
>Live respectfully and peacefully with neighbors far and near across all lands and throughout all dimensions of existence...
>Live respectfully and peacefully with all Life Beings...

~ 1 ~

Welcome, Friends of Old and New Friends soon to be! We are most grateful for your presence and for your willingness to pursue this topic of extreme importance. As many of you already know, the beautiful Island in the Sky, the planet Earth, is in great distress. She needs assistance. Regardless of where one rests on the continuum of believing this reality, the issue of the Earth's changing conditions warrants the attention of everyone residing upon her.

Thank you for taking the time to contemplate her circumstances. The book you are now reading is the result of several old friends who did just that. Although, we initially gathered for other reasons, or so we thought, we soon came to realize that the Earth's declining stability was going to play an intricate role in our futures, as will be true for all others who intend to continue living upon this planet. Because we recently chose to open our hearts to learning more about the truth of Earth's situation, our awareness of her precarious health issues has grown, but there remains much more to learn. Our relationship with this incredible Life Being demands serious reflection.

Perhaps you may wish to reflect upon your own relationship with the Earth. We invite you to do so. Many of you may be surprised by this invitation; however, we believe you will find the experience enlightening. We certainly did when we began sharing our stories with one another. In truth, with the exception of my beloved husband, most of us found the experience rather challenging initially until we finally realized that we did indeed have a relationship with her. This was a surprise to us, because truthfully, we had never given the idea any consideration. Once our hearts opened to the idea, not only did we gain greater understanding of her impact upon our earlier lives, but we also became increasingly more knowledgeable about her influence upon our present circumstances. What a dear, sweet journey it has been. Discovering our individual relationships with Mother Earth has truly been an experience of a lifetime, and we are all most grateful for what we have learned. Accepting our relationships with the Earth enriched our lives in countless ways including helping us to better understand our relationships with one another.

Our journey thus far has been full, and yet, we all know, the journey is just beginning. So much more are we intended to know about our Beloved Earth, and as we come to know her better, so too will we have greater understanding of own truths regarding who we really are. Our lives are intricately linked. She welcomed us into existence when we entered existence, and she assisted and supported us until this day. Now it is our time to attend her needs as she has done for us for so many years.

Dear Friend, this book, *The Answer in Action,* is the culmination of a fictional story that is founded in truth. It has been prepared for a reason. Hopefully, you have already partaken in the two prequels so that you have a greater appreciation for its cast of characters of which I am one; however, if you have not read the prequels, please continue reading anyway. You will find that *The Answer in Action* stands alone in its endeavor to bring the intended message of the storyline forward. At another time you may wish to engage with the prequels so that you can enjoy the company of our characters. I encourage you to do so. Their way, or I should say 'our' way of being, our manner, is worthy of your attention. As we grow and expand throughout the series, so too will you. Similar to the story itself, the characters were also created on your behalf. Like you, Dear Friend, we are ordinary people living ordinary lives until we just happened to encounter an unusual turn of events.

What was desired in creating *The Answer* series was an opportunity to bring forward vitally important information to the peoples of Earth. We believe this fictional story, founded in truth, will be your unusual turn of events.

~ 2 ~

"**W**ellness to the Earth! Dear Readers, this four word declaration came about during our gatherings when we simultaneously realized how often we rely upon the four letter word 'well' to initiate a statement of thought or conversation. What was first amusing became blatantly tedious, and at that point the Circle of Eight, our dear family of friends, decided to alter our intention of the overused word and instead activated a more meaningful expression of it on behalf of the Earth and her current state of health. After great deliberation, Frank and I decided it would be fitting to begin our story with this pronouncement since you will be seeing it frequently throughout the following pages. Hopefully in the very near future this expression will be heard all across the globe. Just imagine how these good wishes, these brief moments of acknowledgement, will impact our beautiful planet. You will learn more about that shortly, but for now, let me focus upon my allotted task. It is my privilege to share the Sandersons' story that began some fifty odd years ago. Frank and I were just youngsters when we decided a hike in the woods might be a pleasant activity. Little did we know then just how adventuresome it would become! Suffice it to say, the day was long, a minor injury was incurred, and we both became very disoriented by our circumstances, which is a polite way to say we found ourselves lost in the woods. What was intended to be an afternoon hike extended into a multiple day life-changing experience that we held close to our hearts for decades. Never once did we share any details about our unusual turn of events with anyone until just recently, when we reunited with our dear friends and they opened the door to the possibility. Because they had the need, and the courage, to explore their own recent unusual experiences, we felt safe to reveal our secret that had been closeted for over half a century.

In retrospect, we wonder what we were so afraid of, but at that point in time, caution seemed advisable. Our list of reasons for remaining silent was long. We do not scold or shame ourselves for our apprehensions; but we do marvel at the determination of those two young people. We were so naïve when we entered into the woods. But we had an unusual experience, you see, and when we came out of the woods, we were different. After the grand adventure was over, we attested our love to one another and also vowed to keep our encounter in the woods a secret. I think it is fair to say that neither

Frank nor I regret our decision. Life has been very good to us, but the decision made separated us from others in ways that we are just now coming to understand. Since we shared our story with our dear friends, we have enjoyed the comfort of their loving support. The relief we felt after sharing our story was beyond description and the blessing of companionship is equally indescribable. Because of this delightful experience, we are now inclined to encourage others to share their stories as well. Our list of reasons for doing so is much shorter than our previous secretive list. Bottom line, Dear Friends, by sharing our stories, we discovered two incredibly important truths. First, we learned that we are not alone, and secondly, we learned that our unusual experiences were not as unusual as we had thought.

Briefly, I will conclude by emphasizing that coming together and sharing our stories has been a blessing for which we will always be grateful.

And now, my New Friends, let me turn the lead over to my beloved husband. Frank will now share his perspective of our unusual event."

"Wellness to the Earth and to all of you who are reading this book. My best friend and dear wife forgot to identify herself in her portion of the story, but I suppose our names are irrelevant anyway. Since Dee and I revealed our ancient incident to our friends, we have discovered numerous other folks with similar, but different unusual experiences. We suspect that there are many more stories waiting to be told. Many names, many places, many unusual encounters! The point is…we are not alone. More importantly, perhaps at this moment in time, it is helpful for you to know that you are not alone. Whoever you are, whatever your story is, you are not alone. Remember that truth please, as you continue to read the stories presented in this book.

Dee's description of our personal experience is accurate, but I will add another factor to the tale that she did not address. The truth is we were scared. Naiveté and youthful arrogance delayed that reality from our consciousness for a while, but eventually we could no longer deny that we were in a difficult situation. I bring the issue of fear to the surface, because it was also a factor in our remaining silent about our experience. We simply didn't believe anyone would believe our story and we were afraid to take the risk. We were already feeling foolish about getting lost in the woods and we didn't want to make the situation worse by revealing our unusual encounter. As Dee reported, our decision felt right at the time, but we now wonder how our family and friends would have reacted back then. There's no way of knowing. Perhaps, some folks would have ridiculed us, which would have been difficult for kids our age, but then again, maybe, just maybe some folks would have believed us. They could have benefitted from our experience and we certainly would have benefitted from their support.

And now I will share another secret with you. Dee and I and all of our friends are a bit nervous about sharing our stories in this format. I won't say that we are afraid, but we are antsy. We have had the good fortune of finding love and support by sharing our stories with one another, and then, by reaching out to others and finding out that there were more stories to be heard. So our optimism is greater than our queasiness. We recognize the relevance of presenting these stories. We know our experiences are important and we believe they must be brought forward. So, Dear Readers, I want you to hear this and know that your story is important too. If your mind is reacting negatively to my statement, just notice its response. You're simply experiencing the doubts that naturally arise in this situation. Take a deep breath and please continue to focus upon the story before you.

This is the truth, as we believe it. The individual unusual events that each of us experienced followed by the unusual events that we shared as a group have revealed to us an extremely important reality of which none of us were previously aware. Not only have we gained greater clarity about our planet's health crisis, but we have also learned about our ability to help her. You will hear much more about this as we continue to share our stories and we believe as more stories come forward, more people will have the same realization as we did. We, meaning all the people residing upon the Earth, have the ability to assist her back to wellness. The Earth's situation is critical. This is a reality that we must all face. We have an opportunity to do something about it, and we must face this reality as well. We have the opportunity and the means to help the Earth, and we must do so. This isn't just an opportunity; it is a responsibility.

We hope you will benefit from our stories, and we hope you will feel safe to reveal your own. We have found that every story we've heard thus far changed our lives and this inspires us to continue sharing our own stories. Your story will change someone's life as well. Each story told will help others to realize that we have the ability to help the Earth. Wellness to the Earth, and to all of you who will share your stories, and to all of you who will willingly listen to someone's story!

I guess that's all I can contribute at this time. Hopefully, there will be more as our stories unfold."

"Thank you, Frank, for sharing your perspective, and as we have witnessed so many times before during our gatherings, your story inspired me to share another aspect of our experiences with our New Friends. Dear Ones, Frank and I are of elder age and we were having many important and difficult discussions about our aging processes before we reunited with our family of friends. We were declining, you see, and it was a time of great uncertainty, and quite truthfully, we were lost in the discomfort of it all. As I say this, I realize how similar this recent sense of being lost was to the time so long ago when we truly were lost in the woods. The sense of hopelessness was profoundly unpleasant, and the concern we had for each other was equally unbearable, because neither one of us wanted to leave the other alone. Young Frank didn't want to leave me alone even though he firmly believed he needed to seek help, and I didn't want him to go off alone for fear he might unknowingly stray further away from our point of entry into the forest. Likewise, in our recent situation, we both worried about the future and the unthinkable thought of leaving our beloved behind. Again, we were feeling hopeless and without options. However, those concerns have fallen aside now. We have been reminded that we are not alone. We learned that lesson in the woods, but during our recent decline, we lost that memory. Our reunion with old friends and the sharing of our stories brought that reality back to the forefront. Again, we approach life with the awareness that we are always accompanied.

Since we became involved with the Earth's difficult health issues, our lives have totally changed for the better. All of this came about because we opened our hearts to sharing our unusual events with our old friends, and then with new friends. We are engaged with life again and we feel guided by a strong sense of a purpose. Our lives are rich, busy, and filled with joy. We have learned so much, and from this new knowledge, we have come to realize that even at our age we have much to offer. We feel useful again.

Dear Friends, we are here because we have awakened to the needs of our planet, and we now know that we have the means to help her. We celebrate everyone who is already assisting the Earth and we desire to join the Earth rescue forces by assisting in a way that complements all the efforts already in progress. I feel comfortable speaking for the rest of our old friends when I say this is why *The Answer in Action* has been created. We want to help the Earth and we believe the information in this book will play a relevant role in her recovery process. We all have a role to play in this vitally important mission of mercy. Hopefully, you too will discern what your contribution will be.

Thank you, Dear Readers, for reviewing our initial remarks. And now, with great excitement and applause, we welcome the Smiths to share their story."

~ 3 ~

"Wellness to the Earth! I open with this particular salutation because it is one that has deeply touched us in recent months. We would like to introduce it to the readers of this book in hopes that you too may find this greeting to be a statement of compassion and loving kindness. My name is Jan Smith and my husband's name is Everett and we wish to share a story with you about a series of unusual events, which profoundly changed our lives. Please understand when these events originally occurred we were not accustomed to such experiences. In truth, we were way beyond our comfort zone. Since then, we have experienced so many additional so-called unusual experiences that they no longer have the same effect upon us."

"Excuse me, dear, but perhaps you might clarify that statement for our readers."

"Yes, of course, Ev. Dear Readers, let me elaborate upon that thought for a moment. We, Everett, myself, and our family of friends, are still amazed every time we encounter another one of these events. Truth be told, I'm not sure we will ever cease to be amazed. However, the frequency of these encounters is now so regular that we no longer regard them as unusual experiences. When the unusual experiences first began, I don't think any of us would have ever imagined that would be possible. We share the reality of our transition with you, because we want you to understand both our initial reactions to these events, and also how we adapted to them. Simply stated, familiarity fosters acceptance."

"Well said, Jan! That describes our adjustment phase beautifully."

"Oh, thank you, dear! Shall I continue or would you like to share our initial unusual event with our readers?"

"I would be glad to take the lead, dear. I too will begin by acknowledging our beloved planet. Wellness to the Earth! May your blessings be many! Dear Reader, our story began on an impromptu trip to an island that we had never visited before. Jan and I are avid travelers; however, traveling to this particular island was in itself unusual. We have a preferred island that we frequently visit, but for some reason still unknown to us, we found ourselves traveling to this new setting. It was a lovely secluded island with beautiful beaches, but being there made us homesick for our preferred island."

"Yes, that's true! In some odd way, Ev and I both felt as if we were betraying our favorite island by visiting this new one."

"We reluctantly left our charming cabana and went for a walk on the most gorgeous beach either one of us had ever seen. It was deserted; we had the entire beach to ourselves. We walked in blissful peace and quiet while we both wondered why we were there. We were so engaged in our own thoughts that we were startled when a fellow in a long flowing white garb appeared in front of us. He appeared agitated and fervently asked us why we were there. He insisted that we must go to The Island. He repeatedly announced this and also proclaimed that The Island needed us. His persistent and intense manner was off-putting. Jan and I were both uncomfortable, but didn't know how to extract ourselves from the situation. We briefly turned to one another with questioning looks and then instantly turned back towards the fellow only to find that he had disappeared. He was nowhere in sight. It was an impossible feat. One moment he was in front of us and in the next moment he was gone. There was no way he could have escaped our view in that brief moment of time. As you might imagine this incident was very disorienting. The fellow's arrival was unusual. His departure was unusual. And his admonishment about The Island in need of assistance was unusual. The perplexing incident hastened our desire to leave and we did. The unsettling nature of the incident weighed heavily upon us for a while, and then life took over, and the incident was forgotten.

Dear Readers, you will soon learn that my beloved wife is a very energetic sort and a wonderful storyteller. I can feel her excitement ramping up now, so I will pass the lead back to her."

"Oh, thank you Ev! And you are right of course, dear, I am very eager to share our next adventure with our New Friends. As Everett commented earlier, we are enthusiastic travelers and the next incident we experienced also happened while we were travelling. Actually, the trip was coming to an end and we were waiting in the New Delhi Airport for our return flight home. We were pleasantly fatigued; the way one feels when you have a particularly enjoyable trip. Both of us were lost in our respective thoughts, each reminiscing about various aspects of the vacation, while at the same time wishing we were already home sleeping restfully in our favorite bed. We have found that traveling makes us very aware and appreciative of the comforts of home, particularly one's own bed. In my silly mind, I was fantasizing about being instantly transported back to our home, as it is so magnificently presented in those wonderful sci-fi movies. Well, as you might imagine, my fantasies did not come to fruition; however, the experience that we encountered does make one wonder about the viability of teleportation.

At one point while we were just wasting time, we were standing near our boarding area and basically zoning out when a well-dressed, gray-haired elder gentleman appeared in front of us. Neither of us remembers him approaching. One moment we were standing alone (in a crowded airport) and in the next instant, there he was before us. Although his appearance and manner were very different from the fellow on the island, his arrival was very similar. And his message was the same theme. He repeatedly said we must return to The Island and emphasized that she was in need of assistance.

Well, as you might imagine, we were stunned by his sudden appearance and equally perplexed by the content of his message; however his insistence did not have the same off-putting affect that we experienced before when we were approached on the island. Clearly the messages presented were the same, but our reaction to the second fellow was different. Maybe we were less taken aback because of the earlier experience, or perhaps, we were more able to hear the urgent request within the message the second time around. I'm not certain why we reacted differently, but I think, although I've never confirmed this with Everett, I think we both were determined to secure more information from this fellow. We wanted to know what was going on?

Similar to our experience on the island, we turned to one another perhaps for reassurance or confirmation that we were indeed going to interact with this man, but when we turned back to face the elder gentleman, he was gone. Everett and I immediately went off in different directions looking for him, but he was nowhere to be found. It was, at the time, inexplicable. We even asked the couple who was standing near us while we were engaging with the fellow if they had seen where he had gone. Neither of them remembered seeing us talking with anyone. Obviously, their response brings out another peculiar factor of this unusual incident.

Needless to say, this experience left us confused and frustrated. Yes, I do think it is fair to say that we were very frustrated by the encounter. Don't you agree Everett? Of course, the mystery of the situation was intriguing as was the incident on the island, but we are people who want to know and understand what is happening around us, and in both of these situations we were left knowing nothing. Even now, as I share this story with you, I can remember the dissatisfaction of not knowing what was going on. Thank goodness, we have since learned a great deal about some of these mysteries. Many aspects of the events are still a mystery to us, but we know so much more now than we did then, and we are very grateful and relieved for this.

Dear New Friends, there is more to share, but I am ready to hand the torch over to Everett."

"Thank you, Jan. Your retelling of the airport event takes me right back to that moment in time, and it's very interesting, dear. As you stated, we've learned a lot since that encounter and because of what we've learned, I am currently reacting to the experience differently. I do indeed remember the frustration we felt, but now, I also recognize we were feeling a sense of desperation because we didn't know how to respond to the elder gentleman's urgent instructions. His insistent command that we go to an unidentified Island that was in great need of assistance was compelling, and complying with his heartfelt appeal seemed to be the appropriate action to take. However, regardless of the sincerity of his intentions, the interaction was too odd and the information was too vague for such a decision to be made. Even though I felt obliged to do something, I simply didn't know what to do. And that brings me back to the frustration that Jan mentioned earlier. The situation was frustrating and also very disruptive to the peaceful state that we were enjoying before the encounter overtook us.

Eventually, we boarded our plane, ruminated most of the flight home, and then found ourselves exhausted and at the end of a mile long queue in the customs section of the airport. Of course, I'm exaggerating about the length of the line, but in the moment, our freedom from the grips of airport bureaucracy seemed to be delayed for another hour at least. This brings us to the third part of our unusual adventures.

While we were slowly progressing in the endless winding lanes of the queue, we heard a couple of women talking in a lane several rows beyond us. Their conversation alluded to an encounter with an elder gray haired gentleman. The teller of this story stated that a stranger, the elder gentleman, had approached her and insisted that she must return to The Island and that he also claimed that The Island was in great need of her assistance. Well, as you might imagine. Oh goodness! There I go using that old four-letter word again. Sorry about that slip of the tongue, but it gives us an opportunity to honor our planet. Wellness to the Earth, Dear Friends! May she grow stronger and stronger with each salutation proclaimed.

Now back to the story. As you might imagine, their conversation grabbed our attention. Normally, we are not people who eavesdrop on someone's conversation, but having just heard our previous story, I'm sure you will understand how our curiosity got the best of us. The woman's story was incredibly similar to our own. We desperately wanted to talk with her, but as she continued to advance forward in her aisle, we grew further and further apart. She reached the customs counter long before we did. As was to be expected, we did not cross paths with her when we exited the airport, but nevertheless, her story validated ours. We realized at that point that something very unusual was transpiring and that we were not the only ones involved. Other people were also having similar encounters to our own. We were in awe. And we wanted more information.

When we finally got home, we felt very alone in this process. Even though we had just overheard this incredible validation of our own experiences, we still remained confused. So we did what we always do when we are mulling over a topic of importance. We retreated to our bedroom where we both jumped upon our bed and situated ourselves in the preferred upright positions that were necessary for delicate conversations. There, in our blessed comfort zone, we pondered what we were to do about these strange events.

We talked until fatigue forced us to stop. Although we made no decisions before falling asleep, we ended our conversation in agreement about our disbelief in coincidences. We had long ago let go of that notion. Although we remained clueless about the incidents transpiring around us, Jan and I were certain that these events were happening for a reason. We had no idea how to pursue more information, but we were determined to do so. Have I reported everything up to this point accurately, dear?"

"Yes, Everett, you've done a lovely job of presenting our story thus far. Shall I bring our presentation to an end?"

"Please do, Jan, and remind our New Friends that the story continues to this day."

"Indeed, this is true, Dear Readers and New Friends. Our story continues; however, I will conclude our story for now by briefly sharing what transpired after that lengthy conversation the evening after we returned from our trip. Needless to say, the desire to know more about the incidents did not fade, and in fact, our frustration and agitation grew because we both felt as if we needed to do something. Even though we didn't know which island was being discussed, we wanted to help. At one point we returned to our favorite island that we have frequented for several decades. Actually we returned numerous times. We walked her beaches, we walked her cliff trails, and we desperately attempted to discern if she was the island that was alluded to by the two messengers from unknown places. I think it is safe to reveal this truth to you, Dear Reader. Everett and I were very unsettled by these events. Our hearts ached. We so wanted to help, but we just didn't know how to proceed. Our distress eventually led us to disclose our story to our dear friends. We were aware they had noticed a change in us, and we could tell that they were concerned, so we mustered up the courage to share our story with them. Thank goodness for that action! It changed our lives. What a tremendous relief it was to share these events with old friends. Not only did we receive their love and support, but we also learned so much more about their lives as well. Little did we know that all of us had stories to share!

We are so grateful to be sharing these remarkable experiences with you as well. Our lives are richer now. It took courage to share our stories. Even though we had years of history with our friends, we were still guarded about revealing our stories. As we look back on those fears, we question why we were so nervous about it, but the truth is we were. The other folks that we have met since then have also shared similar fears. And you, Dear Reader, may be having doubts as well. If you are, please just know that you are in very good company. One of the most advantageous aspects of experiencing these unusual encounters is the camaraderie that has developed from the retelling of our tales. Our relationships have deepened, our outlook on life has expanded, and the joy that we feel from participating in this work is as indescribable as were the encounters themselves. We are so grateful to be a part of this important project.

As Everett said earlier, there are many more stories to share; but for now, I hope you have a better understanding of who we are and why we are pursuing this project of reaching out to others with similar experiences. We are committed to helping others and we are committed to helping our Mother Earth.

Oh goodness, I just realized there are still two more tasks for me to address. First, Everett and I wish to thank you for reading our stories. We hope you have benefitted from the experience and we welcome any feedback you may wish to share with us. My second task, Dear Reader, is not really a task at all. It is a privilege to have the opportunity to introduce you to two of our dearest friends. We are certain you will be as amazed by their story as we were. Bill and Pat have been in our lives for many, many years and we are deeply grateful to be sharing this incredible life experience with them. So without further ado, please welcome the Joneses. Enjoy the read!"

~ 4 ~

"**H**ello and welcome to another chapter in the lives of the Circle of Eight. If you haven't yet been introduced to this term of endearment for our group, suffice it to say, we are eight old friends who have found ourselves in the middle of a remarkable mystery that is filled with oodles of so-called coincidences. Even though none of the eight involved believe in coincidences, the mystery, or better said, the mysteries have captivated our attention.

Our group initially came together because each of us was seeking counsel about an unusual encounter that we had experienced. It was only natural that we would turn to our dearest friends to discuss such a sensitive matter; however, we were all taken aback when we found that each of us had experienced a similar unusual incident. Since we came out to one another regarding these unusual events, we have gathered many times to explore more information about these situations, and much to our surprise during our gatherings, many more unusual events unfolded. We presume we have been given the designation of the Circle of Eight, because of our frequent meetings and our fervent desire to understand what is happening. Whether our presumption is accurate or not, we are not certain. Nor are we sure who afforded us this designation, but that is another uniquely puzzling mystery that demands a chapter of its own. Stay tuned for that episode of the ongoing saga of the Circle of Eight!

Dear Reader, my name is Bill and I begin the Joneses' story in this manner because it is important that you know that my dear wife, Pat, and I are not people who typically get carried away by unusual events. We've lived a very quiet, ordinary life and it never occurred to us that we would some day be wrapped up in this type of adventure. Having said that, I cannot fully impress upon you just how happy and grateful we are to be a part of these exciting times.

I think I've said enough for the moment, so I'm going to turn this over to the real storyteller in our family."

"Thank you, Bill. Hello, Dear Readers, I am Pat and I am so delighted to share our story with you, but before I jump into that, let me first address an extremely important matter. Wellness to the Earth, and to you as well, Dear Friend! We like to take advantage of every opportunity to extend good wishes to our wonderful planet. Bill and I try to acknowledge her several times a day and we also address her recovery process every day. More about that later. Actually, I will say a little more about the Earth's recovery process at this point because it is the primary reason for the development of this book. We will be delving more deeply into that topic shortly, but for now, let me say that all of us, meaning all the members of the Circle of Eight, are committed to doing a minimum of at least one healing meditation a day on behalf of the Earth. We believe intentional acts of kindness can effectively improve her present state of health. It is one of the simple ways in which we and everyone else across this enormous planet can immediately take action to assist her. There is so much more I would like to share with you, but I am getting ahead of the story. Let me return to task.

Bill and I had our first unusual experience after visiting our son's family. Our grandchildren are growing up very rapidly, and as is typical for grandparents, we selfishly want to spend as much time as possible with them before they become so busy with their own affairs that they won't be interested in hanging out with the old folks. We're near that time already; they are so involved with school events, after school events, weekend events, etc., etc. We had a wonderful time with everyone, but Bill and I sensed when it was time to leave, not just for us, but for the kids as well. So we decided to make the drive back home a real road trip, the kind you take when curiosity is leading you around every bend in the road. We hadn't done a trip like that in a long time, but we were enlivened by the idea. In fact, the more we discussed the itinerary, the more excited we became, and soon our enthusiasm over shadowed our sadness about leaving the kids and grandkids.

So off we went on our adventure, and goodness, we did have a lovely time. We saw so many beautiful sights. We drove miles and miles, stopping here and there along the way, always attempting to secure the best possible photos, when we came upon a scenic overlook, which had received great reviews according to our guidebook. It did indeed look very appealing from the road, and we were both in need of a snack by this time so we decided to take advantage of the opportunity. It seemed too good to pass up. When we pulled into the parking area, we were a bit dismayed because no other cars were there, which made us wonder if this really was the special scenic overlook advertised in the guidebook. Once we got out of the car and walked up to the railing, we knew we were at the right place. To say the view was stunning would be the biggest understatement of all time. This may sound odd to you, Dear Reader, but Bill and I both felt as if we lost time while we were standing there. It could have been a few minutes or an hour or more. We don't really know, but it was an unusual feeling that we still remember to this day. At some point, Bill pointed to our left towards a stand of large boulders resting at the edge of the canyon. He mentioned that they seemed to be seeking our company and suggested we change locations. These huge ancient structures had the appearance of a stately family graciously welcoming guests to enjoy their meals while also consuming the remarkable views. Needless to say we succumbed to the temptation. As Bill grabbed our brown bag lunch from the car, I meandered over to the chosen dining and viewing area. What an exquisite setting it was! The natural formation of the landscape provided a comfortable sitting area, where one could leisurely take in the miles and miles of panoramic views. When Bill joined me, the vista recaptured our attention again. My Friends, this planet is absolutely gorgeous. It is so sad that we do not intentionally take time to notice her, but we did in that moment. We quickly situated ourselves side-by-side on Mother Earth's beautifully developed surface, peered out over the canyon view, and once again seemed to lose time. No words were spoken; we simply took in the magnificence of this remarkable Life Being. Time passed, although we do not know how much so.

Eventually, long deep breaths were simultaneously taken. The synchronicity of our bodily rhythms could not go unnoticed. We embraced one another, enjoying the moment of heartfelt connection. When our eyes returned back to the views, we were stunned once again, but this time it was not the countryside that grabbed our attention. In between the boulders and the railings at the canyon edge stood an impeccably well-dressed gray-haired elder gentleman with the most engaging smile either one of us had ever seen. I repeat we were stunned. There he was dangerously positioned with his back to the canyon seemingly oblivious to his precarious situation. Where had he come from? His attire indicated that he was not a hiker who had quietly trekked in front of us. Bill remembers quickly glancing towards the parking lot to see if another car had arrived without our notice, but none other than our own was there. As you may imagine, we were very confused. Questions filled our minds, but before we good say anything, he proclaimed a most unusual message. Gently, yet firmly, he informed us that we must return to The Island, and emphasized that The Island was in desperate need of our assistance. Except for this ominous message he was delightfully pleasant. He even referred to us as Old Friends, and if circumstances had been different, we might have agreed with that sentimentality. Even through the context of our encounter was so peculiar, we did in truth feel a sense of connection and peacefulness with his presence. Unfortunately, neither of us had any idea what he was talking about. He did not identify the island in question, nor did he elaborate upon the assistance that was needed, and when we attempted to gather additional information from him, it was not forthcoming. Instead, conversation came to a close and another unusual event transpired, as if his sudden appearance wasn't enough. I think it is fair to say that his departure was as equally theatrical. One moment the elder gentleman was there before us, and the next, he was gone! Needless to say, we were flummoxed, bewildered, and mystified…you choose the word that suits you. Each one is applicable.

Most importantly, Dear Reader, we were changed. This is very difficult to explain. Even though the experience was mindboggling, Bill and I both knew that we were being called to do something. Obviously, we didn't understand what the 'something' was, but we just knew from deeply within that our lives had taken a different course.

Our road trip ended at that canyon's edge. We both became very quiet and just wanted to get home. No more photos were taken and no other scenic overlooks grabbed our attention. The drive home was similar to a dream state. We remember very little about it; we were both lost in our own thoughts. When we finally got home we went straight to bed and slept for twelve hours. The next day we awakened in a daze. It took us several hours to remember our experience, and to realize that we had forgotten another part of our story, which we will share with you at another time. Suffice it to say, we had a life changing experience. And in the following days, our anxiety about our experience heightened. We knew that action needed to be taken, but we had no idea as to how to proceed. It was maddening in many ways, and yet, there was a sense of purpose that was indescribably resonant. We knew, without knowing how we knew it, that we were here for a reason, and that sense of purpose still resides within us to this day.

We live in gratitude every day for what has transpired in our lives. Even though we still do not understand everything that is being asked of us, we are committed to participating in acts of kindness and support of the Earth. What we have learned about her situation demands that action be taken. And what we have learned about our ability, meaning humankind's ability, to help her demands that we access these abilities on her behalf. Dear Friends, we are here to invite you to read our stories, and to share them within anyone you may feel it appropriate. We do not believe we are the only ones who have encountered these unusual experiences, and in truth, we have already met numerous others who have their own remarkable stories. Our hope is to bring the stories out into the open, so that everyone knows what is going on.

Bill, is there anything more you would like to add?"

"Yes, Pat, I would, but first let me thank you for presenting our story. We did indeed have an experience that profoundly changed us, didn't we, dear?

As, you can tell from my dear wife's wonderful tale, we have had quite an adventure. And because of it, we are more than we were before. Please let me elaborate upon that odd statement. The truth is I'm not sure anyone would even notice any changes in us. We're still just Pat and Bill. We look the same and for the most part our behaviors probably are not noticeably different except to those who truly know us. But we're different on the inside, and that's the point I really want to make.

Dear Readers, we've learned that there is more. So much more than we ever imagined! Some of you, hopefully many of you, already are aware of this truth. We were not, but our hearts are open to this reality now. And we are so, so grateful for this awareness. Our so-called unusual experiences have enriched our lives, and we hope by sharing our stories, others will also benefit from them. Thank you for reading our stories, and we look forward to hearing yours as well."

"Bill, we still have one more item to address. Dear Friends, we are happy and honored to introduce you to another dear friend of ours who is also a member of the Circle of Eight. Marilyn Brown has been in our lives for decades and we are so grateful she has been a part of this journey. Marilyn has a calming way about her that helps center our gatherings. Please continue reading, Dear Reader. You are in for a treat! And let me thank you again for reading our story."

~ 5 ~

"**W**ellness to the Earth and to you, Dear Reader! My name is Marilyn Brown and I would like to begin my story with a meditation. Will you please join me? I know it is difficult to read and meditate at the same time, but I'll proceed slowly so you can participate in both.

Please position yourself comfortably, Dear Friend. Whether you are presently lying down or sitting in your favorite chair, or wherever you are at this moment, please take a long deep breath. And live into it. Just be with your breath. Close your eyes now and just be with the expansiveness of your precious breath. Take the lead now please, and return to the next paragraph when you are ready.

With another deep breath, Dear Friend, open your heart to infinite possibilities. No need to think about this; just allow all thoughts to drift away. Open your heart to whatever may be. Close your eyes again, and allow your precious heart to be your guide. Return when you are ready.

Take another breath, Friend, and move to a place of gratitude. Wherever this thread of intention takes you, just be with the overwhelming awareness of deep heartfelt gratitude. Breathe this in, and remember! Remember how the presence of gratitude feels in your body. Remember this, please. Now close your eyes again and rest in the presence of your own inspired gratitude. Follow your own leadership and return when you are ready.

Welcome back, Dear Friend, and thank you for participating in this meditation with me. I am most grateful that you are here sharing this time with me. I am so excited about sharing my story with you and I'm grateful for your willingness to read about my personal journey.

As you may imagine, I have given this a great deal of thought and had to manage my fears and doubts to actually get to the point where I could muster the courage to share my experiences with you. The truth is this is not an easy task to approach until you are ready to do so, and then, it becomes another part of the journey.

I do believe it is important to share all aspects of this experience, including the reality of the doubting mind. Like it or not, there is a part of us that feels anxiety about sharing these unusual stories because we are afraid of being judged. I'm sure most of you can relate to this in some form or fashion. While I do not need to expound upon this part of the journey, I do want you know

103

that all of us in the Circle of Eight had moments of doubts and fears about coming out with our stories. We first had to face this when we shared our experiences with one another and then we faced it again at our first outreach gathering, and now we are facing it once more as we brace ourselves to put our deep heartfelt experiences down in writing for the world to see. I felt a tremor when I first faced the keyboard of my computer, and then I just knew it had to be done. I realized how important it was for us to communicate with others. We all believe that we are not the only ones having these experiences and we assume that these other people are as nervous about these experiences as we were. Our group is so blessed to have one another's support. It made this process easier. We hope by sharing our stories that others will find the process easier as well.

So, Dear Readers, here we are! And now, I must begin. So please excuse me, while I take another long deep breath. A moment for centering, no matter how brief it is, always assists me in whatever I am doing. Thank you!

I want to begin by sharing a secret with you. For a very long time, I have longed for something more. Although I didn't really know what that actually meant, I knew something was missing in my life. Having said that I must also acknowledge that my life was good. I had wonderful friends. My work was deeply satisfying. And my home was a personal sanctuary that gave me great pleasure; and still, there was an ache within me for something that I could not identify. Unfortunately, when one does not know what they are looking for, it is difficult to know how to pursue what is missing. Of course, I read many books and went to many workshops in attempts to find the mysterious missing piece in my life. Sometimes these efforts were briefly inspiring, but more often than not, the hunt for the unknown answer just left me feeling empty, and the ache deepened and became more intrusive than before.

Fortunately, one of my dearest friends is remarkably intuitive. Even though I had not brought this topic up in any of our conversations, one morning as we walked one of our favorite paths, my friend challenged me with a most curious question. When are you going to pursue your spiritual journey, my friend asked of me. The question posed was life changing. You see, Dear Reader, I had no idea there was such thing. I had never heard that term used before, so the question ignited a flame within me. My friend encouraged me to visit my favorite bookstore, which of course I did as quickly as was possible, and much to my surprise I did something I had never done before. I departed the self-help/psychology section that I knew so well, and boldly...actually that is an exaggeration. Truth be told, I timidly stepped into the New Age/Spirituality section of the store. The titles were intriguing. I remember feeling excited and nervous at the same time. Part of me wanted to grab every book that came into focus and another part of me was hesitant. I was shocked by my interest in these, yet to be read books. This isn't me, I thought. Well, in the upcoming days and weeks, I consumed dozens of these titles, and still craved more.

My curiosity was soaring. I felt as if questions finally were being answered but with each answer came dozens of more questions. Because of my friend's question, my heart was opened and the ache that I was so accustomed to became a friend rather than a nuisance. Of course, I still wanted to know more about The More I was seeking, but that question about the spiritual journey changed my outlook about the ache. I finally understood that I was on a journey, and even though I had no idea where the journey would take me, I knew my process was moving forward. What a precious gift that was! The ache of despair transformed into excitement and anticipation about life, towards life, with life. It was exhilarating and it remains so to this day.

Oh, Dear Reader, I am not articulating this well, but I hope you are grasping the beauty of realizing that there is more, and that the more is worth pursuing regardless of the moments of confusion. Now, when an inexplicable moment comes up, I am more inclined to giggle about it than to be concerned. Life is remarkable, Dear Friend, and we are just one of the many fascinating parts of the Greater Life that comprises the universe. How fortunate we are to be aware that we are indeed part of this magnificent mystery called Life. My life isn't really much different than it was before my friend asked the perfect question for the moment, and yet, life is so much better. And it is so much better because now I am aware that the 'More' that I ached to be with is ever present, everywhere, at all times. I am not alone, Dear Friend! Isn't that a wonderful awareness?

Dear Reader, my Dear Friend yet to be, life is so much more if we allow our hearts to open to all the countless possibilities that surround us. I invite you to open your hearts and I ask you the same question that my friend asked me. When are you going to pursue your personal journey? My Friend, you are a spiritual being in human form. And you are perfection just the way you are!

Why not pursue who you really are and discover the wonder of you?

Thank you for allowing me to share my story with you. It is an ongoing, never-ending story. Each day brings new opportunities for me to preview and to incorporate into my present way of being. And each day, more is learned about the more that we are a part of. It's a very comfortable place to be. Goodness, I realize before I bring this to a close another part of my story must also be shared. As you well know by now, we, the Circle of Eight, have enjoyed a most delightful experience together, which is why this book is being composed. Similar to my friends, I also am grateful to include my encounter with the elder gentleman who has shared so much with us about the more that I have attempted to share with you. His wisdom has been and continues to be profound. And his presence brings one to another level of awareness. Perhaps, that sounds odd, but it is true nonetheless, and you will experience it for yourself someday if you haven't already had the pleasure. My initial encounter with him was a life long dream come true. There are no words that will ever adequately express the heartfelt connection that was felt. I am so grateful for the experience because his presence was proof of the more I desire to know. Although I am embarrassed to admit that I wanted proof, the truth is, I did want proof. And I now know this experience of connection is not rare. It is available to everyone! Because of our connection with this amiable fellow, our group now understands so much more about the circumstances of our Beloved Earth, and because of this new awareness, we are committed to providing assistance to her. We can to do this, which in itself is a gift to know. We are healers, Dear Friends, but we forgot about these innate abilities long ago in our evolutionary development. But the skills still exist within us, and with these skills, we can assist the Earth back to good health. There is much more to know about this topic and it will continue to unfold through the pages of this book. Please open your hearts to this opportunity, Dear Readers. Your assistance is needed as well.

I hope to meet you soon and I look forward to hearing about your story. Peace to you, and to the Earth!

Oh, goodness! I have one more task to address. Before we part company, it is my pleasure to introduce you to the friend, my walking buddy, who asked me the question that changed my life. I hope you are as fortunate as am I to have such a good friend. Good luck with your journey, Dear New Friend."

~ 6 ~

"**W**ellness to the Earth! And to you, as well, Dear Reader! I hope this moment in time finds you filled with curiosity, hopefulness, and peace of mind. Regardless of your current life circumstances, these three powerful attributes will sustain you during your present situation and also in the adventures that lie ahead. Dear Friend, it is a privilege to be in your presence, and I am most grateful for your willingness to participate in this story about the stories of ordinary people living ordinary lives.

As you read these stories, you may wonder if they are real or fantasy and the answer to both of the questions is yes. Each story encompasses the adventures of real people who call the Earth home. And each story is also one that many have fantasized about, but not yet realized in their present life experience.

Most people desire more. They may not understand this feeling residing deeply within them, but at some level there is an inkling of awareness that they need more. And of course, I am not speaking of material things. Most of us have far too many things already. I am referring to the existential need for the inexplicable more. Hopefully, more people will come to this realization of their need 'for more' by their participation in reading this story, which is a true story about the planet Earth. In learning about her health crisis, one also learns more about their own place in existence. Dear Friends, there is so much to learn, and we will do so, as we participate in one of the greatest stories every told. As the Earth continues to struggle for her life, everyone who resides upon her will be needed to provide her with support and assistance. Fortunately, we have the ability to do this. Although this may be news to a large sector of the population, we do indeed possess an innate ability with which we can assist her. Of course, some will find this idea ludicrous, but the Earth does not have time to wait on those who thrive on denial. Eventually, everyone will realize the truth, but in the meantime, she requires assistance now. Even though we are speaking of a skill lost ages ago, the skill still exists and it is operational in every living being. So, we must focus our intentions and reignite our innate ability back to its maximum efficiency. Every effort we make on her behalf is beneficial. Even as we practice re-engaging with our ancient abilities, she will be aided. The point being, dear friends, we have the ability to heal her and even as beginners our efforts will help sustain her.

The beauty of this reality is that every person on the planet can participate in this action without costs and without relocation. The infusion of energy from one person to another or to a very large Life Being demands nothing more than sincerity and intention. This healing aspect of humankind exists, and by accessing this ancient skill, we can help restore her back to full health. This contribution does not override or interfere with any other efforts presently underway. It is an ancillary service of extreme potential. Needless to say, Earth is a very large Life Being, and one dose of energy will not be enough to cure her ailments. But magnify one contribution by over seven billion contributions and you can begin to imagine the possibilities. The effort required to transfer energy to another is an insignificant amount of time and effort. Anyone can do this. Just imagine everyone on the planet participating in this every day, several times a day. As we do this, there will be more time to complete sustainable operations to maintain her future well being. This is doable! Dear Readers, open your hearts to this. Access your curiosity, your hopefulness, and your peace of mind. These three factors can alter the Earth's decline.

This is the scenario of the Earth's story. The question is how will her story end. So little is asked of us, and yet, so much we can achieve. Ponder this, Dear Friend. Much more will be said about this as we move forward with our personal stories.

What you just read now flowed through me as I addressed the task of writing about my experiences. I would love to say it was of my own making, but the truth is, I am reading it as it unfolds upon my computer screen just as you are reading it now in front of you. This unusual ability is new to me, and I am coming out about this now as I share it with you. This is just one of my unusual experiences, but it certainly is a favored one. I cannot express how humbling it is to participate in such a transmission of information. For many, this will sound ridiculous, but it simply is what it is. I am grateful to be a part of this fellowship and am doing my part by showing up, quieting myself, and listening with the ears of my heart. As you might imagine, I was taken aback when it first began, but my faith assured me that it was real and I trusted that this guidance was true. So far, what has come forward through me are some of the most significant messages I've ever been privileged to hear. They are loving, compassionate, and important for everyone. Clearly, these messages are meant for everyone, not just me. I am merely the receiver and the presenter of these words of wisdom.

My Friend, for a very brief moment, I was enamored with this process.

Why me, I wondered? Why now? These questions and many more filled my mind, but the answer to all the questions was the same. The time is now. The time is now for the messages to be presented. The time is now to take action. The time is now for the peoples of Earth to realize the truth regarding their existence in existence. The time is now! And I am just one of many, many people on the Earth who are receiving similar messages. This ability that seems to have appeared from out of nowhere is not unusual, even though it appears to be. The truth is that everyone has this innate ability, but for reasons that I am still unclear about, the ability is somehow triggered in some while others are still in process. Perhaps it is similar to the blossoming of spring flowers. Some begin the path of new beginnings before others do, but all are capable of blooming when their particular time arrives. I have no more words about this other than that simple analogy. The point is, one day I was unable to receive messages. In fact, it never even occurred to me that it was an option. And the next day, the messages came forward. It was a surprise. And once I got over the concerns, the doubts, and the fears that I was losing my mind, I accepted the reality that I had finally found the true mind that exists within all of us. After dealing with this for some time now, I can truthfully say that this is one of the most remarkable opportunities that I have ever experienced. To say the least, it is fascinating. To elaborate a bit, I will add that it is also the most healing experience I've ever had. The intimacy, the deep heartfelt connection that one feels when participating is this process is indescribable. Many unusual experiences have occurred recently that transformed my life, but this one stands alone for me personally. Gratitude is awakened in every cell of my body.

My unusual experiences also include an encounter with an elder gray haired gentleman, whom I am sure you've heard about from my dear friends. When I first heard about him I was extremely curious, and then, the story of his appearance repeated itself with several other friends and from numerous clients as well. I felt as if he was appearing to everyone but me, and I must admit I was a bit out of sorts that I was the only one who had not encountered him. Then one evening as I walked about in the neighborhood pondering his unusual appearances, I came face to face with him. He was the most delightful jovial individual anyone could ever hope to meet. We sat down on the curb side by side, and we talked and laughed, as time stood still. At one point, I asked him if anyone else could see him sitting beside me, and he replied that it was unlikely. We laughed again, noting how curious that would be to a passerby who saw me sitting there alone talking to and laughing with empty space. At that point we agreed it would be wise for me to communicate from within. At first, I wasn't certain how one might do that but soon found it was as natural as speaking aloud. Many other such conversations have happened since then, but that one is very fond memory of mine.

He, our elder friend, is a frequent visitor to our gatherings. Sometimes he comes in visible form and sometimes, he does not. We have come to understand that it requires a great deal of energy to manifest form and sometimes that energy simply isn't available. Obviously, we prefer to see his effervescent smile, but his presence, visible or not, is the essential connection that we long for. All of us are equally skilled in existential communication now, so his invisibility isn't an issue. We simply enjoy his presence. We have learned so much from him. And the time is now for us to share what we have learned. The time is now for action to be taken.

My Dear New Friend, we are ordinary people. We have no more skills or abilities than any other. We are simply good friends who found ourselves wrapped up in a remarkable set of circumstances that brought us all together to confront an issue of extreme importance. We are here for a reason. And so are you!

The Earth, our beautiful planet, is critically ill, and she cannot continue to support us in her present state of being. She demands attention and she needs it now. If she is to continue to be a residence for all of humankind, then humankind must come to her aid. The evidence of this reality is inescapable even though there are many who prefer to ignore and deny the truth for reasons that are purely founded in selfishness. There is no longer time to discuss the irrational behavior of those who refuse to accept the truth about the Earth's decline. The reality is this. She requires help now and the only way she will survive, as she is presently known, is for the civilization of humankind to come to her aid. We are not talking about the pragmatic efforts of sustainability that are already in progress. Those essential efforts must continue to expand and grow globally, but those efforts will not transpire quickly enough to alter the Earth's decline. They will aid her in the future, but they will not correct what is already happening in time for her to recover on her own.

The assistance that is needed requires the participation of every human on the planet. An act of generosity is needed and the people of Earth are the ones who must initiate this action. So little is asked of us. Within each of us resides the innate ability to heal self and others. We unfortunately lost awareness of the ability long ago in our evolutionary development, but the ability still exists within us. If your mind is currently creating doubts about this possibility, please ask your mind to be quiet. The ability exists. We are capable of relearning how to use this ability. And the process is so easy that there is absolutely no reason for anyone to resist this responsibility. I use the word responsibility because it defines our role in this process of saving the Earth. For millennia, she has provided us with residence and asked nothing in return. Now, she is in need, and it is our responsibility to assist her as she assisted us since we came into existence. She gave everything to us while putting herself in jeopardy. All that is asked of us is that we share our energy with her. That's all that is required. Once a day offer a particle of your energy to her. Consider this to be a prescription for a dose of medicine that will assist her recovery process. Dear Reader, this only takes a few minutes of your time. In fact, it is so easy that one can participate in this process more than once a day. She is such a huge Life Being. She will require many doses, and we will need to be patient, for she is very ill. Her recovery will not happen over night, but she will recover if we participate in this act of generosity. Just imagine that, Dear Reader. Just imagine the opportunity to help the Earth. What a privilege it will be! And in so doing, we will also be assisting humankind, because we cannot continue without her. That is a thought that no one wishes to face, and if we act now, we will not have to. We have the ability to heal the Earth, Dear Friend. And it is our responsibility and our privilege to do so.

Dear New Friend, I am so grateful for this time together. Thank you for reading my story and for facing the truths that were brought through from messages that were received during and before this story was written. I so look forward to meeting you in the future, and thanking you in person. Please continue reading, for it will take so little to learn how to tap in to your healing abilities. In peace be, Dear Friend. And wellness to the Earth!"

~ 7 ~

"*P*eace to the Earth and to all the Children who reside upon her! Greetings of peace and good will are my privilege to present to you. I am most grateful to be in your presence, as you turn the pages of this book that was created on your behalf. Perhaps this is an unusual way for us to meet, but as you have learned from the previous stories, the first encounter is typically experienced as an unusual event. I am most grateful for this opportunity and hope that it will expedite our next encounter, which will preferably be in person.

I am the one that the story refers to as the elder gray haired gentleman. Indeed, that description is accurately presented. It is an appearance that pleases me, and one, which has been claimed for many lifetimes now. I hope when we meet in person that my appearance will feel familiar to you.

As I read the stories with you, I am deeply touched by the emotions relayed by my Old Friends. I too have enjoyed our encounters, as well as the many experiences we have shared. It is most gratifying to be in their company. Fond memories enliven my spirits. One cannot adequately express the joy of being with those most loved. Gratitude overwhelms the senses and one's voice is momentarily silenced. Suffice it to say that I am where I am intended to be and the opportunity is deeply satisfying.

My colleagues in the Circle of Eight refer to the readers of this book as New Friends Yet To Be. That is a lovely sentiment and one that rings true; however, I must refer to you as Old Friends, for this is our truth. As the Circle of Eight are Old Friends to me, so too are you! Thus, I must acknowledge how happy I am to be with you once again, Old Friend. It is good to see you again, and I look forward to the moment when my appearance is available to you. What a delightful encounter that will be!

So, Old Friend, there is much work for us to do! As you have already read, our Beloved Earth is in peril. I speak bluntly because it must be done. There is no longer time to mull over this terrible news. We are beyond the time for discussions, debates, and denial. And we are beyond the time for pondering actions. Action must be taken now! Old Friend, please listen with the ears of your heart. The news of the Earth's condition is not new, but many have chosen to ignore the truth, so hearing it spoken so bluntly may be disturbing. I apologize for the shock of this reality, but the truth of her situation is upsetting and whether this is the first time or the thousandth time of hearing about her decline, the news remains incredibly *alarming. Breathe, my Old Friend, and know that you are not alone. The peoples of Earth must unite as One to face this crisis. You are not alone with this tragic situation, nor are you incapable of managing it. Please continue to read, Old Friend, for there is reason for hope!*

When existence came into existence, all existence was infused with the energy of the original existence, and that energy remains within all in existence to this day. The energy that created existence brought life into existence, and that energy, Old Friend, exists within you and all others in existence. Read this information over again, please. Read it and accept it for it is the truth that you and all of your fellow beings must accept. Humankind has the energy to revitalize the Earth. Old Friend, this is a truth about existence that must be accepted. For the sake of the Earth and for all who reside upon the Earth, this reality must be understood and accepted.

Another matter regarding this truth must also be accepted and this may be problematic for a species that has believed they were superior to other species, but the truth is truth nonetheless, and it is time for humankind to face this reality as well. All Life is infused with this original energy, not just the human species. All Life means just that! Ponder this, Old Friend, and again, realize that you are not alone. In addition to the enormous population of humans, there are far more Beings on the planet than just the human species and every life force is capable of assisting the Earth. Those who are considered less than human by humans are already striving to help her. Now, the human species must do their part. Old Friend, again I urge you to breathe into this. Open your heart and your mind to the truth that is provided, for it remains the truth regardless. As said before, there is no longer time for debates or for proof of what is presented. Action must be taken now. We pray that humankind will accept what is provided and will recognize the potential that exists within them.

Many from other locations are also here to assist, and we hope this will be comforting rather than alarming. The Earth is a Beloved Life Being who is highly regarded and cherished by other members of the Universe. These from other locations have been working on her behalf for a very long time, and intend to continue their efforts; however, without humankind's participation, the necessary change in her energy field will not be accomplished. Humankind must participate. They must come to her rescue.

The ability to heal her resides within you. This is not a joke. It is not a gimmick to sell books. It is a reality, and it is so simple. So little effort is needed. Each of you can help her from the comfy chair in your own living room or from any other location you choose. The point is that you have the ability to heal the Earth.

We are aware that this claim will be ridiculed and dismissed by many, but the appeal must be made anyway. And we do so now. What will you do, Old Friend? Will you shrug your shoulders and declare that this claim is impossible? Or will you stand up for the Earth? Will you give her a moment of time and relearn how to access and use your healing power? Will you give her the attention that is needed…just a few minutes of your time daily? Will you help? Will you participate in an act of generosity that can restore the Life Being Earth back to good health?

Please do not rush away from these questions. Please do not feel that you are being asked to participate in an impossible task. Old Friend, the healing power existing within you is a reality. This is not a ruse. You are more than you appear to be, and yet, you are as are all others. This truth is one of the most significant realities for humankind to recognize and accept. You are all One. No one is more than another nor is anyone less than another. You are all One, and you all share the unique ability to heal self and others.

For ages, humankind has distanced itself from one another. Rather than accepting your brotherhood and sisterhood, you focused upon and defined differences as reasons for separation, while ignoring the extensive similarities that you share. You chose status and greed over compassion and connection and the painful consequences of these ill-fated decisions are factors in the declining health of the planet. Each act of unkindness and cruelty created a negative energy that polluted the Earth, and as the meanness and violence grew, so too did her illness. She experienced every injury perpetrated upon one of her residents. When her forests were decimated, she screamed in pain. When the whales were slaughtered, she wept in despair. And when humans chose wars over compromise, the agony was unbearable. She endured every act of unkindness that transpired upon her. No wonder she is so ill. Not only have her resources been stripped from her, but she has also witnessed more cruelty than anyone can bear. The negative energy of humankind can no longer be tolerated. It is destroying the planet and everyone who lives upon her.

To heal the Earth, humankind must also heal themselves. By participating in healing the Earth, the energy of humankind will also change. As stated before, the innate healing ability is capable of healing self and others. You cannot restore another's well being without benefitting from the healing process. This is truth of the Earth's crisis and the crisis of humankind. They are intricately linked. One cannot survive without the other.

Dear Reader, Old Friend, the truth is told, and now action must be taken. The people of Earth must accept their role in this unthinkable situation, and they must come forward and be the good people they are intended to be.

The Answer trilogy was prepared and presented to the peoples of Earth so that you will understand your role in this situation. You are responsible for the Earth's declining health and you are the Answer to her struggles. You can restore her to full vibrancy once again. Please accept this information about your innate ability and pursue recovering and revitalizing the ability within you. The task is easy. For the sake of the Earth and self, please take action.

My Friend, you are not alone. Many are here to assist and one way in which we will do this is by completing this book, which is intended to assist you in regaining access to your innate ability. Please continue reading, and invite your family and friends to do so as well. The Answer resides within these pages, and more importantly, the Answer lies within you. As you learn more about your skills and practice accessing these skills, your energy frequency will strengthen, empowering you to be of greater assistance to the Earth. Each time you offer a particle of your energy to her, she will benefit. Every time you think of her with love and kindness in your heart, she will benefit.

Compound this notion of sharing clean healthy energy to the Earth by a minimum of seven billion people and you will begin to comprehend the possibilities of your simple act of kindness. Every person that participates diminishes the negative energy produced by humankind's actions of ill will. Acts of kindness produce kindness within. Imagine the Earth filled with people who are behaving kindly towards one another. By changing the energy within the peoples of Earth, we will change the energy within the Earth.

Old Friend, there can be peace on Earth, and you can make this happen.

And now, I must bid you adieu. It has been an extreme honor to be in your presence. I am grateful for your time and attention and I hope you will give careful consideration to the plea of Those Who Came Before You. We are but a breath away."

~ 8 ~

"Wellness to the Earth! And to all the Life Beings who reside upon her! Hello again, Dear New Friend. This is Frank Sanderson speaking on behalf of the Circle of Eight. We hope you are still with us. You've been given a crash course in unusual experiences, truths about our existence, and the fate of life, as we now know it. What a read, uh? Welcome to our journey!

We are so hopeful that you will join our Mission to save the Earth. Sounds rather grandiose, doesn't it? In truth, it's just taking one more action a day, a few minutes of your time that will benefit her and you as well. As you have learned from reading this book, we are ordinary people who were blessed to have an unusual encounter with an unusual fellow with an unusual story. And we are so, so grateful! Navigating through all the new information was challenging at first, but that passed quickly; and then, it was a matter of living into this new information. I'm not saying that we are handling our commitments perfectly, but we're trying, and I think it's fair to say that we are improving. What I mean about commitments is this. We all agreed to take on this responsibility to assist the Earth. So each day, we make her a priority. We hold her in our thoughts and prayers, and we send energy to her a minimum of once a day. It a small thing to do, but it's powerful. I think each of us would say that participating in this act of generosity, as our Friend refers to it, has changed our lives. Dee and I both feel we have a purpose again and that makes us feel good about ourselves and about our lives. We've also noticed a change in our interactions with others. We're kinder, less impatient, and more appreciative of our friends and other acquaintances as well. Our view of the world has definitely changed for the better. We notice goodness first now, rather than targeting the nonsense of humanity. It's a shame that acts of cruelty are sensationalized while acts of kindness are ignored. We still keep ourselves informed about the daily news, but we no longer allow it to consume us. We're very careful about that and we also are diligent about focusing our intentions upon the goodness in the world. That totally shifts our viewpoint about the future. We are happier than we've ever been. In fact, I think we are joyful. Although our lives have always been good, I'm not sure joyful was a descriptor that ever came to mind, but it is now. Life is filled with joy. We look to the future with hopeful optimism now. Isn't that amazing? Even though we have greater understanding about the Earth's situation, we are now more hopeful than ever, because we know we can help her. It's very comforting to know you can help someone else. Yes, we are very pleased with our lives and with the outlook for the future.

We hope you will be too, Dear Friend, once you have had time to adjust to the information you've just received. It takes a while to wrap your brain around the Earth's failing health, but knowing that you can help makes all the difference is the world. Literally, Dear Friend, you can make a difference. We all can! Yep, I find that very comforting.

Does someone else wish to speak up now?"

"Yes, dear, I would love to have a few minutes of our Reader's time. It's me again, Dee Sanderson, just wanting to offer a few words of encouragement. I would love to tell you to take your time and sort through everything you've read, but I just can't do that. We don't have the luxury of time. So instead, what I want to say is this. Trust yourself! Trust that you can tell the truth, when it's being presented to you. The truth about our Beloved Earth is difficult to hear, but it certainly isn't the first time you've been apprised of this. I think you can feel and sense the sincerity of this message. And even if you still feel skeptical about the notion of possessing a healing ability, please don't immediately reject the idea. Open your heart to this, please! Having positive thoughts about the Earth certainly cannot do any harm. So have a little faith! Wish for the best! Hope for a complete recovery! Whatever way you can phrase this opportunity to make it work for you, please do it. We need your help, New Friend. The Earth needs your help. Please open your heart to new beginnings for humankind and for the Earth. I could say to you…take the risk, but there is no risk involved here. We are simply asking you to join us in focusing our intentions on healing the Earth. Please consider it.

I guess that's all I need to say…for now. Does anyone else wish to chime in?"

"Well, I see that my walking buddy is giving me the nod, which is her way to nudge me forward, so let me gather my thoughts please.

Peace to the Earth! And to all who are present! Dear Reader, New Friend Yet To Be, please just be with us for a moment. The Circle of Eight would like for you to gather with us as we prepare to send energy to the Earth. This requires only a few minutes of your time. If you cannot do this at this time, please take a break from this reading experience, and return later when you are free to be with us.

Dear Friends, let us begin as we always do with a long deep breath so that we can settled ourselves for this opportunity to be of service to the Earth.

Do so now, please. Take your deep breath and quiet your mind to outside interferences. Take several elongated breaths to facilitate the stillness that is desired. Close your eyes, Dear Reader, and rest with the peace that you are creating. When you are comfortable with your quiet space, return again for the next step of our exercise.

Friends, we are gathered to send a particle of the healing energy that resides within us to our Beloved planet Earth. Only one particle is necessary. Do not deplete your own resources, for another opportunity to aid her awaits. So visualize the healing energy resting within you. Perhaps, you sense it in your abdomen area, or in your heart space, or in the palms of your hands. The choice is yours. In actuality, your entire form is comprised of this healing energy. The visualization is simply to facilitate the conveyance of energy from you to the Earth.

So imagine your energy activating and becoming stronger with each breath that you inhale. And when you are ready, practice emanating the energy from your body and sending it outward to a nearby location of the Earth. It maybe a backyard, a garden, a lake, an ocean, or any place of your choice. Simply visualize your energy moving from your body outward towards a selected place. Release your healing energy to the Earth and breath deeply as you recover from this expense of energy.

As you rest from this act of generosity, allow yourself to feel the gratitude of Mother Earth. As she receives your gift, often a wave of her gratitude will rush through you. The intimate connection cannot be denied. The power of her gratitude is restorative. As you give to her, she returns the favor.

And now, Dear Friends, gift yourselves several more deep breaths as you return to the present.

Thank you, Dear Ones, for that act of generosity and for the pleasure of your company. The camaraderie of our combined efforts was most pleasing.

Marilyn, would you like to take the lead now."

"Yes, I am happy to do so. And thank you for guiding us through that energy session. So, Dear Reader, unless you are already an energy worker, I suspect this is your first exploration of being a healer. I wish you were here in person so that we could discuss your experience with you. If your first experience was similar to ours, you probably have many questions circling about in your mind. Just know this is to be expected. We still have lots of questions that surface after an energy exchange. Let's face it, Friend, this is a bit mind-boggling!

But I'm going to follow the lead of my walking buddy and encourage you to breathe into this. Your questions will help you to grow into these new experiences. Don't be afraid of the questions, but at the same time, don't give them more attention than they deserve. I personally found that my doubting mind was the biggest factor that I had to contend with when I first engaged in energy work, but it was easily overcome when I chose to be open-minded and curious instead. That gave me time to simply marvel about the mysteries of energy work rather than trying to understand every aspect of it. At some point, I finally realized that I didn't have to know everything about the process to accept that the results were positive, sometimes inexplicably so, but positive nonetheless.

And over time, my participation in sending the Earth healing energy has convinced me of the efficacy of this simple, yet unusual process. Perhaps it is described as unusual because it is difficult to explain; however, there comes a point when you know with absolute certainty that you have made contact with this incredible Life Being, and you sense her appreciation. You feel it, hear it, and know it all at the same time. It's like receiving a huge download of confirmation from her. Dear New Friend, I realize how odd this must sound, but it's my truth. I wish there were some way of transmitting this download to you, so that you could actually feel it as well. Wouldn't that be a hoot? Trying to explain these experiences is difficult, but all we can do is try. I look forward to the day when you can share your download experience with all of us.

I hope you will continue reading, New Friend, and also continue practicing your newly found healing ability. Keep sending energy to the Earth. You develop a rhythm after a while, and it becomes as easy as taking a deep breath. Thank you for participating.

Would someone else like to address our reader?"

"Oh, yes! My enthusiasm is running away with itself. Jan Smith here, and I just want to say how happy and grateful we are that you are reading *The Answer in Action*. That in itself is exciting, but the idea that you participated in an energy session with us brings joy to my heart. I cannot tell you how pleased we are to know that others are going to join us in this process.

Obviously the Earth needs a lot more doses of energy than the eight of us can provide, so your participation is a dream come true. If you're still reading this book, I assume you are as concerned about the Earth as we are. You don't have to be a scientist or a physician to know that she's really struggling. Her symptoms are blatantly obvious. You must recognize this as well, and that is very comforting and reassuring. Your presence reminds us that we are not alone. Oh, thank you so much for joining us. My heart is filled with gratitude.

Everett, dear, do you have any words of wisdom to share?"

"Goodness! Words of wisdom! Hmmm! I doubt that, dear, but I do have a thought to add to this gathering. Our Circle is growing! And I find that incredibly satisfying! In my mind's eye, I see the healers of the Earth growing in numbers until we actually encircle the planet. Just imagine that! The Children of the Earth standing side by side, hand in hand, from all over the globe. Standing together on her behalf and combining our efforts to generate enough positive healing energy so that she will recover from her illness and return to full vibrancy! The thought brings tears to my eyes. Imagine the peoples of Earth coming together to save the Earth. What an incredible act of kindness and generosity! The vision brings peace to my heart.

Dear Reader, New Friend, thank you for being a part of this Mission to save the Earth. Thank you for your kindness and your willingness to participate. I really look forward to meeting you some day soon."

"Thank you, Everett! The image you just shared is breathtaking. It warms my heart just thinking about it. This is Pat Jones, Dear Reader, and I just want to welcome you to our group. You've arrived at a very good time. As you can see, our gatherings are eventful. Someone always brings some revelatory idea for us to ponder, and Everett's vision is stellar. I see a beautiful poster in the making! This imagery really depicts the purpose of our story. We need people all around the planet to stand up and infuse her with their healing energy.

Everett, I'm going to incorporate this image into my meditations for the Earth. I believe it will intensify my efforts. The notion that all those other people will be participating in this process with me feels empowering, and I believe this state of empowered well being will enhance my abilities to share my healing energy with the Earth. I am so excited about this. I can hardly wait for the next session. Thank you so much, Everett.

And thank you, New Friend, for reading the book and for participating in the healing session with us.

Bill, do you have any thoughts to add?"

"Yes, Pat, I do. I must admit that this is an unusual session, Dear Reader, but in truth, most of our sessions are unusual, so this really isn't anything new, except that it is. I find it odd to be talking with a Reader of a book that we haven't even met, and yet, it seems right to do so. The truth is we feel very strongly about our responsibility to assist the Earth, and part of that responsibility is getting the word out about the innate healing ability that resides within humankind. As you might imagine, this is quite a surprise to all of us. Just a short while ago, we weren't even aware of this innate ability, and now, here we are presenting a book for the entire world to see. And that's exactly what we hope will happen. We hope everyone around the globe will read the book and get on board with this Mission to save the Earth. Again, I say, this is quite a surprise to all of us. But here we are! And here you are reading the page before you, and all I can say is Thank You.

My friends and I have already addressed many of the ups and downs of our unusual encounters and experiences. There are more, I can assure you, but I think you have a sense of what this process has been for us. We hope that you may learn from our advances and our mishaps, and that you will have compassion for your own vulnerable moments when you encounter them.

In general, I think all of us would agree that this period of life is incredible. And specifically, we are all eternally grateful for the experiences we have shared and for the opportunity we have been given to assist the Earth.

We welcome your participation, Dear Reader. You are needed! Please keep reading, because more information regarding the healing process will be presented soon. Thanks again!"

~ 9 ~

"**W**ellness to the Earth, and peace to all who inhabit her! Dear Readers, it is time for us to address you as the plurality that you are. You are not alone. As you read *The Answer in Action,* so too are many other readers all across the planet. Each of you has chosen to participate in this project intended to save our beloved planet Earth. We are most grateful for your presence, Dear Readers, and for your willingness to learn more about the innate healing ability that resides within each of us.

The Circle of Eight has learned much about this process in recent months, but we do not consider ourselves experts in this field that is as new to us as it is to you. Our goal is to share with you what we have learned, as best as we can, and also to facilitate communication between you and those who have provided us with this information. We recognize that this is an odd situation, and we appreciate how puzzling it must be. It was for us as well when it initially began to unfold; however, at this point in time we trust what is happening and we are comfortable with the exchanges that have transpired. The truth is, Dear Readers, nothing but goodness has happened as a result of our connection with the elder gentleman and his Companions. We agree with you that this appears to be an incredibly unusual experience, but it is one worth pursuing. Please stay with us.

We will begin by turning the lead over to our elder friend."

"Greetings, my Dear Friends! It is most delightful to be in your presence once again. I ask that you assist me in making our connection more deeply experienced. Please imagine me in your mind's eye to be in your presence. Perhaps I am in your home sitting in a chair next to you as you read these pages, or perhaps we are sitting on a preferred bench or a large boulder overlooking a favorite scenic view. Regardless of your present location, please envision me near you. I am smiling at you, Old Friend. Please feel the warmth of affection that is emanating from me, so that our relationship melds more quickly, and the reality of my presence strengthens within you.

I am real, Dear Friends. Even if you are incapable of seeing me at this particular moment, I am real, and it is a joy for me to see you once again. I selfishly hope you will be able to see me soon as well. So satisfying it is to be seen by those who are most precious to you.

My Friends, we are here for a reason. In truth, each of you is here for a variety of reasons; however, in this particular time at this particular place, we have come together for the purpose of saving the Life Being Earth. She is a cherished member of the Universe and she is intended to continue for all eternity. Her present situation is incomprehensible. Never has anyone given so much for so many. To see her in this condition breaks the hearts of Those Who Are Her Oldest and Dearest Friends. This was not intended. She is not intended to fall into dormancy.

Dear Friends, we need not repeat the messages regarding her declining health again. You already know the truth or you wouldn't be reading this book. So, let us discuss why we are really here. Each of us has been drawn here for a reason. Whether you are clear about this or not is irrelevant. The fact is you are here now, reading this book, because at some level of awareness, you know that you are intended to assist in the revitalization of the planet. You also know at this point that the revitalization process is dependent upon you and the innate healing ability that exists within you. Indeed, this is the reality that humankind must face. Each of you is responsible for her decline and each of you must actively participate in her recovery process. Fortunately, the solution to her problem resides within you.

My friends, we can save the Earth. As simple as this statement is, it purports a profound truth. The people of Earth can save this Life Being. Indeed, there are many actions that humankind will have to pursue to become model citizens of the planet. Many behaviors of greed and callous indifference will need to be faced before the Earth can reach a level of sustainability for future generations. However, the Earth cannot wait for humankind to change. Countless appeals have already been made, and still, the aggressive, offensive perpetrations continue.

The Earth requires immediate assistance. Her ill health must be stabilized and revitalized now. This is our priority, Dear Friends. This is why we are here. By accessing our innate healing ability, we can stabilize her and with persistent treatment, she will return to a state of renewed well being. Again, I say to you this is the priority.

In the meantime, all projects that are currently addressing matters of her decline must advance forward. Sustainability issues for current and future generations should be treated as priorities as well, and moved forward as quickly as possible. Those who are already working on the Earth's behalf must valiantly continue. Your contributions are invaluable. Those who deny her situation and who continue to contribute to her decline must face the insanity of their actions. Why do you continue to destroy the planet upon which you live? Do you not understand that your life depends upon her well being? If she does not recover from your brutal mistreatment of her, your species will not survive.

My friends, I regret having to speak so bluntly to the peoples of Earth, but the truth must be heard and accepted. If sanity prevails and steps are immediately taken to heal the Earth, then new options will present themselves. After the Earth's situation is stabilized, behavioral patterns will be challenged and addressed. People will recognize their shortsightedness and they will embrace change. Little tolerance will be had for selfish and foolish misconduct. The Earth's failing health will bring out the goodness in humankind. How sad it is that an unthinkable tragedy was required for this to happen.

Dear Friends, we are here for a reason. Together, we must act on behalf of the Life Being called Earth. I will now turn the lead over to the Circle of Eight. Perhaps, there is a need for a moment of reflection. In peace be, Dear Friends."

"Well, dear ones, we've had another adventure with our elder friend, haven't we? This is Dee Sanderson again. Dear New Friends, I suspect you have many thoughts about what just transpired. I wish you were here with us now so that we could all have a good discussion about this experience. I can assure you that his words were difficult for us to hear, as I imagine it was for you as well. We do not take his words lightly. We trust him and we know he speaks the truth. I can't exactly explain how or why we are so confident about what he tells us, but we are. Somehow, deep inside, we simply know he speaks the truth.

I so wish we could see you, New Friend. I wish we could look into your eyes and try to allay your fears. As I hear myself saying this, it makes me have greater appreciation for all the experiences we shared with our elder friend. The visual presence of another makes connection and communication so much easier. My point, New Friends, is this. There is reason for hope. Even though the Earth's situation is precarious, there is reason for hope. Oh my goodness! We must all remember this! We have the ability to help her. Isn't that amazing? We were gifted with this ability when we entered into existence, and now, in this critical moment in our existence, we are gifted with a reminder that we possess this innate ability. This is not a coincidence! Please don't dismiss the beauty of this significant awareness. Humankind has enjoyed so many blessings in our brief time in existence, and we are experiencing another blessing now as we face our futures together. My goodness, how sweet this is!"

"Indeed, it is, Dee! This is Frank again. New Friends, the truth is the encounter you just experienced with our elder friend is not unusual. He joins us regularly, and needless to say, he has been the impetus for our participation in this rescue mission. As Dee said, we trust him, and we depend upon his guidance. Sometimes, perhaps we rely upon him more than we should, but he's been very wise about helping us to own our individual leadership abilities. He's been an incredible teacher. And a friend, as well. We've been very fortunate.

Dee, maybe this is a good time to for another practice session. What do you think?"

"I believe we could all benefit from a moment of peace and quiet. New Friends, I hope you have time to join with us. We find resting in the silence a very restorative activity. This will only take a few minutes of your time. While you think about this, I'm going to turn to our friend who is so exquisitely skilled in leading our meditations. Dear One, will you take the lead please?"

"Of course, Dee, I am happy to do so. Well...oh goodness. There's that four-letter word again! Wellness to the Earth, Dear Friends! And peace to everyone who is here with us today! We've just had another reminder of the work that remains ahead of us. As always, it is challenging to hear the truth spoken so bluntly, but it is necessary. Unfortunately, the news about the Earth is not easily digested, so our attention goes to other topics that are less stressful and foreboding. We have refused to hear the truth for too long.

For some of you, this may have been your first reminder. Rest assured it will not be your last. Over time, we came to realize how quickly our attention can go elsewhere. We make commitments to assist the Earth daily and our intentions are sincere, but in a few days, the impetus to fulfill these commitments wanes. This is not a behavior that is easy to admit, but it is the truth and a reality that we must all face. Even though I trust myself to honor my commitment to the Earth, I must acknowledge my good intentions are easily distracted by life's ordinary happenings. One of the reasons I am so happy that our group meets regularly is because it curtails my forgetfulness. Because of our connection, we remind each other that we are here for a reason. Hopefully, New Friend, this will not be an issue for you, but in case it flares up, please be kind to yourself and remember you are not alone.

Dee, I would like to return to what you mentioned earlier. There is reason for hope. I so appreciate your saying that because it is the truth, and it must be remembered. There is reason for hope, and each one of us is a significant part of that truth. We must remind ourselves regularly about this truth as well.

So Dear Friends, far and near, let us begin our meditation with a deep breath. Be with your breath for a moment, and notice how you are situated. Are you comfortable? Are your surroundings, as you prefer? Give yourself time to assess your situation. If anything needs to be adjusted to improve your setting, please do so now.

And when you are ready to continue, enjoy another long, deep inhalation. Do not hurry your breathing exercise. Adjust your rhythm and pace to satisfy your needs. This is your time to hone your meditative skills. Breathe in when you prefer. Breathe out when you prefer. Mastery of this practice will come from your own inner wisdom.

Please continue to practice your breath work. Notice what works best for you, and what needs to be improved. Simply notice your process, without any criticism or judgment and when you are ready to do so, make the adjustments that you discern are needed.

As your breath work takes you deeper within, allow your mind to quiet. Release your thoughts. Release outside distractions. And enjoy the rhythm of your own inner being. Be with this as long as you desire. Dear Friends, I invite you into the Silence. Enjoy the luxury of the Silence that is opened to you. Just be. Nothing more is required of you. Just be with the Silence and know that you are not alone. Never, Dear Friends, are you alone. Always, you are in the company of Those Who Came Before.

My Friends, when you are ready to return, I will be here to welcome you home. Take your time. You are in command of your inner journey.

Ah! How nice it is to be with you again. Oh, Dear Friends, how I wish you were here with us now, so that we could all benefit from each other's travels. The stories we would share. New Friends, we look forward to the possibility of such a gathering some day soon.

Until then, we will hold you in our hearts and keep you in our prayers. May your blessings be many! Thank you everyone for participating in this brief meditation.

Dee, would you like to take the lead?"

"Actually, I will pass this time, dear, but thank you for the meditation. It was wonderful, as usual. I believe there is another who wishes to take the lead now."

"Well, it appears that my lovely wife as been eavesdropping on my thoughts. Not surprising! She is very good at that. Yes, dear, I would like to chair the gathering for a bit. I have a suggestion to make. Perhaps, this isn't the time, but I'm going to do it anyway. We've had a busy exchange today, and maybe it's time for everyone to put this book down and get some rest, but I think we would be remiss if we did so.

In case you didn't notice it, I began my reply to Dee with the four-letter word that we now use as a reminder to honor the Earth. I actually did this on purpose because I wanted to remind everyone who is reading this message right now to remember her throughout your day. Hold her in your heart and think of her with loving-kindness. Would you do that please? She needs our messages of good will. Wellness to the Earth! Silently repeat that phrase over and over again in your mind. She will hear you! And it will warm her heart. And her spirits will be raised by your good intentions. It matters, folks. Every positive thought matters.

So, before you close this book, wish her well. And keep sending her positive energy and messages of hope until we join again. In peace be, everyone! And wellness to the Earth!"

~ 10 ~

"Hello, Dear New Friends, we are most pleased to be in your presence again. As this is being written, I imagine you here with us. 'Here' refers to the home where we most frequently gather. The owner of this wonderful house, as you well know from reading *The Answer* series, is a Dear Friend, whom we all respect and cherish. The house is most pleased with its owner and delights in their conversations, even though they are, shall we say, one-sided at this point. The owner praises the house daily, which deeply pleases the house, and the house always responds with gratitude and a fastidious manner; however, the owner is yet to hear the house's responses. Each is in a state of anticipation. The owner anticipates an answer, while the house anticipates being heard. I'm certain this anticipatory state will resolve itself shortly.

New Friends, I have forgotten my manners. This is Dee Sanderson again and it is my pleasure to welcome you back. We are grateful you are here and we are eager to begin our discussion about the Outreach Program we are initiating. So without further ado, here's our dear friend Marilyn."

"Thank you, Dee! I believe it is appropriate to begin our discussion with a moment of silence for our Beloved Earth. Please do so now.

Thank you! Wellness to the Earth and to all of you who are participating in this project of good will! As you well understand by now, the Earth needs our help. She cannot survive without our assistance and we will not survive if she doesn't. Clearly our futures are intricately dependent upon the other, and even if this were not so, we cannot turn our backs to another Life Being that is in distress. How could we possibly live with ourselves if we acted so inhumanely? Coming to the aid of this planet is the only course of action that is acceptable. Many approaches can and will be taken, and with each contribution made, a spark of life will be reignited within her. Each effort made will be of assistance.

New Friends, when our group came together and shared our unusual experiences with one another, we were of course dumbfounded by the similarities of our stories. Our reactions were many. We grew from our discussions and it was through these conversations that we gained clarity about our role in assisting the Earth. Each of us has made an individual commitment to learn how to access his or her healing ability so that we can personally be attentive to her care and revitalization. And as a group, we decided to initiate an Outreach Program that will hopefully assist and inspire others to take actions as well.

We are aware that we were extremely fortunate that we had each other for support during these unusual experiences. Looking back on it now, I am so grateful that I was not alone during that initial phase. Please don't misunderstand me. I never felt that I was in jeopardy, but the experiences were odd, and I am someone who prefers to discuss what is going on in my life. I find the camaraderie of exchanging stories and ideas with others both satisfying and expansive. And I believe everyone in our group would agree that we grew much faster because we benefitted from each other's stories.

As the idea of outreach came to the surface, we recognized how vulnerable we each felt before we shared our stories with one another and this was the impetus for moving forward with the program. We didn't want others going through similar experiences alone. Obviously, everyone's experience is unique and some folks may not feel a need for support or collaboration, but for those who do need support, we want to create a network of support that will be easily accessible.

We initiated our first outreach attempt before focusing upon this book and it was remarkably successful. The experience energized us and solidified the idea of bringing a book forward that hopefully might be of assistance to others. We agreed that preparing the book was a priority. We hope it will serve as a model for you and others to begin your own support groups. Essentially, we thought the book would distribute the messages regarding humankind's healing ability more quickly than we could do on our own. And we are even more hopeful about that now.

New Friends, in recent months each of us has encountered people who have had similar, yet different experiences. These moments were delightful, intriguing, and confirmation for our own experiences. Crossing paths with these individuals has enriched our lives, and in each situation, we were struck by the wonderment of it all. The beauty of being in the right place at the right time so that a story could be shared, heard, and affirmed makes us smile to this day. One can accept that such an encounter may happen occasionally in one's life. You meet someone, you share a moment of time and feel a connection with this person, you marvel about the experience for a while, and then you go on with your life. I imagine everyone remembers some type of encounter like this somewhere in their past. Occasionally is acceptable; however, when these encounters begin to happen on a frequent basis, you begin to raise an eyebrow. You shake your head and wonder what on Earth is going on. Then you find out that your dearest and most trusted friends are having similar experiences. At this point, you see a pattern happening and even though, you may not understand it, you know that something curious is going on, and that it is happening for a reason. As you well know, Dear New Friends, the members of the Circle of Eight don't believe in coincidences.

We don't believe we are the only ones having these extraordinary experiences. Actually, in our humble opinion, we believe we are being assisted. Our elder gentleman friend is certainly our primary reason for this deduction. And we believe we are crossing paths with these other wonderful folks because the Earth needs our help, and we are being gathered together so that we will take action. Our way of taking action now is by producing this book. The messages we've received regarding the state of the Earth's health crisis and how we as ordinary citizens of the planet can help her are critically important to our future. Our encounters with other individuals have validated the messages we've received. Although we did not need this validation, it was certainly gratifying to hear. Dear Readers, Dear Brothers and Sisters of the Earth, we have a solution to Earth's crisis. We are the solution. Each and every one of us is the solution.

A truth about our evolutionary beginnings has been provided to us. The truth reminds us that we came into existence with an innate ability to heal. For reasons, yet to be understood our memory of this ability was lost over time. Although it is hard to conceive that we are actually capable of healing another, this information has come forward at a critical time in our evolutionary development.

Although some individuals in various areas around the planet have been aware of this reality for a long time, I think it is fair to say that most of us have not. Some of us may have heard stories of an individual participating in acts of healings, but these stories are rarely believed and quickly forgotten. For reasons that are unclear to me, humankind has not been open to or accepting of the idea of healing powers. Even those whose faith adheres to the teachings of healing practices find the idea difficult to accept in our modern world. Too many of us regard it as impossible, which is actually a lack of faith in our own abilities.

Dear Readers, we understand why people will doubt the pronouncement being presented in this book. We certainly did. But we had the luxury of experiencing unusual events that gave us reasons to believe. We hope the story that has been presented to you will give you reasons to open your heart to this possibility. As our dear elder friend often says to us, let me speaking bluntly, Dear Friends. We have been presented with an exceptional gift, the gift of memory, a reminder of the truth of who we really are. We are Life Beings innately endowed with healing powers, which enable us to heal other Life Beings. Is it not stunning that we would be reminded of our ability at this critical moment in time? There are no coincidences, My Friends. We have been purposefully informed so that we will take appropriate action. We are intended to come to the aid of the Earth in her hour of need.

Perhaps, you're wondering if this is really a gift or a preposterous joke? My Friends, we don't have time for jokes. Our future is at stake. This is no joking matter. The Earth's hour of need is ours as well.

Dear New Friends, the reality of Earth's state of decline is sobering. We must learn to hold this truth in our hearts and at the same time remember that there is reason for hope. People around the planet are waking up to the truth. Significant positive actions are already underway. And now, we have even more reason for hope. With this new knowledge about our healing capabilities, every citizen of the Earth can participate in her recovery process. No cost is involved other than a small amount of our time on a daily basis. The idea that I can participate in healing our planet gives me great joy. And when I think of this act of generosity being multiplied by billions of caregivers, it brings tears to my eyes. I imagine children in schools all across the globe taking a few minutes during their day to send energy to the planet. Isn't that a lovely vision? I imagine similar activities occurring in churches, business meetings, conferences, sporting events, retreat centers, and more. And I envision people all over the world coming together and forming small groups, and gathering in homes for the sake of Earth's well being. Just imagine this my friends. People coming together on behalf of the Earth and actually getting to know one another as the process unfolds. Imagine that!

Everyone can and must help. Don't be afraid of this, Dear Friends. It is so easy to participate in these healing sessions and so fulfilling. I personally feel better after every session. That's another reason for having hope. As the Earth grows stronger and healthier, those who are assisting her will as well. She will benefit from our assistance and we will benefit from the process.

The idea for our Outreach Program came about because we wanted to help others move through their own awakening process quickly and easily. We remain deeply grateful that we had each other's support during our awakening phase, and we would like to provide similar support for others. We hope *The Answer* series will serve as an impetus for growth. We hope it will help you to believe in yourselves. We hope it will help you to learn how to access your inner abilities and that it will comfort you and support you during your expansion process. You really are a person with healing abilities, Dear Friends. Even though that still may be difficult to accept, it is your truth nonetheless.

Through our many gatherings and conversations, our group became excited and optimistic about the idea that sharing our experiences might possibly benefit others, and that assumption was validated when we had our first outreach meeting. And as you might imagine the benefits were mutual. We gained new information from the stories our guests shared and they benefitted from our stories. We've learned so many lessons that we would like to share. We hope the ones already shared have been helpful.

Obviously, the most important lesson we've experienced was the practice of assisting the Earth by sharing our own energy with her. Rest assured, we were doubtful and somewhat hesitant, but we were also very curious. We all wanted to help the Earth, but declarations expounding upon humankind's healing abilities didn't particularly convince us that this was a viable option for saving the Earth. Thank goodness curiosity led us to make the right decision, as did our trust in one another. Dear Readers, we opened our hearts to the possibility that we might actually be able to help the Earth. Do we have scientific data to provide you as evidence of our efforts? No, we don't! Can we see that Earth benefitted from our healing sessions? Not yet!

But we all know what we felt when the energy transfer took place, and that makes us believe in this possibility. Each of us in our own way experienced a deep heartfelt sense of gratitude rush through our bodies that was undeniably real. Immeasurable for sure, but real, nonetheless. There are times, Dear Friends, when one must believe without the luxury of proof. This is one of those times. We were not told, nor do we tell you that the Earth can recuperate immediately from these transfusions of energy. She is not well. To expect an immediate return to complete wellness is unrealistic. However, success can be anticipated and accomplished with repeated treatments by many, many caregivers. There is reason for hope!

Shall we practice now, Dear Friends? Each time we do so, we learn something new, and we gain confidence in our ability to participate in this exercise. Like any type of meditation, practice improves the process and deepens the experience. By practicing together, we hope you will gain more confidence in this process as well. We also hope you will become more comfortable with the idea that you are a person with healing powers. Just be open to it…it takes a while to grasp this reality.

The other opportunity we would like you to have is to experience these sessions with different facilitators. Each of us has our own style of engaging the Earth and facilitating the energy transfer. We find that beneficial as well. We learn so much from one another. So, Dear Friends, please make yourself ready. If this is not a good time to begin for you, please return when you can. So, as I am speaking to you now, my companions are making themselves comfortable in their preferred chairs. Preparation for these healing practices is important. You learn what is most amenable for you to have an exceptional experience, and what isn't. So if you will, please prepare yourself. Experiment if you are so inclined. Perhaps, you may enjoy the company of a favorite selection of music or a scented candle. Whatever is your preference; by all means make your setting as accommodating as possible.

At this time, I would like to invite Frank to lead our session. His deep connection with the Earth has inspired all of us to pursue greater connection with her both during the sessions and also on our own. We are very grateful for his facilitation skills. I think you will really enjoy this experience."

"Thank you, Marilyn. You must have been reading my mind. I've actually been pondering what I would say if given the opportunity and I guess the best way to begin is by saying Thank You, Dear New Friends. I wonder where you are located and I wonder about your relationship with the Earth. I hope you have been as fortunate as me. My relationship with Mother Earth has been long and precious. My Father introduced me to the idea of tending the Earth, when I was just a youngster. That was quite a while ago! I won't elaborate on the number of decades. Suffice it to say, it was the greatest gift my Dad gave me. The Earth is a Life Being, Friends. Remarkable in every way and generous to a fault! Her ongoing, never-ending hospitality has put her in jeopardy. She cared so graciously for her inhabitants that she gave too much of herself, and now, she is suffering the consequences. She needs our help. She deserves our help. And now, we've learned that we can assist her in ways that we never knew were possible. I am so grateful that there is still time. New Friends, we can do this! Please join me now, as we practice our newfound skills.

Please take several long deep breaths everyone. You already know this part. So do what you need to do, and while you settle in, I will ask Mother Earth's permission to impart a dose of energy her way. Dear Old Friend, I know you're listening and I hope you are open to receiving an infusion of energy. We have guests today, Old Friend, who are just learning how to do this. They come from all parts of the world and they are interested in being on your caregiver team. I hope you with allow us to assist you at this time. I will wait for your answer.

Dear New Friends, continue your breathing exercises, reaching more and more deeply within. Find your place of serenity and release all the issues of the day. Simply rest in the stillness and know that you are not alone. You are one among many from around the globe who are practicing this exercise at the same time. You are one of a team of assistants waiting to infuse the Earth with healing energy.

Envision the spark of energy within you now, and with each breath that you take, see the spark growing stronger. Imagine the sparks growing brighter around the face of the Earth in anticipation of serving the planet.

She welcomes your assistance, and opens herself to receiving your spark of life. New Friends, take another deep breath and when you are ready, share your energy with the Earth. See it move from you to her and feel her inhaling your life-assisting infusion of energy.

Rest, as she consumes the energy that has been transferred from all of you who are participating. Feel her gratitude as you quiet yourself after this activity. Your assistance is essential, and she is so grateful.

Now, Dear Friends, gently detach from the Earth and fully return to your own body. Please feel good about your contribution. You have helped her. And each day, you can do more on her behalf. So little time is required to participate in this act of generosity, and so much is accomplished. Trust this, Dear Friends. Trust that your participation matters. What a privilege it is to participate in this healing experience. What a blessing! Thank you all for participating.

When you are ready, take another long deep breath and return to the present, knowing that you have been an instrument of good will.

In peace be, Friends of the Earth!"

"Ah! My goodness, Frank, you outdid yourself. That was a wonderful experience. New Friends, it is Marilyn again. I so wish you were here with us now, so that we could share our experiences of this session. Perhaps, it would be helpful if you heard the responses from some of our local Friends. Would anyone like to take the lead?"

"Yes, I would like to respond to the question that's floating about in Frank's head. He wants to know if he honored the Earth appropriately. Oh my goodness, Frank! Your love for the Earth pours out of you. At one point,

I imagined she was blushing. When you are facilitating Frank, my heart feels pure, because your heart is pure. And I am totally confident in this process. I know it is real and I know we are truly helping her. I know this because of your confidence and your faith. My friend, you are an inspiration to us all. Thank you!"

"Wow! That's high praise coming from the owner of this house, Frank. Hope you're taking every word in. Anyone else want to share?"

"I do. Everett Smith here. Frank, you're remarkable. I felt more connected to the Earth during this session than ever before and it's because of the way you communicate with her. It's so natural, which of course, makes sense because you've been talking to her for decades. I'm just really grateful, Frank. This was a very important session for me. It will take days for me to process everything, but I'm looking forward to doing the work. Thanks again, Frank."

"I'll go next, if it's okay. Jan Smith speaking. Frank, that was exceptional. I'm not sure how to explain this, but I think I felt joy coming from the Earth. When you shared with her that others from around the planet were participating in the session, I think she was deeply touched, surprised, and happy. Joyous! It was a wonderful sense of connection and I don't think this was imagined. I really think I sensed her feelings. This is big, Frank. Thank you so much!"

"Bill Jones here. I think we're witnessing another oddity of human nature. Frank just led an incredibly meaningful session, and a part of him doubted his facilitation skills. I'm glad we're able to provide some reassurance about that. Frank you did good! It was very helpful and I am very pleased with our contributions. We all did good! Thanks, Frank!"

"I'll go next. This is Pat Jones speaking. I went away during the experience. Don't know how to explain that other than what was just said. One minute I was listening to Frank's voice and the next I was gone. My focus was still upon assisting the Earth, but it seemed as if I were viewing the planet from above, like I was in outer space looking down upon her. And I could see sparks of light igniting all about the globe. In fact at one point, it seemed like I circled the Earth to see if there were more sparks of light and there were! They were all over the place. It was so exciting! I believe somehow, in some way, I was shown a glimpse of what was actually happening. Although I cannot explain this, if it is true, if what I saw was real, then, we had a very good turnout. My goodness, Friends, we really can amass the necessary numbers to make this work. Frank, thank you for making this possible."

"Well, my love, you were superb! This husband of mine is someone very special. I've known this for a long time, but he's oblivious to the truth about himself. I have a lot of witnesses to back me up now. I'm so proud of you, dear. Thank you!

As you can see, New Friends, our group is very loving and supportive of one another. We wish this for you as well. Initiating such a group may seem like a stretch for some of you, but we encourage you to consider the possibility. I'll let someone else broach that topic.

Marilyn, dear, would you like to continue facilitating or would you like to pass that on to another?"

"Let's ask for a volunteer, Dee. I think it is so important for our New Friends to have an opportunity to get to know all of us. Who feels energized and ready to take the lead?"

"I cannot believe my hand is raising up and acting as if this is something we, my hand and me, really want to do. Hello, New Friends! It's me again. Pat Jones. I'm the one that just circled the Earth from outer space.

Actually, I do want to talk about this topic, but let me take a few deep breaths first so I can settle myself. New Friends, what you're witnessing currently is just one of the reasons people are reluctant to participate in groups whether it is as a participant, a facilitator, or the creator of the group. We all have our gifts, and most of us also have some limitations. Shyness is definitely one of my challenges. On a good day, it isn't a problem, but on a vulnerable day, it can seem paralyzing. I'm sure some of you know exactly what I'm talking about, and those of you who do not, please count your blessings.

When Dee and Marilyn brought up the suggestion of initiating a group, my heart sank. And yet, the eight of us are in the process of creating outreach groups. Obviously, it is something that I am very interested in, and still, the thought can take my breath away. So I think it is important to share a few tidbits with you.

Before we actually started meeting on a regular basis, we went through a period of sizeable agitation. Each of us had encountered an unusual experience, and even though we needed to talk about it, doing so was not an easy matter. The list of fears was endless. Will they believe me? Can I trust them? Will they think I'm crazy? Will they tell my story to someone else, and what will that person think of me? Will this change their perception of me? Will they still like me?

Can you imagine our stress levels? We were in the company of our dearest friends, and still, these doubts and fears overtook us. And these insecurities arose again before our first outreach event. We are hopeful that these tedious moments will pass as we become more comfortable sharing our experiences with others. Actually now that I think about this, I understand why we were so tenuous about coming out to our friends. They are the ones whose opinions matter the most to us. Oh my goodness. This makes sense, doesn't it? We didn't want to lose their respect and affection. And of course, that was the primary factor when dealing with our adult children and grandchildren. We certainly didn't want to upset our relationships with our family. So essentially, what I've just deduced is that it is easier to share these stories with strangers than it is with people with whom we are very close. Well, this is information for us to take under consideration.

New Friends, and present company included, thank you for allowing me to think out loud. I think there is a reality that must be faced when coming out with news that may create controversy. There will be some people who will be sympathetic to the stories that are shared and there will be others who are not. It's just that simple. And we must proceed regardless of those moments that may be disappointing.

We are here for a reason, Friends, and we must do our part. Each time a flame of awareness is ignited in another, the Earth benefits. The interconnectedness between humankind's dilemmas and the Earth's declining health demands our attention and consideration. Both the human race and the Life Being Earth are intended to continue. Extinction is not our destiny. However, for both to survive, cooperation is essential. She has done her part. We must now do ours.

For reasons, we may or may not remember, we, Dear Friends, have awakened to the Earth's situation and we have been asked to assist her. We cannot walk away from this. We cannot allow our fears to keep us from doing what we are intended to do. We are here to help the Earth. And we can do this by sharing the news about our healing abilities with everyone we encounter. We must keep our commitments to send her energy every day and we must invite others to participate in this act of generosity. So we must share our stories and encourage others to share their stories as well. We will proceed with our outreach attempts and we hope others will do the same. And we will spread the news through this book, and perhaps, more will come forward. The point is, my Dear Friends, we must take action and we cannot allow our fears to prevent us from doing so.

Geez! I'm not quite sure where that all came from, but hopefully, it made sense. I think I'm done now. Thank you for listening. Wellness to the Earth!"

"Wow! Good job, Pat! New Friends, this is Frank speaking and I just want you to know that Pat just demonstrated her courage and strength. Her comment about her shyness is real. She has struggled with this all her life, and we've been blessed to witness her moments of indecision, as well as her determination and perseverance. You've just seen what a powerhouse she can be once she gets started, and I hope this inspires all of you. The truth is, everyone in our group has moments that cause us to hesitate. We see it in ourselves and we witness it in each other. It's normal. We just have to learn to push through it like Pat just did. We can do this folks. Just remember, you're facing your fears for the sake of the Earth.

Thanks, Pat! You really did an outstanding job!"

"Oh, yes! Pat, thank you so much. Listening to you just warms my heart. I'm so proud of you.

Sorry, folks, this is Jan! Pat and I share the shyness issue. We've talked about this topic for years and it still creeps up on us. But as you just read, New Friends, Pat is confronting it well.

Your message really was inspirational, Pat!"

"Well, New Friends, you are truly having an opportunity to witness the benefits of having a community. By the way, this is Dee again, and I'm aware that the four-letter word just slipped into the conversation. Let's just say that I did it on purpose, so that we would all have the privilege of greeting the Earth. Wellness to the planet! And thank you Old Girl for everything you have done for us! We are so grateful!

Back to Pat…I hope you're taking in all this wonderful feedback, because you deserve it. And we are all benefitting from this! First we had the pleasure of your inspirational message and now we get to see the impact you've had. This is exactly the type of situation we want to present in our outreach programs. Well done, Pat!

I'm going to hush now and turn this over to our quiet friend. She's pondering about something. I can tell because her house is getting excited."

"You rascal! Your telepathic abilities are shining! And now, you're even tuning into my house. What next, Dee? And of course, you are right. I am having a myriad of thoughts.

Pat, thank you! I too am deeply moved by your willingness to share your heart and soul with us. It's very healing to be in the presence of someone who has the courage to connect in this manner. The depth of intimacy that transpires when someone is communicating at this level is absolutely precious. It opens the heart of those who are listening and helps the listener to reach into his or her own heart and discover more about their own mysteries. You've given us a gift, Pat. And you've demonstrated one of the goals we were striving for via the outreach groups. Connection at a deep heartfelt level changes the energy of those who are present and beyond. This type of energy can create great change. One's heart is full when you connect at this level and peace engulfs the speaker and the listeners. And it awakens the desire for more of the same.

Imagine everyone coming together to connect in this way. We would actually get to know one another. We would see the goodness in others and our hearts would open to new friendships. My mind is in whirl just thinking about the possibilities. Oh, Pat, thank you so much. There really is reason for hope."

"Dear One, can you elaborate on your comment about changing the energy of those and beyond? Our New Friends may be confused about this."

"I can try. As you well know, Dee, this is a complicated task. However, there is an easy way to discuss the topic and a curious, yet very intriguing way to approach it as well. I will begin with the easiest. So, let me think for a moment. How shall I begin? Hmm. I have an idea.

It is very common in this house of mine for the telephone to ring very early in the morning. And when I say early, I mean early. You see, my walking buddy is as eager to greet the sun in the morning as I am and we often rise early for that reason. Our commitment to one another is to call when the urge arises, which it frequently does.

Now, let me share with you the impact of those phone calls. They absolutely brighten my day. I know when that phone rings that my Dear

Friend desires my company and this thrills me. I know that we will have some wonderful, interesting, and heartfelt conversation from which I will greatly benefit, and I know that the rest of my day will unfold in lovely ways because of the interactions that she and I shared. Our connection enhances my energy and as a result everyone that I encounter during the day benefits from my heightened energy level. This is the gift of heartfelt exchanges. And I am confident that some, if not all, of the folks that I engage with during the day will also have an uplifting positive energy experience that they too will pass on to others. This chain of exchanging goodness is unlimited. It makes me wonder how far one act of kindness can travel and how many lives can be changed by an initial effort of reaching out and touching someone's life. We probably will never know what our outreach in any situation will be, but it's wonderful to think that a morning's walk with a Dear Friend might actually have long reaching positive effects. The thought of this makes me smile and it solidifies my desire to be a part of this outreach program. Imagine what might happen if the same potential for connection plays out with our New Friends who are committed to saving the Earth. It could result in worldwide connections of people transferring healing energy to the Earth. That's exciting.

Now, let's address the more complicated aspect of my task. As you can see in the scenario above, beyond can certainly refer to those folks beyond our range of awareness. One conversation can travel from one person to another and from places to more places while we have gone on with our day and have absolutely no idea of the impact of our presence upon another. That's one reality about the notion of beyond, but there are other realities as well. And our elder gentleman is a good example of the latter.

Our friend, whom some of you may have already met, resides elsewhere. We don't exactly know what that means, but perhaps it is best said that he travels more expansively than we do. For those of you who have already read the prequels to this book, you are acutely aware that he comes and goes in the most delightful manner. I cannot speak the truth about our Dear Friend, because I do not know it, but I can share my thoughts about his comings and goings.

I personally believe that our Friend is someone who once lived an embodied life here on this planet. At some point he passed from that lifetime to another, and now he continues to help the Earth and her residents via his new form. We have witnessed him materialize before our eyes, and we have also witnessed him disappear. In fact, we have become accustomed to his unusual arrivals and departures. I must admit it is still a hoot to witness this, but I simply accept it now as a natural way of being for his present state of existence. He is evidence that there is more in existence than we allow ourselves to imagine.

And New Friends, we also know that there are more Friends beyond our elder. We know that he facilitates messages from others, and even though we have never seen them, we trust our awareness that they do exist. I hope that you will believe what I am saying. This is one of those times when one is given an opportunity to trust without proof. If you don't, I will not take it personally. I will be the first to say that seeing our elder friend is truly gratifying. I believed my friends' stories about him, but I ached to see him for myself. And when he appeared I was ecstatic. Just remembering the moment brings joy to my heart. Oh, how we giggled together! What a gift it is to see the gift before you.

New Friends, the members of the Circle of Eight believe that there is more, and we have certainly experienced that reality through the relationship we have with the elder gentleman. We find this belief is very comforting and we also believe that more will be revealed as we continue to pursue our efforts of saving the Earth. We so hope you will join us, and that you will invite others to join as well.

Thank you so much for listening to me, New Friends. I am very grateful to be in your company. In peace be."

"This is Bill Jones, again, and I would like to make a comment or two if you don't mind. First, I want to thank everyone for their contributions to this discussion. I hope our New Friends are benefitting from this conversation as much as I am. Every time we talk about these recent experiences, I learn something new. One would think that retelling these stories would become monotonous, but that has not been the case. It seems that another aspect of a repeated story always unfolds, which takes us to another level of understanding. I think it's important for us to remember the importance of sharing our stories, even if it begins to seem routine for us. What's happened to us is significant and I really want our New Friends to hear this. Your experiences are important, Friends, and people will benefit from hearing them. At our first outreach event, we learned as much if not more from the experience as our guests did. I believe it is fair to say that our guests felt validated and relieved by the stories we shared, and we found their stories riveting. Our shared experience inspired us to pursue more outreach opportunities and it also inspired the participants to do the same. We hope the Readers of this book will have similar aspirations.

I would like to change my focus now and share my perspective about the 'beyond' topic that was just discussed. The idea that there is more was really a stretch for me. To be honest with you, in the past, I never gave it much thought, and when the topic came up in conversations, I wasn't particularly interested. I'm sure there were times when I was outwardly dismissive about it. Well, our encounter with the elder gentleman forced me to give the issue some thought. Actually, that experience resulted in a great deal of thought. Let's face it, when someone disappears right before your eyes, it gets your attention. It took me a while to get over my old beliefs, which were founded in nothing more than judgment and the idea that everything must be substantiated to have any merit. Repeated encounters with this fellow forced me to open my heart and mind to what was transpiring around me. I urge you, New Friends, to open yourselves to this wonderment. There is more! Whether you want to believe it or not is yours to decide, but the truth remains the truth regardless. There is more! Enjoy the reality of this truth and open your heart to the path of new discoveries.

By the way, I am aware of my use of the four-letter word that has taken on a new meaning in our vocabulary. Graciously serving as a reminder for attending the Earth, let us take advantage of the moment. Wellness to the Earth! Old friend, we are grateful for everything you have done for us. With your permission, we stand ready to offer you a boost of energy. New Friends, and all who are in listening range, please join us. It is time for another dose of healing energy for the planet Earth. Wherever you are located, please prepare yourself to share a particle of your pure healing energy with her. Make yourself ready in the manner that is most comfortable for you. And when you are ready, offer your energy to her. Allow her to consume the energy, and then give her space to rest. Each particle of healing energy matters; you serve her well when you participate in these brief moments of connection and energy exchange. Feel her gratitude.

Thank you everyone for participating in this act of generosity. And for listening to my ramblings."

"Thank you, Bill, for your comments, and for leading us in another healing session. I am so glad that we are integrating these sessions into our conversations. I hope everyone is realizing how easy a healing practice can be. It requires so little of us, and yet the impact is immeasurable. New Friends, this is Dee again. We are so grateful to be in your presence, and we hope our conversations are helpful. We would, of course, prefer that you were gathered here with us in this lovely living room, but we are extremely happy with the connection that we presently have. Thank you so much for reading this book. In so doing, you are taking action, and for that we are all very grateful.

Marilyn, Dear, it seems that it may be time to bring this conversation to a close. Would you like to facilitate that?"

"I would be happy to do so, Dee, but first let me check in with our group. Does anyone have anything more to add to our outreach discussion? Hmm! It seems that several of my companions are pointing their fingers at me. Perhaps, they know something that escapes me. Let me be silent for a minute and see if I can figure out what is going on here.

Okay, message received. New Friends, the members of the Circle of Eight have become increasingly more in tuned to our telepathic abilities. Frank and Dee are particular skilled in this area, and the rest of us have been enjoying opening ourselves to the process. We still find it very fascinating and often wonder how this actually happens. The truth is, it is happening whether we understand it or not, and it is happening more and more frequently. We are simply trusting the process and enjoying our newly found skills. It seems that these skills have been heightened by our experiences with our elder friend. We assume the development of our telepathic abilities is relevant to the mission of healing the Earth. So, this is the message I just received from my dear companions. It seems that numerous ideas were running about in my mind during the outreach discussion and they are encouraging me to share these thoughts with everyone.

I am deeply touched by what is transpiring through these pages. We are connecting with one another, Dear New Friends. I cannot express the joy that this brings to me. Just knowing that you are there, somewhere on this beautiful planet, willingly reading this book and learning more about the immediate needs of Mother Earth. I am so hopeful, and I think it is appropriate for me to say that all of us here located in our Friend's living room are filled with hope and possibility. We can save the Earth! If anyone had told me this a few months ago, I would have shaken my head in disbelief. But now I truly believe it is possible.

Hopefully, each of you participating in this reading experience is learning how easy it is to connect with her at a heart level. That first step is more significant than we allow ourselves to believe. Imagine how she feels every time someone stops just for a moment to acknowledge her presence. That small gesture must in itself have healing implications. Remember a time, New Friend, when someone acknowledged your presence; remember how it felt to be treated with respect and affection. When I remember such a moment, it warms my heart and brightens my day. Similar acts of kindness can do the same for her, and that matters, Dear Friends. Even though the effect is immeasurable, it makes a difference. And now that we are accepting the reality of our healing capabilities, our potential for assisting her has skyrocketed.

I remember some time ago in the early days of my quest to establish a meditative practice, a very wise woman said to me, 'If you aspire to seek the Silence, you must practice meditating every day.' Truthfully, New Friends, at that point in my life, I had no idea what I was seeking and I certainly didn't understand the concept of the Silence. However, her wisdom has served me in many ways, and it is applicable to our present situation. If we want to learn how to access our healing abilities, we must make the effort. Practicing daily is not a huge request. As you have seen from our various exercises, the process is easy and can be achieved quickly. We purposefully wanted to impress this upon those of you who are very busy and who erroneously presume that you are not able to take on another task.

The manner in which you approach your practice is yours to discern. There are times when I revel in the opportunity of sitting quietly in a meditative state for thirty minutes or more. Those times rejuvenate me and often bring forward awareness that I may or may not have been seeking. The point is, at that particular moment in time, I preferred a longer meditation. On other occasions, my time is restricted by responsibilities and/or obligations and I need an alternative way for quieting myself. I personally enjoy using my time in the shower as a brief meditation. Incorporating some peace and quiet into my walks is always a delight, while some times, I just need to pause and take some deep breaths to center myself. The paths are endless; it is just a matter of being creative. One of my friends, who loves to knit, finds that activity a time of worship. She meditates, does her centering prayers, and simply rests in the Silence while she knits some beautiful article of clothing that she will lovingly gift to someone. Our dear friend, Frank, whom you have come to know through these chronicles, finds his escape in the workshop while he is communicating with some wonderful piece of wood with whom he is collaborating. From what I hear from others, runners, bikers, and walkers frequently use their preferred activity as a time for contemplative opportunities.

New Friends, you will find your own ways of seeking inward, and in the process of doing so, you will also find that some avenues are less satisfactory than others. These are not failures. Each option that does not bring you closer to peace of mind is simply information that steers you in another direction.

For the sake of clarity, let's distinguish between meditation that is solely for the purpose of free entry into the silence, and meditation that has an intentional purpose. The former is meditation for meditation sake. This path encompasses the goal of freely entering into the meditative state without intention or anticipation of a desired outcome. It is a passageway to the inward realm of existence and it is an adventure of self-discovery, and more. I invite you to think expansively regarding the mysterious four-letter word *more!* So much more awaits the seeker who freely enters into the world of Silence.

Our healing meditations on behalf of the Earth are a wonderful example of mediation with an intentional purpose. In these sessions, the goal is to clear your heart and mind of distractions and to focus solely upon the needs of the planet. In so doing you purposefully access the healing energy within yourself and transfer that energy to the Earth. The purpose is to enhance her wellness while not depleting your own good health. You will find that each time you practice this transmission of energy that you will hone your skills and your methods of doing so. You will learn to trust the procedure and you will come to recognize the importance of even a moment of positive intention. There will be times when you prefer to devote more time to the Earth, and in those moments you will have the luxury of connecting more deeply with her. You will feel the benefits of those precious times more richly and completely. But on those days when you are rushed and harried, send her energy quickly and efficiently as has been demonstrated in some of our exercises. Your intentions matter! Perhaps, you can spare a brief moment while commuting to or from work, or both. Or take time while you are brushing your teeth. My point is this. Snatch any free moment you can, and offer that time to the Earth. Let her know that you are sincere about helping her and send her a dose of your healing energy. Every good intention matters! Please remember this. If you delay assisting her because you think you do not have ample time for a healing session, then you are functioning from a place of misunderstanding. Obviously, it is preferable for both you and the Earth to have longer encounters, but please do not minimize the effect of a brief session. The power of your healing energy is inestimable. Longer sessions enhance the relationship between you and Mother Earth, which is a sustainable aspect of your healing presence, but the actual transfer of your healing energy is equally powerful regardless of the amount of time spent during the healing session.

New Friends, we do not consider ourselves to be experts in the field of energy transfusions. We're not even sure how to explain the dynamics of such a thing, but we do know from our experiences that this process is important. Each time we participate in an energy transfer our confidence in this procedure strengthens. We know we are assisting the Earth, we know the potential for rejuvenating her is possible, and we also know that we cannot do this alone. With your help, her chances for recovery improve. As more and more individuals recognize their healing abilities and willingly participate in her healing process, her potential for a full recovery increases. Dear New Friends, we so hope you will open your hearts to this mission of rescue and that you will help spread the word to others. I imagine that you are shaking your heads and questioning the validity of this proposal about now. We understand your doubts and confusion. We certainly went through that phase as well, but eventually, our individual and group experiences could no longer be denied. They were the evidence we needed to accept this truth about ourselves.

At one point, I remember thinking, what do we have to lose? The Earth's crisis is real and rather than just feeling helpless about it, why not do something. People pray when they are concerned about a loved one. This is an acceptable approach for billions of people. Well, focusing one's intentions upon the Earth's healing process is also a form of prayer that incorporates the healing energy with which we are divinely endowed. Now that we have been reminded of this ability, why would we not use it on her behalf? Why would we not at least try? Personally, I made a decision to do just that. Before the unusual events became prevalent in my life, I felt frustrated and helpless about the Earth's circumstances. I didn't know what to do to improve her situation. Of course, I participated in water conservation and tried to be mindful about recyclables, but that didn't seem like it was enough. I wanted to do more, and now, I am. My involvement in these healing efforts is very gratifying. It makes me feel useful, and I truly believe my efforts, our efforts, are assisting her back to good health. New Friends, participating in healing the Earth is a privilege. Every time my energy merges with hers, I know with all that I am that the transfusion of energy was successful. I feel the boost of energy that she feels and I feel her gratitude. It is a remarkable experience. I so hope that everyone will have the opportunity to experience this soul connection. It is certainly mutually benefitting. As we supply her with healing energy, her increased vibrancy heals us, as well.

How humbling! Even in her declining state, she continues to help the peoples of Earth. My Friends, we owe her so much. Will her crisis be the factor that finally unifies the people of Earth?

Must we have a global tragedy for us to recognize that we are all Brothers and Sisters? Questions to ponder.

Hopefully, Dear Friends, we will find harmonious solutions that will accelerate her recovery. Hopefully, we will come to recognize the wonders of this remarkable Life Being, as well as the beauty in one another. Hopefully, we will become the peaceable beings we are intended to be.

Join me everyone, please. It is time to honor the Life Being Earth and to express our gratitude for everything she has done for us and for all those who came before us. Old Friend, we are humbled to be in your presence. Words will never adequately express the sincerity of our gratitude that radiates from our hearts. Please feel our gratefulness and carry this memory with you. We are here because of your gracious hospitality and we are finally realizing all that you have provided us. Thank you, thank you, thank you!

Please allow us to offer you a breath of assistance now as we gather on your behalf. Friends from far and near ready themselves, as do your Friends throughout the Universe. You are loved, Dear Friend. Please prepare yourself to receive.

Take a deep breath, Friends of the Earth. Ignite your healing energy on her behalf and may your Light be an inspiration to all. Continue your deep breaths until you are ready to transfer your Source energy to her. Do this at your own pace; this is for you to discern. When you are ready release your healing energy and intentionally send it to her.

She will graciously receive what is offered. Stay with her as your energy merges with hers so that you can enjoy the experience of her emanating gratitude. Let it wash through you. Experience the joy of unity with this amazing Life Being. Once you feel this heartfelt connection you will never be the same again. You will understand the connectedness that exists between you and you will begin to grasp the concept of Oneness. As you, Dear Reader, experience this connection, realize that countless others are also experiencing the essence of unity and Oneness. How sweet this experience is for everyone involved! How gracious the Earth is to provide this opportunity for everyone. Regardless of where we are located, we are all One.

Thank you, Dear Friends, for participating in this healing act of unity. In peace be!"

~ 11 ~

"Hello, Dear Friends. Welcome back from your journey to assist the Earth. We hope the experience was a positive one. This is Dee again, and we are eager to discuss several other outreach topics with you at this time. We hope you are ready for another discussion. If not, take a break and return when you are ready to be fully present.

When our gatherings first began, it was because of a sense of urgency that our group members were experiencing. As you well know, there was a period of unrest and uncertainty until we began to share our stories. It was extremely comforting to discover that we were all sharing similar unusual events. Doubts diminish quickly when you realize that other people whom you admire and respect are also having inexplicable experiences. You are much less inclined to consider insanity as an option for yourself if someone you know is also having a questionable experience. We found such comfort in sharing our stories. And this has been a driving force in our desire to create a network of outreach programs that will provide similar support, as we were fortunate to enjoy.

We've also continued to gain more information about ourselves because of our frequent meetings, and this also propelled us forward to initiate contact with other folks who may have similar needs. We would like to share some of our thoughts and ideas with you now, if this is a good time for you.

As you may expect, each of us developed in our own unique ways, which will of course be true for you too, Dear Readers. By sharing our experiences, we all have had the opportunity to learn more, and to do so more rapidly. So, we believe it would be beneficial if we address with you what has evolved for us during this period of growth.

I'm going to call on the Smiths first, since they were the ones who initially opened the door to all that has followed. Their courage inspired the rest of us to share our stories as well. So, Jan, Everett, will you take the lead now?"

"Yes, Dee, we're ready. I'll go first if that's okay with you Everett. Hello again, Dear Friends. Hmm! Isn't this interesting? It seems we have shifted how we are addressing you. When we began, we referred to you as New Friends, and now we are simply calling you Friends. Isn't that lovely? Our connections have deepened.

Just a quick reminder! Everett and I are the ones who encountered the fellow in flowing white gowns on the beach, and also, the well-dressed elder gentleman in the airport. Those two incidents profoundly changed our lives. Each of those men begged us to assist The Island. They repeatedly stated that we must go to The Island; she needs us. Needless to say, both of us were deeply affected by their appeals. Even though we had no idea which island they were referring to or how we could possibly be of help, we felt compelled to do something. We talked about the unknown island incessantly. We had dreams about it nearly every night and our first conversation every morning focused upon this island we knew nothing about. We felt helpless and agitated, and as our discomfort grew, we became more and more in need to discuss our situation with someone. We weren't exactly sure who that might be, but we knew the time had come to share our story.

Fortunately, one morning on the trail we crossed paths with our dear friend here who provides us with this lovely meeting space. Thank goodness we did, because Everett and I were in a state. We could not contain ourselves. We desperately needed to talk and our wise friend invited us to sit beneath that gorgeous old beech tree with the huge canopy. There we shared our story for the first time. That experience also changed our lives and it seemed to set off a chain of reactions. One by one, each of us in what is now referred to as the Circle of Eight shared our stories. It was such a relief. Before that, we had felt so isolated by these experiences; and then suddenly, we were all in this together. What a blessing that was!

Our gatherings, which quickly became frequent events, were an essential part of our development. The conversations shared in our group sessions and the encounters we continued to experience with the elder friend naturally led us to look more deeply within ourselves. I must admit this was not an ordinary practice for Ev and me. We are thinkers, always have been! Our style is to discuss things endlessly while making lists of pros and cons, and then, by starting all over again and analyzing the situation up one side and down the other. This has always been our modus operandi. Truth is we enjoy doing this; however, our preferred approach was not suitable for the inner work that we needed to do. Our lists simply were not helping us to discern what role we were to pursue in helping The Island. Obviously, once we learned that The Island referred to the Earth, our desire to be of assistance intensified even more. As we learned more about the healing energy that exists within us, we also learned about accessing and dispersing that energy through the assistance of meditative exercises. Previously, neither of us had been inclined to pursue a meditation practice, so we knew very little about the activity. It was initially a challenge for our over-active minds, but we were determined to learn how to meditate for the sake of the Earth. As you might imagine, we are so grateful that this practice was introduced into our lives. We feel good about the progress we've made and plan to continue honing our meditative skills. Meditation has already helped us in numerous ways. We are now effectively able to access and distribute our healing energy quickly and easily, and we are able to travel within to learn more about ourselves. Through our meditation experiences, we gained clarity about how we want to help with the healing of the Earth.

In addition to transferring her energy on a daily basis, we also want to participate in the outreach program by traveling to other locations that may wish to set up similar support groups for addressing the Earth's crisis. Because we are avid travelers, visiting other settings and interacting with other folks would be something that we would really enjoy doing. Essentially, we feel called to spread the word about the truth of Earth's situation and we would like to help by sharing what we have learned about humankind's healing abilities. We anticipate encountering people, similar to ourselves, who will be interested in learning how to access and utilize their own abilities, and when we do, we will offer to assist them. We will remind them as the elder gentleman did us, that these healing abilities can save the Earth. Our desire is to tell everyone that there is reason for hope! And we also want to solicit their help. Dear Friends, the truth is we feel that we should do what the man on the beach and the elder gentleman in the airport did for us. We should speak the truth to everyone who will listen. We remember how confused we were when we were initially approached, so Everett and I plan to practice how to deliver these messages in ways that people will most likely be able to hear them. We hope to minimize confusion, facilitate discussion, and inspire hope. This is a tall order, but we are willing to try our best. The Earth needs us, and we want to help her.

Everett, dear! Would you like to take over now?"

"You've just about covered everything, Jan, but I will elaborate a bit on a couple of items. I feel a need to be very candid about how agitated we were, or at least I was, with our initial experiences with the beach person and the elder gentleman. The incident on the beach was disconcerting. I remember feeling very protective of Jan and also worried about the man whose stability was questionable. Our perspective of that encounter is different now, but at the time, it was upsetting. He startled us, which probably influenced my reaction, but the point is we do not want to have that kind of impact on the folks we meet. Obviously, our situation is different in that we will not have the disappearance factor to contend with, as we did with both of our unusual encounters. Even as amiable as the elder gentleman was, his sudden appearance followed by an equally sudden disappearance was a bit unnerving. We're comfortable with his comings and goings now, but initially we were not.

Perhaps, one of the reasons it is important for us to participate in spreading this information about the Earth's circumstances to others is that we are here in the present. When we arrive at a new setting, it will not be an unusual event, and because our goal will be to facilitate interactions and discussions with the people we meet, our departures will not be sudden or unexpected. We will have the luxury of time to engage with New Friends and they will have time to get to know us. Hopefully, Jan and I will finesse an approach that is openhearted, sincere, and informative. I know we will be nervous the first time we reach out to folks, but we're optimistic that we can grow into this outreach work. We know that these events will be mutually benefitting. Hopefully, the participants will learn something from us and we're confident that we will learn more from them.

The other topic Jan addressed that I wish to tag onto is regarding the development of a meditation practice. I was reluctant to even try meditation because of a misunderstanding that had somehow developed over the years. I don't know if I had heard or read that this discipline was very difficult to master, but somehow the idea evolved in my mind that I would never be able to be proficient at meditating. My Friends, I know you have encountered this saying many times before, but it is absolutely applicable for this occasion. If I can do it, so can you!

Once I got over my anxiety about mastering this alleged incredibly complicated task, the experience was a pleasure. Mediation is a journey! Each opportunity is different and best faced without judgment or criticism. Enter each occasion with an open-heart and wait and see what unfolds. I think you will be delighted with the process.

I guess that's about all I have to say. Thank you for listening and good luck with your own decisions regarding how you will assist the Earth."

"Thanks, Everett! And thank you all for reading about our deliberation process. It took a while for us to discern how we might best help the Earth. Now, we are eager to move forward. You will find your own way of assisting her soon, but in the meantime, let us not lose sight of her immediate needs. She needs infusions of healing energy daily, and preferably more than once a day. You can help now, Friends. Just focus your intentions upon her and send her love and positive energy. Your assistance will make a difference.

Join us in this mission to save the Earth. Please help her. Wellness to the Earth and to all who reside upon her!"

"Thank you, Dear Ones! I can just see the two of you traveling here and there and making New Friends wherever you land. People will be so fortunate to be in your presence. I don't have any doubts about your abilities to spread the messages in a warm and coherent manner. Your presence will open people's hearts to these new, yet ancient ideas. The same way our elder friend opened our hearts to the truth, so too will you have a similar impact upon others. Thank you for being an advocate for Mother Earth.

And now, let me invite the Joneses to take the lead. Bill, Pat, will you please share your story of discernment with others?"

"Of course, Dee, we are excited about sharing our story with everyone. Dear Friends, we are so grateful for everything that we have experienced and learned in recent months. Encountering the elder gentleman was and remains one of the most important encounters either of us has ever had. The news of the Earth's precarious health was difficult to hear, but we are glad we know the truth. And the reminder, as he called it, about humankind's healing abilities is a life-altering experience. How could we be so blessed to be a part of this remarkable turn of events? We marvel at the changes that have occurred in our lives in such a short period of time. It is unbelievable, and yet, it is true. Bill and I are filled with gratitude and we begin everyday by thanking the powers that be for allowing us to participate in this incredible moment in time. We are thrilled!

The only factor that has been problematic for us is family, which of course is significant. As unusual events unfolded for us and around us, we became increasingly more interested in understanding exactly what was going on. Our interest never waned. However, each time we learned more about the Earth's declining health, our concern for the children and grandchildren grew. We felt conflicted. We wanted to share everything we were learning with them and at the same time we were afraid to do so. We did not want to burden their lives, but we believed they needed to know the truth. Fear, many fears erupted within us. I didn't want to frighten the grandkids. It's so unfair that they must grow up with these unthinkable circumstances. I just kept thinking that we, the older generation, have failed them. And Bill didn't want lose the children's respect. He was afraid they wouldn't believe our story about the elder gentleman and that they would be concerned about our involvement with these so-called unusual experiences. The longer we fretted about our options the more distant we felt from our kids and that was intolerable. We simply couldn't handle the disconnection that we were feeling and realized action had to be taken.

So we did. We broached the topic with them. That in itself was a challenge. We debated how to do it and when. Should we do it by phone or should we travel to them and do it in person? We were so concerned about causing them harm that our deliberations over how to tell them delayed the process. We eventually led with a phone call announcing that we had news to share with them and that we preferred doing so in person. Of course, they were immediately concerned that something was amiss and thought that one of us was having health problems. We reassured them that we were both fine, but they were still pensive. I share this with you now only to prepare you for your own encounter with family matters. No matter how long or thoroughly you plan this discussion, or any other for that matter, there will always be glitches that arise that you didn't anticipate. So, at that point we decided we would simply proceed from a place of kindness.

We intentionally arrived on a day when we knew the grandkids had evening activities. That gave us some quiet time to share our stories with their parents. Needless to say, they were taken aback by our encounter, but they were respectful and listened attentively. Interestingly, they were not shaken about the news of the Earth's situation. Unfortunately, I suspect this is true for most people. We've grown so accustomed to hearing about climate change and global warming that the news has become mundane. If a headline manages to catch our attention, we momentarily feel the reality of the Earth's decline, before quickly moving into a state of helplessness. And then life goes on. This reaction of inaction, I'm afraid has become the norm for most of us.

Bill cleverly took advantage of the moment to discuss the commitment we had both made to take an active role in helping the planet. He began by identifying the various actions we were taking around the house and in our community to become better citizens of the Earth before moving into the topic that we really wanted to discuss. Broaching the topic of humankind's healing abilities was not easy for either of us. Our fears of being perceived as nutcases were looming large, but Bill handled the situation beautifully. He quietly and carefully shared the experiences that we were having with our oldest and dearest friends in conjunction with the mysterious elder gentleman. He spoke of the doubts that we all had in the beginning and how overtime our experiences led us to open our hearts to the possibilities that the information we were being introduced to was indeed worthy of consideration.

Naturally, the kids had many questions, some of which were based in curiosity and others that were founded in concern for us. Bill did a wonderful job fielding their questions. He was calm, openly responsive, and readily acknowledged when he didn't know how to address a particular inquiry. The kids demonstrated great maturity throughout the entire interaction. We were very proud of them, and relieved.

It was helpful that they know and trust our friends. These are people they have known all of their lives. It was so wise of Bill to include them in our story because their presence and participation in this tale of oddities added validity to our story.

Fortunately, our children were grateful that we had shared our experiences with them and really appreciated how we had carefully orchestrated the visit. They said that they needed time to process all the information we had shared with them, which was a reasonable request. And they particularly wanted time to make decisions about sharing our information with their children. I could see that their deliberation process was already in progress. What would they tell the kids, when, how, etc. My immediate compulsion was to advise them not to tell the grandkids. All of my anxiety about bringing this information to their attention rushed forward again, and for a brief moment, I regretted our actions. Bill undoubtedly intuited my thoughts. He gently placed his hand on mine and thanked the kids for listening to our story and reassured them that we would accept their wishes regarding any actions they chose to take. The four of us agreed that more conversations were necessary and that we would keep each other informed about any decisions that were made. We returned home feeling good about our visit.

I'm sure Bill has much more to add, so let me turn it over to him now."

"Thanks, Pat. As you shared our story, the emotions from those times surfaced again. I must admit that I was really concerned about approaching this situation. I did not want to jeopardize the relationship that we had with our children and I truly was afraid of losing their respect. Now, I realize how disrespectful I was of them. I wasn't giving them the credit they deserve. My fears interfered with my good judgment. Obviously, they needed time to adjust to all this new information the same way we did when it was presented to us.

This is a critical aspect of outreach that we must all remember. We must be where the person in front of us is. Our elder friend is a wonderful role model for us. His participation in assisting the Earth has, shall we say, been extensive. The truth is we have no idea how long he's been working on her behalf, but he certainly was and remains much more knowledgeable about her unwellness than we are. However, in all our encounters with him, he has always provided the information as graciously and kindly as he possibly could. He honored where we were in the moment and gently educated us to our current reality. And he nudged us forward when he believed we were ready, even when we didn't think we were ready to hear any more news about the Earth's declining health. He trusted us to be able to handle the situation and he lovingly pushed us along so that we would be ready to assist her.

When we were debating how to approach the children, we lost sight of his methodology. Now, that we speak of this again, I realize that we needed to have faith in our children's ability to manage the situation, and we must remember this when we encounter newcomers in the future.

I also realized as Pat was expressing her concern about our grandchildren that they probably know much more about the Earth's circumstances than any of us. They're in school, for goodness sake, and they are learning about this daily, while we pick up information when we watch the news. We must trust that the children of our planet are more informed than we are and that they are the ones who will make the greatest difference in assisting the Earth. I suspect the healing energy of the youth is more potent than the energy of our generations. Hmm. That's a very interesting thought. I wonder where it came from. Pat, we must bring this up the next time we visit with our elder friend.

Dear Friends, Pat and I feel very strongly that outreach can happen more rapidly by including one's families in the conversations. Our family is multigenerational, so any information that is discussed among us has the potential for spreading more rapidly to various sectors of the population. We also believe discussions about the Earth's health can have unifying effects within the family system and throughout the community at large, and our vision of community extends globally.

Based upon our own experiences, I think we must face the reality that difficult topics are uncomfortable for people to bring up whether you are among family, dear friends, or strangers. But the Earth cannot wait for us to resolve our many issues regarding our fears and trust. We simply must nudge ourselves forward for her sake and our own. We were fortunate to have a positive outcome with our children. Our group also had a successful outcome with our first outreach attempt. And there will be more positive experiences. We must focus on these positive results and live more fully into our commitments. When we find ourselves obsessing about potential pitfalls, we must quiet our fears. In our zeal to find the perfect approach, Pat and I created more anxiety for ourselves and delayed the necessary action that needed to be taken.

Dear Friends, far and near, let's focus on the end goal. The Earth needs our assistance. She is our priority, not our fears. Wellness to the Earth!

Thank you for listening to our ramblings. We are grateful for your time and presence.

Be faithful to yourself and to the Earth."

"Thank you, Dear Ones. You are such wonderful parents! I'm certain your experiences will be extremely beneficial to many of our Readers. Your thoughtful, tender care for your children and grandchildren warms my heart. And I am so grateful for the wonderful reminder you provided all of us. We must be where the person in front of us is. My friends, that is stellar. Thank you.

And now, I wonder who would like to go next. Perhaps, someone is ready to volunteer."

"Well, Dee, maybe it's time for us to share our story. I'll go first if that suits you."

"I thought you were ready, Frank. I am too. Let's go for it! And yes, I would be delighted if you went first."

"Most of you already know that Dee and I have enjoyed a very long relationship with our well-dressed elder friend. He's played an instrumental role in our lives, since we were youngsters lost in the woods, but his influence of late is what I wish to talk about.

Dee and I were in a very different place a while back. To put it bluntly, our longevity was getting the best of us. I was feeling my age more than I wanted to admit, and my beloved was struggling with some memory issues. We were each worried sick about the other. Many long discussions were had about the future. Plans were made and forgotten and then the conversations repeated themselves. It was a trying time. I was terrified that I would pass before Dee. The idea of leaving her alone was more than I could bear. Neither one of us wanted to be left behind, nor did we want to go first. Both options were unacceptable and there were many, many talks about leaving together. That was the only solution that was satisfactory to us.

I share this reality with you, Dear Readers, because I know that my beloved and I are not the only ones who face this unpleasant situation. This is a part of life, we said to one another. That quip didn't resolve anything. We were still left worrying about the other and wondering when we should take steps to sidestep the inevitable separation that we were facing. That's a confounding decision to make when you're feeling good, and an easy one when you are feeling bad.

Life, as we know it, is difficult to say goodbye to. Particularly when you don't know what is waiting for you after the decision is made. Oh, we were definitely blessed during that period. Our family of friends rallied around us and offered to assist us when the time came. That was extremely generous and comforting, and it calmed the sense of urgency that we were feeling. But then we worried about them because we didn't want to put these dear friends through the hardship that we imagined it would be. As I listened to Bill's talk a while ago, I realized that we should have trusted our friends' sincerity and their ability to take care of themselves. Their offer of assistance was an incredible act of generosity. And we both remain very grateful for their willingness to stand by us.

That's where we were before the elder friend came back into our lives, but things have changed considerably since then. We both feel useful again. Passion has been reignited and everyday is filled with interesting possibilities. It's amazing how wonderful one feels when you are participating in life. We're not obsessing about end of life issues anymore because we are too involved in the present. We know the inevitable lies ahead of us, but for the time being, we are focused on the here and now. Our time with the elder has reminded us of a truth he shared with us some fifty odd years before. The existence of life is a never-ending process. It changes its appearance from time to time, but the essence within never ceases to exist. Dee and I lost sight of that for a while, but we're over that fretful time. Life in the present is too rich to miss even a moment of it worrying about a fate that is not intended to happen.

Dee and I are in a very good place with our perspective of eternal life, and we are also excited to be living at this particular time in history. We are here to assist the Earth. We want to assist the Earth and we are grateful that we still have the strength to do so.

Thank you for listening, Friends! I'm sure Dee has much more to add. Peace and wellness to you and the Earth."

"Thank you, Frank. You spoke eloquently about our trying times. We were indeed in an uncomfortable place back then. Unfortunately, the burden of our circumstances fell upon Frank. My memory was playing havoc with our lives and he was the one that held us together. I'm so grateful that we came out of that dark, desperate time. We temporarily lost ourselves to worriment, but things turned around when purpose and meaningfulness reentered our lives. It was fascinating to witness what I will call our return to life. Frank's creativity surged forward and my memory came back. We became physically and mentally more active again. I don't mean to brag, but we became functional, sharp people again. It was wonderful to think clearly and to remember what had just transpired minutes before. And you cannot believe the activity that was stirring in Frank's workshop. Oh my goodness! His collaboration with the fallen wood he collected was producing incredible results. It was marvelous. We were alive again! My goodness, what a blessing it was!

Dear Friends, our story is not unique. And neither are we! We are just ordinary people who enjoyed life fully until we allowed fear to take over. I bring this topic up because one must learn to recognize fear. Few of us perceive ourselves as fearful individuals, which allows fears to sneak in without our awareness. Oddly enough, when fear is blatantly obvious, it is more easily navigated because we are aware of its presence. However, when fear is obscure, it can be and often is an insidious companion. It lurks within us without our notice taking advantage of the moment to insert its dastardly misguidance. During these misadventures, we are typically unaware of its presence, much less, its impact.

My Friends, fear is! It simply is and when you accept that it simply exists then you are the master of your fear. When our family of friends came together to discuss our unusual experiences, we acknowledged many different feelings. We expressed suspicion, doubtfulness, anxiety, excitement, puzzlement, curiosity, confoundedness, and many more descriptors that now escape me. The point is we were aware of many different emotions, but the subject of fear didn't initially come up. That emotion escaped us. When one finally recognizes that many of our emotions are founded in an underlying fear that we are unaware of, then we can truly understand what is going on within us. Then we are able to manage our fears and regain command over our own decision-making process.

As I speak of this, I wonder if you are curious about my choice of topics. Why am I talking about this, you may be thinking. If I were in your shoes, I would be having these thoughts. There is a point to my ramblings, my Friends. The truth is: exploring the unknown can inspire fears to surface. So be it! Fear is nothing to be afraid of if you simply accept that it is a part of your makeup. Once you acknowledge this to yourself, then you have changed the dynamic of your relationship with fear. Somewhere in our history, we were led to believe that we should fear our fear. This makes fear the enemy. I would rather have fear be my friend. It has much to teach me. And because I am an eager learner, I would rather take advantage of this teacher than reject it for reasons that are unclear to me. My friends, I invite you to open your heart to your fears. You will learn so much more about your true self if you do, and your life will be less complicated.

Another thought comes to mind, Dear Friends, about the notion of the unknown. I use this term to describe our adventures, because most people will think of our experiences from this perspective. We certainly did in the beginning, and it's true that we are now acutely aware that there is so much more to learn about the unknowns that surround us. We know with all that we are that there is more; however, exactly what that more is remains unknown to us. But we are not afraid of this unknown! We are excited about learning more about the unknowns with whom we coexist.

This is the message that I wish to impart to you. There is more, Dear Friends, so much more. Be open to this! Open your hearts and embrace every opportunity that comes your way. We are not alone. I find that the most delightful notion to ponder. Yes indeed, I find this fascinating, and I hope you will as well.

Dear Friends, may you find peace in the days ahead. Wellness to you, to the Earth, and to all those who you are yet to encounter! Thanks for listening!"

"Well done, Dee! I'm glad you introduced those topics, an important reminder for all of us. There's another point to make related to fears, Dee. Remember what happened when we all realized that fear was challenging us. Not only did we grow wiser individually, but we also grew collectively. There were and still are times when one of us will sink into a fear state without knowing it, and someone else in the group will immediately recognize the symptoms and take action. We've been able to help one another quickly move through that unpleasantness.

I agree with Dee's observation about fear. It simply is a factor of the human condition. It's nothing to be ashamed of, but life is easier when you take charge of it.

So, I guess it's time to move on. Who wants to take the lead now?"

"I would like to go next, please. This is Marilyn again. Frank and Dee's love story always manages to stir up many emotions for me. I picture young Frank carrying Dee on his back up and down the hills of the forest, and I am in awe. What a way to start a relationship! First, the accident, and then the encounter with the elderly well-dressed gentleman. And then many years later when they found themselves in another complicated situation, guess who shows up. What a remarkable story! Hearing about the concerns and fears that came up for you during those difficult periods is helpful for me. We really must have more compassion for ourselves.

Each one of us had issues concerning coming out about our unusual encounters because we were afraid of being judged by someone. Isn't that sad? Here we were having these incredible experiences in our lives, and we were afraid of telling anyone. And the more we gave into the fears the more fearful we became. Thank goodness we had one another!

My Friends, this is one of the points I would like to make. Having a community of friends is a blessing. We were very lucky that our friendships were of long standing. Some of you may not have that readily available to you, but open your heart to the possibility. Think long and hard about this before you choose isolation over connection. What I've witnessed during these times of exploration is the potential connection with strangers. I came into this adventure in that way. Before I had my own experience, I knew about what was happening because of being in the right place at the right time when a friend, soon to be, needed to share her experience with some other person. I am so grateful I was available. It is such a privilege to hear these stories. It's important, Friends, that we remember how difficult it was to reveal our unusual experiences with others. We must remember so that we have compassion for those who are in the midst of that experience. Our familiarity with these types of events makes us ideal candidates to serve as listeners and as a support team for those just introduced into this area of the unknown. We were so blessed. Perhaps, we can be a blessing for someone else.

As I look back upon an experience I had while sitting on a bench with a previously unknown woman, I realize it was indeed an encounter. Listening to her story apprised me of the mystery that was unfolding around me. I was fortunate to be the listener, and I was so excited about what I heard. Her story opened my heart before I even had my own unusual experience. And there's more to this as well. Her story gave me hope! Even though I didn't really understand what was going on, I was so envious. I wanted to have an unusual experience as well, and this tagged onto my life long desire to know more about the more that I was absolutely certain existed. Even has a child I pondered thoughts about the Universe, about existence, and about God. Big questions and ideas sparked my imagination and raised more questions, more ideas, and more wonderment.

So, I am grateful for the opportunities to hear other people's stories. They broaden my awareness and validate my own beliefs. Our group has often talked about the importance of being willing to share our stories, and the equally important privilege of being a listener. How sweet it is to be the recipient of someone's story. This is one of the ways I feel called to serve. As a listener I can assist the storyteller by holding their stories for them as they adapt and adjust to the reality of their circumstances. I also believe that I am here to hear stories from others who are from distant places. Not quite sure what that means yet, but I'm eager to learn more about that possibility.

Dear Friends, I am so grateful that you are here participating in this grand event of connection that is occurring on our planet. What we've learned so far is that people are gathering to assist the Earth energetically. Isn't that wonderful? No matter where one is at any given time, we are able to assist her. We can help her individually or we can join with others. The choice is ours, and hopefully, we will be inclined and available to participate in many activities. I have a dream that we will have global energy sessions on her behalf. Just imagine that…people all over the planet joining together at a designated time to send her healing energy. Wow! This is possible! We can facilitate such an event. Oh, New Friends, I am so glad that you are here. Thank you for reading this book and thank you for helping the Earth."

"Thank you, Marilyn. Your words are an inspiration to all of us.

As I listened to each of you speak of your experiences, my heart was full. So much has happened in such a small amount a time, and yet, it seems as if a lifetime has been lived during these brief, but precious moments. Each experience we shared with one another was an extraordinary gift. I am so grateful, which brings up yet another essential element to review.

The state of gratefulness has been a significant factor during these remarkable times. I've often heard that living in the present and living in gratitude go hand in hand. We can certainly attest to that. One of the most vivid memories I have about our ongoing gatherings is the ever-present expression of gratitude. Repeatedly during all our interactions words of appreciation and tender heartedness were spoken. Sadly, I don't think this is the norm for most folks, but it certainly became commonplace among us. And I am grateful for that! What a warm, loving setting unfolded during our exploration of our unusual experiences.

I have come to believe that gratitude is contagious. Whether it is verbalized aloud or spoken quietly within, the expression of gratitude begets more gratitude, and this has a stabilizing effect upon everyone involved. We've witnessed this repeatedly in our gatherings. We've become more attentive to one another and more compassionate about each other's feelings and reactions. I believe we've become kinder and better people. We, meaning the Circle of Eight, our family of friends, have found that living life from a place of gratefulness is a healing experience. And of course, this brings us to the reality that we are beings with healing capabilities. What a surprise this is for all of us to hear!

Dear Friends, I truly hope you are listening with the ears of your heart as you read these pages. The most important information we've learned from our unusual experiences is the truth about our healing abilities. This is definitely the primary message that is being presented to all of us and it is the message that we are intended to pass on to others.

As you might imagine, we were anxious about bringing this message forward. Even now as you read our story, we have no idea how you may react to the idea that humankind is endowed with healing abilities. We are hopeful that you will be as excited about this reality as we are, and we are also hopeful that you will choose to pursue your gift.

My friends, I do not believe it is a coincidence that we are being reacquainted with these ancient skills at this time. The Earth needs help and we are the solution to her crisis. Whether you believe in coincidences or not is irrelevant. We've been given a reminder that is critically important to our ability to provide assistance to the planet Earth. When faced with such an opportunity, why would we not accept this timely offer? To do so opens the door to the future; to decline leads to a disaster that was never intended. The choice is ours.

Our toxic energy is the primary cause of the Earth's decline. Obviously, our disrespect and mismanagement of her natural resources and our endless perpetual greed also are responsible for her state of unwellness, but the state of ill will that festers within humankind is the primary factor that must be addressed. This is a harsh reality that is difficult to face. My Friends, many will read this and be shocked by the insinuation that the negative energy generated by the peoples of Earth is the primary cause of the planet's decline. No one wants to think that his or her energy is negative; nor do we want to believe that our energy has disabled her. It is a shocking reality with which to contend. In typical human fashion, we will blame someone else for the problem. Surely, 'those people' must be the ones responsible for this! The truth is, my Friends, we do not have time for more of the same. Shaming and blaming simply increase the toxicity levels that the Earth is already enduring.

For those who wish to cling to the idea that their energy is pure, your assistance is needed. For those who readily accept that their energy is a factor in this problem, your assistance is needed. And for all of those people around the world who are confused about this proposal, your assistance is needed as well. Everyone's help is needed.

Dear Friends, Dear Readers of this most unusual book, we are all needed. The planet Earth is in great need of assistance, and we are the answer to her precarious situation.

We invite you to accept the reality of the Earth's situation and we implore you to pursue your healing abilities. Within each of us lies the ability to heal self and others. Now, we must come forward on behalf of a Life Being who is essential to our own continuance. We cannot do this alone, for the Earth is too large and she is too ill for the energy of a few to restore her to good health. Fortunately, we are not alone. Every living being on this planet is capable of participating in this act of generosity. What is asked of you requires nothing but your good will. You are not asked to relocate, to spend large sums of money, or to relinquish great amounts of your time. You are simply asked to focus your intentions upon the wellness of this remarkable planet a few minutes of each day. When, where, and how you do that is for you to discern, but your participation is essential.

As each of us focuses upon her healing process, we too will heal, and as we heal, her healing will continue. The process is so simple that it seems impossible, and yet, the truth remains the truth. Healing energy inspires more healing energy and the cycle of healing that emerges from combined healing energies results in transformation.

Dear Readers, *The Answer* series was created for a reason. It is a reminder to those who remain upon the Earth to care for her. Although those who remain are far fewer than those who came before, we, you and I, who still remain, are the keepers of the Life Being Earth. Though we no longer remember the agreements made between the Earth and those who requested residence upon her, we are the descendants of those who came before, and as such, the responsibility for her well being falls upon us. She has served well and asked nothing in return; however, now her circumstances have profoundly changed. That which was never intended to be lost is being lost. That which was never intended to happen is happening. A crisis of unthinkable proportion has developed as a result of the Earth's generous hospitality. As said before, she needs help and those who initiated the crisis must be the ones to bring the crisis to an end. This can only be done by an act of extraordinary generosity. This sounds as if the act is more than anyone can fathom, but in truth, it is merely an act of kindness offered by those who benefitted from her since they came into being.

Dear Friends, we are those who remain upon the planet Earth. We are the answer to her crisis. We are the ones who must offer acts of kindness. We must stop our incessant fighting with one another. We must stop committing acts of meanness and cruelty to one another. We must stop sickening the Earth with our sickening ill will. Our behaviors need an adjustment. Improving our behavior towards self and others is necessary for her good health and for ours. We cannot continue to be as we have been. A transformation of our way of being is needed for our sake and for hers as well.

If you, Dear Reader, are feeling dubious about humankind's ability to change their behavior, please question your doubting mind. Do not waste your time wondering about the other seven plus billion people on the planet. Time is of the essence. Focus upon your own behavior! You are the one who has dominion over your ability to change your ways.

Please imagine for just one moment the possibility that you are a person endowed with the ability to heal another. What might you do with that ability? Is there someone in your life presently who is in poor health that you would love to assist? Would you rush to that person and offer your time and healing energy to them? Just imagine being able to assist another person back to good health. Imagine that, please, Dear Friend. And then take a deep breath and remember the truth that was revealed in this book. You, and all other beings, are endowed with healing abilities.

Indeed, it may take a moment or two for you to adjust to this reality, but get on with it, Dear Friend. Accepting who you really are will be the first act of kindness that will precede a parade of acts that follow. Choosing to accept that you are a being with healing abilities diminishes the inclination towards of acts of unkindness. Choosing to accept the responsibility of aiding others with one's healing abilities also greatly alters the tendency towards negative behaviors. As you grow into the reality of who you really are, the old behaviors of meanness and unkindness will fall aside and the misunderstandings underlying these behaviors will be released as well. As your behaviors incorporate goodness into your daily activities, the positive energy that you emote will assist the Earth in her recovery process.

Dear Friends, Dear Readers, we can change our behaviors, and in so doing, we will change the impact we have on the Earth. By deliberately and consciously choosing to pursue our healing capabilities, we will improve her health, and by actively transmitting healing energy to her, she will recover from this terrible state of ill health.

Remember, Dear Friends, focus on your own behavior. It is not our privilege to focus on another's behavior. Each of us must work on ourselves for our own sake and for the sake of the Earth. We cannot change another, but we can change ourselves. As we each change for the better, so too will the Earth's health, and as we find peace, so too will she.

My Friends, we, the Circle of Eight, are so grateful that you have taken the time to read this unusual book. What was revealed through this fictional story was the truth of the Earth's declining condition and it was the truth of humankind's potential. We hope you will accept that this book has crossed your path for a reason.

Please accept the truth about your healing abilities, Dear Friend. There is no more time for delays. The Earth needs your help now!

~ 12 ~

"*Beloved Children of the Earth, we are most pleased to make connection with you through the means of this unusual story. Perhaps you may wonder why we chose to approach you in this manner. Your thoughts, Dear Friends, deserve a response and an explanation for the purpose of this unusual encounter with a book devoted to a tale about unusual encounters and experiences. As the book suggested opportunities for outreach, so too is this book a means of outreach from Those Who Came Before to Those Who Still Remain upon the planet Earth. We attempt to connect with you in a manner that hopefully will not create chaos or arouse endless controversy regarding the legitimacy of the book's formation or its intention. As is often stated within 'The Answer' series, there is no longer time for delays. The imminent crisis demands attention now.*

We come forward for the sake of humankind and for the purpose of saving the beloved Life Being Earth. She, who graciously offered herself as a haven upon which a civilization could evolve, was never intended to sacrifice herself on our behalf, and yet, she has valiantly done so. What she has done for us, now we must do for her.

Our civilization has existed many lifetimes upon her surface, and always she willingly allowed us to express ourselves in ways that were not always in her best interest. She persevered through our growing pains hoping that one day we would reach a level of greater understanding about our ways and about our impact upon others. We have not demonstrated the level of growth that was hoped for or anticipated. Instead, an infection of great misunderstanding grew amongst our peoples leading us to ways that were selfish, untrusting, and uncaring of others. The decline of our good will led us down a most unfortunate path of unconsciousness regarding the consequences of our misdeeds.

What has happened has happened, but we can no longer linger in this state of willingly continuing our misguided behaviors. The truth of our ill will is unbearable to ponder, and yet, the evidence of our ways is undeniable. Each one who reads this statement will, of course, have his or her personal reactions. We urge you to be both gentle and honest with yourself. What is done cannot be changed, but what you do from this moment forward can create remarkable change.

You, Dear Friends, are more than you appear to be. We speak of the reality that you came into existence from pure source energy. All in existence are created in the same manner, and as such, you are more than your appear to be. You are indeed the one you view in your mirror, but you are much, much more, because within you resides the pure source energy that resides within all others. You are One and You are Many. Equally endowed are all others in existence. This delightful way of being also includes the innate ability to heal self and others. While this concept may be difficult to accept, it is the truth nonetheless. This has always been the truth of all in existence. Believe it or not, Dear Friends, this is your truth, and it is a truth that you must accept. Your survival depends upon it.

The ability that exists within you is capable of altering the course of the Earth's decline. With the cooperation of all humankind, our peoples have the ability to stop her decline and to restore her to full vibrancy once again. Dear Friends, this is your reality, and it is the task that lies before you. The news of the Earth's failing health is not new to you. However, what you do not know is the speed at which the calamity is progressing. There is no time for you to deliberate about the truth just provided. You must take action now. The title of this final book of The Answer series is prophetic…The Answer in Action. You, Dear Friends, are the answer and you must take action now.

Dear Friends, you are not alone. You are a cooperative of over seven billion members and you are more. Those Who Came Before also remain in existence. We come forward now to remind you of our existence and to reassure you that we are also here to assist with the rejuvenation of the Life Being Earth. And there are more than the beings of Earth who stand ready to aid her.

Many have accumulated on her behalf, but our resources cannot override the willful negative energy created by humankind. This task is yours to address. The choice to change your ways is yours to make.

Dear Friends and Families, we take no pleasure in bringing these messages to you, but we must. For the sake of all involved, we must speak the truth. For the sake of All Those Yet To Come, we must implore Those Who Still Remain to change your ways. The acts of goodness that are necessary to change the course of this impending catastrophe are so easy to achieve. Take care of one another. Be kind to one another. Treat each other as the brothers and sisters that you truly are, and above all else, do no harm to anyone for any presumed righteous reason. Every act of unkindness harms the Earth. Please do not cause her anymore distress. Love her as the Mother that she is. So much she has done for so many. So little is required of you. Simply be the person of goodness that you are intended to be.

Dear Friends, please take action. Devote several minutes every day to healing Mother Earth. Numerous examples were provided throughout 'The Answer' series, but these are not the only ways of expressing your concern for the Earth. What is important is the effort that you make on her behalf. These moments of intentional care for the Earth are so easy, and yet, so remarkably powerful. The more you can contribute, the more rapidly she will recover. Please do not be dismissive of these small acts. Your thoughts, your intentions, your prayers are ways of correcting the ramifications of the past. Each moment of goodness and loving kindness that you share with her enhances her ability to rejuvenate her own well being; however, she cannot recover on her own, nor can she recover as long as the behaviors of wrongdoing continue.

Dear Friends, you are more than you appear to be. You are the answer in action. Please respond to the innate ability that resides within you and focus your healing energy towards the Earth. With good intentions, this act of kindness will achieve success. With daily persistence, the goal of saving the Earth will be accomplished.

Throughout The Answer trilogy, you witnessed the formation of our characters as they came to grips with the reality of their healing powers. You experienced their doubts, their fears, and their reluctant hopefulness. We attempted to portray the process as accurately as possible, and we hoped that you would also experience their various reactions as they unfolded in the story, as if you were part of the story itself. It seems that the human condition demands such a developmental process to validate that a point being proclaimed is actually legitimate and sincere. Dear Friends, we hoped by presenting our story in this manner that your willingness to accept the truth about your own healing abilities would be enhanced. As so often stated, there is no longer time for endless conversations about the Earth's situation. Fortunately, many on the planet have already taken action on her behalf, but these efforts are not enough and they are not happening as quickly as is needed. More is needed! And you are the answer!

We urge you, Dear Friends, to move forward as if you totally and confidently believe in the idea that you are a person of healing abilities. Choose to believe this. Act as if you believe this. And everyday, insistently and persistently, focus your intentions upon healing the Earth. If you are unsure exactly how to do this, do what you do whenever you approach a situation that is new provided in this text. Choose one or create your own. There is no exact way of attending another who is in need. Those of you, who prefer to follow your preferred ideas of prayer, please do so! Make the Earth the focus of your intentions, and pray earnestly for her health, every day, several times a day if possible. She will deeply appreciate your prayers and she will heal from your good intentions. Others of you may wish to review the energy techniques specifically discussed within our story. If you feel drawn to this option, please hone the process so that it suits your style. Regardless of the method, holding the Earth lovingly in your heart will successfully aid her during this critically important time of need.

Please, Dear Friends, do not make the mistake of believing that the act of healing is a process that is too difficult for you to achieve. This is not the truth and we do not have time to dispel this old way of thinking and believing. The opposite is the truth. Healing is actually a simple act of kindness that only demands the participation of a loving heart.

Our beautiful Earth requires the assistance of many, many loving hearts. You are one among many who will be working on her behalf. The more who participate, the faster she will recover. This reality must be understood as well. A Life Being of the Earth's size requires everyone to participate in her healing process. Not only are we needed to send her positive healing energy, but we are also required to alter our negative approaches to life. We will achieve this way of being by changing our own personal behaviors. What is requested of us is small compared to what the Earth has done for us. In addition to entering into existence with the innate gift of healing powers, we were also endowed with a loving heart. We are all that is needed to save another Life Being. We are all needed to save the Life Being Earth.

Dear Friends, we are most grateful to be in your presence. Although we have always been near not all of you have been aware of this reality. We assure you that we are indeed here and we are already working towards saving the Earth. With your assistance, she will be restored to her full potential. Thank you for reading our unusual story and for recognizing the truth beyond the fiction. In peace be, Dear Friends. Your survival is dependent upon your loving ways.

In peace be!

Printed in the United States
By Bookmasters